the girls'
ALMANAC

the girls'*
ALMANAC

EMILY FRANKLIN

AVON
TRADE

An Imprint of HarperCollins*Publishers*

Some of these stories appeared in the following journals and anthologies:

"Come to Iceland," *Mississippi Review*
"Early Girls," *Small Spiral Notebook*
"A Map of the Area," *Carve Magazine*
"In the Herd of the Elephants," *Literary Mama* and
Before: Short Stories About Pregnancy from Our Top Writers
"43 Lake View Ave.," *Pindeldyboz*
"Defining Moments in the Life of My Father," *Heat City Review*

HarperCollins books may be purchased for educational, business, or sales promotional use. For information please write: Special Markets Department, HarperCollins Publishers Inc., 10 East 53rd Street, New York, NY 10022.

FIRST EDITION

Library of Congress Cataloging-in-Publication Data

Franklin, Emily.
    The girls' almanac / Emily Franklin.—1st ed.
        p. cm.
    ISBN-13: 978-0-06-087340-0
    ISBN-10: 0-06-087340-X
    1. Female friendship—Fiction.   I. Title.

PS3606.R396E36 2006
813'.6—dc22   2005057202

06 07 08 09 10 RRDH 10 9 8 7 6 5 4 3 2 1

For my dad

Acknowledgments

So many thanks are due to: Faye Bender, who loved *The Girls' Almanac* right away; Jennifer Pooley, for her brilliant editing and belief in this book; Grandma Bev and Papa, who read so many of these stories before I completed them and whose constant love and support of me and my writing is a huge part of my life; to Jack Harris for physics and math assistance; to Kristin Pape, who wrote the poem upon which "Residency" is based; Heather Swain for support, humor, and encouragement; my mom; my children; my brothers; Kathy for her early reads; Heather Woodcock for careful notes in those first drafts; the Strauss Family; the writers who gave their support with blurbs; and my own group of early girls. And of course, always, Adam.

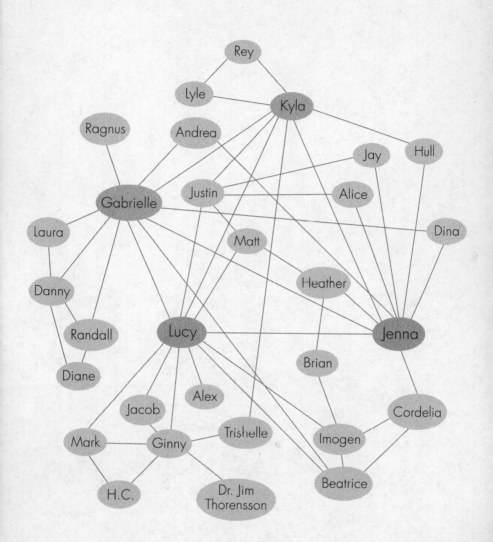

tips for gardening

Early Girls

At the gym, Lucy uses a yoga ball to stretch. Large and blue, the rubber globe has teats to hang on to, and Lucy does, all the while envisioning the bright-hued cow who might have the ball as an udder. In the locker room, she doesn't bother to shower but notices the skin all around her in various stages of sagging and figures herself somewhere in the middle. All of the imperfections—moles and hip-flanking stretch marks, the puckered folds of back skin—all seem wonderful to Lucy. After Matt had proposed, they'd lain still in their swimsuits on the lakeshore with his hand like a map's x on her belly.

"I love this part of you," he'd said, touching the pigmented splotch below her ribs. Like something melted, the spot spread each time she breathed out. "I wonder if it will get bigger when you get pregnant."

They'd speculated, tried to guess which state outline the birthmark might resemble as her body changed. Propped up on her elbows then, Lucy had looked at the smooth plane of water, watching for fish ripples and feeling her newly ringed finger. Matt had kept his hand on her as they stayed there, paperweighting her as if she might become airborne at any moment.

When she thought about that day, she could make any of the objects huge in her mind—the birthmark splotch could seem to take over her belly, or the striped beach towel they were on could enlarge to blanket size, but usually the water took over, breaking out of its lake-hold and seeping onto them. The ring never grew, though. Once, in a dream, the diamond band had actually become minute, baby-earring size and then the size of a small-fonted o. When Lucy woke up, she went to the box on her dresser where she kept the engagement ring and checked to see if it still fit.

On the back deck are the flats of pansies and new strawberry plants Lucy will earth later in the day. She walks past the small bobbed flower heads and tangled stems to the back door, going inside to change into nonathletic clothing, something her mother would call "an outfit."

"It's hard to say," she says into the phone to Kyla. "I feel like it should feel weird, but it doesn't."

"Maybe you're just blocking it out," Kyla says, the slur of highway noise and radio coming through.

"I hope you're using your earpiece." Lucy picks at dirt under her thumbnail and then, unable to flick it out, uses her teeth, feeling the sand grit on her tongue.

"It's called an earbud, Luce," Kyla says.

"I know. It just sounds gross—like an earwig or something that's going to bite you or something. Anyway, I think I'm just going with the black pants, white top."

"Good," Kyla says. "You'll look like a very stylish waiter."

At Unveiled, the bridal boutique in downtown Boston, Lucy steps in the door, only to have the sensors go off.

"I'm not even holding anything," she says, trying to make light of the loud buzzers and the tomato-shaped and colored lights flaring atop the electronic gate. One of the saleswomen comes with a key to unlock and restart the device.

When Ginny, Lucy's mother, arrives with her black binder full of bridal ideas, Lucy tells her about the sensor incident, saying, "It's like even they know I'm not supposed to be in here."

"Don't be ridiculous," Ginny says and splays her bridal book onto the counter. "Now, let's figure out some options."

Two saleswomen, "bridal assistants" they call themselves, peck and hem at Ginny's book, fondle the fabric samples she's pinned inside, and remark about the work that went into the collection of torn magazine pages, clipped tapestry samples, articles about shoe dyeing.

One of the assistants turns to Lucy and says, "Can I just do one quick thing?" Without a response, the assistant sticks her hands into Lucy's hair and fluffs out the matted locks. Lucy is so grateful for the touch that she doesn't react.

Ginny nods as if there's been some conversation that Lucy's missed. "I know, her hair has always been baby fine. No body—wouldn't even hold a perm. Granted, this saved her from those giant mistakes some of the girls made." Ginny holds her hands several inches from her own head as if she's trying on an invisible helmet. Then she turns back to Lucy. "She looks so nice when it's just been cut, though. A blunt cut to frame the face."

Lucy rolls her eyes; she's heard the hair speech many times before. She suspects the pale-skin talk will follow, but before Ginny can tell of the way a tan suits her daughter's coloring, the assistant says to Lucy, "Now, tell me—will you wear your hair up or down for the ceremony?"

"Actually, my mom's the one getting married," Lucy says, which prompts instant fussing from the assistants, who cover up their assumptions by fawning over the bridal binder again.

They self-correct and distract by saying to Ginny, "Well, this makes much more sense. The designs you've picked out are far more suitable for a more mature bride, the closed sleeve for example."

Lucy wanders to the garment racks by the bay windows. Unveiled prided itself on being less a store than an elegant town house that just happened to house hundreds of bridal gowns, tiaras, and corsets. Sifting through the hangered dresses, Lucy wonders if her mother will wear white or settle on something more common for the déjà vu bride.

"How about celadon?" Ginny shouts across the room, holding up a wrap the color of treacle.

Lucy nods and then, to make sure she seemed enthusiastic enough, nods again, emphatic as a seizure. The gowns are set on the puffy silk hangers that make Lucy think of ballet slippers, trickling ribbons, the old poster she had in her room of a ballerina with torn tights and bruised knees. Shopping with her mother when she was a girl, Lucy would lose herself in the racks of clothing, stepping into the center or underneath the displays. She wants to do that now, not just to remove herself from the tea sandwiches and tiara talk but to feel the cool satins and rustling crinolines against her skin. She imagines sitting under one of the wide bell skirts like one of Mother Commedia's children in the *Nutcracker* who suddenly bursts from the fabric folds and dances. Just then, Lucy remembers that the role is danced by a man, and this makes her sad. She would like to have the company of tiny children, huddled around her, tucked into the umbrella of the skirt. She goes to find Ginny in the dressing room and sits watching her mother being buttoned into a cream-colored gown that casts a pink hue in the light.

"Well," Ginny says into the three-way mirror. "The color's no good. I feel like a cheap wine. But I do like the style, I must say."

"It's very popular with our second-wedding brides," the assistant says. She touches the waistline and adds, "It's very flattering through here."

"Yes," Ginny says. "I'm small so, you know, I have to be very particular about the cut of my clothes."

Lucy likes to refer to her mother as short, since it annoys her that Ginny will say only "small" or, rarely, "petite."

"My whole family is short," Lucy says. In the mirror, she allows herself a glance—she is the same as she was freshman year of high school, dark blond hair, breasts bulbous as eggplants, nearly betraying her otherwise small frame.

"The women are small, that's true." Ginny twirls around. "And with poor circulation to boot." She holds up her mottled hands, pressing to show how slowly the spot under the skin refills with blood. "But we live a long time, so that's what's important."

Ginny always connected her circulatory issues with the fact that her mother and grandmother lived past ninety-six, and it never made sense to Lucy, who also had blotchy blues and purples on her toes and whose hands were always cold. The comment, though it is family lore, makes Lucy feel worse, mainly because her mother should have known better.

"My grandmother always said to marry for height," the assistant says.

Ginny instantly looks to Lucy—they both are thinking about how tall Matt was—about his extralong shirtsleeves and size thirteen feet.

"You look nice, Mom," Lucy says, goes back out into the living room section of the store, sits, fairly shrunken, on the love seat, and assumes her mother is telling the Matt Story. No doubt the bridal assistants would be riveted as Ginny told of her daughter's courtship, engagement, and then prewedding widowhood after Matt's drowning two summers before.

Lucy didn't enjoy overhearing her mother talk about it, but she found she would deconstruct the way the story was told—Was the emphasis on their meeting? The beach proposal on Cape Cod? The son-in-law Ginny almost had? Lucy barely spoke of it now, but she found that when she did—to Kyla, or to some old man next to her on the subway who wondered why a pretty girl like herself hadn't been snatched up yet—she rushed through the beginning and middle of her time with Matt and zeroed in on the end.

There was the last time she'd seen him, at the ferry port on his way to Block Island, the grease stain he'd had on his shorts and hands from fixing his slipped bike chain that had left a waxy thumbprint on her shoulder, the scab on his forearm where he'd scraped himself on an upturned trowel in the garden. Lucy liked to pick at Matt, look for blackheads on his nose or pluck the stray hairs that he missed shaving, and she found that if she talked enough or if Matt were tired enough, she could dig at a hardened scab for a couple of seconds without making him wince or hold her back from scratching at his skin with her thumbnail.

She'd wondered about the scab when she found out Matt had been tangled in the sea reeds and drowned. The casket was closed, but Lucy had put her hands to it and thought about checking to see if the scab was still there. The drowning part, or the way she'd watched the ferryboat take Matt away from the mainland and out toward the island where he would two days later die, was the section of their relationship Lucy focused on. Ginny was wrapping it up now, Lucy could tell. She could make out her mother saying something about other fish in the ocean, not even realizing the tasteless- ness of her expression. She'd said it once before, and Lucy had said, "If there really are other fish in the sea, I hope they're live ones."

Then Ginny usually went on to say something about moving forward, about Lucy joining a law practice in town, maybe. Ginny still introduced Lucy as a lawyer though she'd never practiced, never even passed the bar—even when Lucy took a part-time job at the bookstore café in town.

Lucy's interest in being a lawyer had been faint to begin with, tempered by the thought of having a private country practice—a swinging sign by the front porch while Matt's garden flourished.

Lucy visited her brother, Jacob, in Connecticut for a weekend of respite after Matt's funeral. "You can have two more crackers and that's it," Jacob warned his toddler, Maddie. "Five," she countered, her small fist clutched around the Wheat Thin she already had. "I said two," Jacob said and threatened to take the yellow box from the table and stash it in the cluttered closet he used as a pantry. "Three," Maddie answered, waited a beat, and raised her eyebrows. Jacob nodded. "Three." Lucy watched as he lay the tiny squares on the table in front of his daughter. "She'd make a good lawyer," Lucy said, her arms over her chest, then flapping useless at her sides. Jacob turned to his sister. "Yeah, that's what Julie and I call it—lawyering. The barter system of two-year-olds."

Maybe then, maybe later—Lucy knew she wouldn't take the bar, wouldn't practice. She'd only just received her degree when Matt had asked her if she minded spending Memorial Day apart. His friend—now their friend—Justin had a boat out on Block Island, and they were planning on fishing the shallows for the bluefish that invaded the reefs and rock piles. Lucy had agreed— weren't you supposed to give men their space, show them that you were a self-sufficient woman? Lucy said she was sure Matt would have fun and figured his time away would be impetus for her starting her bar exam studying with nothing to distract her but the sounds of the garden at night. Sometimes Matt would lead her to the window and they'd peer out at their plantings as if they could catch them in the act of growing.

Ginny had liked Matt. She would say sometimes, since he had been in agriculture, just setting up his own organic farm, that her future son-in-law had grown on her. Matt laughed at the joke every time. Of course, she'd assumed Lucy would marry someone from the law school in Cambridge or maybe an engineer. But she'd watched Lucy and Matt in the garden together, seen them turning the soil, watched them lay pine branches loosely over the broccoli plants they'd grounded to protect them from the late-season snow. As she stamped snow and dirt from her boot soles, Lucy's cheeks would be cold and ruddied, and while she assumed Ginny, who might have popped by for coffee, was studying her daughter's mismatched layers of clothing, Ginny was really over-whelmed by how much the outside suited Lucy, how appropriate she was among the curling vines and stalks that bent, boneless, over the swollen zucchini.

Ginny goes to sit on the love seat next to Lucy and puts her hand on her daughter's knee. Lucy defends the milk stain on her black pants immediately. "They were clean, seriously, but then I spilled something on my way here in the car."

"It looks like milk," Ginny says and points to her daughter's white shirt. "Too bad you didn't spill it on your shirt."

"Kyla said you'd think I look like a waiter," Lucy says.

"Waitress, yes," Ginny says. "You do, a bit." Ginny shakes her head. "Poor Kyla, she's just saying that because she *is* a waitress."

"Don't start, Mom," Lucy says but is glad to deflect the cri-tique onto the nonpresent friend.

"Lulu, I asked you to come with me today because I kind of needed the support." She gestures to the assistants hovering by the dressing room. "They're too much for me. I need your opinion, someone who knows me." Lucy nods.

By the dressing room, Lucy inspects the two gowns Ginny is deciding between. "This one has the dip in the waist that I like," Ginny says, moving her hands across the garment like a game show host displaying a new leather luggage set. "But this one has the boatneck, which I think is very becoming on someone my age."

Lucy agrees with this last bit and says, "I think the boatneck works. And you should get it in cream, not white."

"Not lilac?" Ginny laughs. "The color of old ladies?"

"You're not old, Mom," Lucy says and touches the gowns again. She wants to touch her mother but doesn't. Then, right when Lucy is set to leave the moment, her mother—without fixing her hair, without letting her gaze wander to the stain on her daughter's clothes—looks at Lucy straight on.

"Neither are you," Ginny says.

It's late spring by the time Ginny's wedding outfit is stitched and fitted. She picks it up from the tailor and hangs it, sheathed in plastic, from a hook above the passenger-side window of her car. In the back of the Jeep, spread out on flat black garbage bags, are flats of tomato plants she plans to deliver to Lucy.

Along the dirt driveway up toward Lucy's house—the house she and Matt had only just put an offer on that is now only hers—small lights shaped like Chinese boat hats are still on, confused by the day's dark clouds. Prestorm, in the hush of the blue spruce trees that back the garden, Lucy slips her feet out from her red plastic garden clogs and sets the clogs by a bag of Nurseryman's Preplant fertilizer. Far off, eggplant-colored clouds suspend from thinner gray ones, looming bulbous and full.

Rooting into the loose dirt with her bare feet, Lucy thinks about Matt's lips, about the way he kissed her first on the side of the mouth and then looked at her, surprised, as if the action had come before the thought. She thinks about what they would have been doing on this day two years ago—were they planting the Early Girl tomatoes that were the first full-sized ones to ripen in the summer? From inside the kitchen she used to watch Matt pick the small, deep red ones, mouth one, and collect the rest in a shallow basket and bring them to the counter. Lucy would have drizzled

maple syrup, Worcestershire sauce, and lemon juice on a plate.
When the Early Girls were halved and put open side down onto the
plate, Matt and Lucy would stand there, staring at the tiny red
bluffs in a darkening sea.

Lucy was the first to give in, to pluck a tomato half and eat it.
The Early Girls had a slightly tough skin with a rich and sugary
juice, and Lucy liked them best of all. After the drowning, she had
forgotten to change the location of the tomato plants, though, and
cutworms had invaded, despite the aluminum foil wrappers she'd
put around the bases of the seedlings.

Lucy enjoys thinking about Matt. Not what they might have
been doing if he were alive, breathing in the dark lull of the raked
dirt, but what they had done at an exact moment two years before.
Maybe this was the day they'd gone to the fair on the town green
and been caught in tacky caricature, balloon-talking love to each
other from grotesque mouths. Each day could have been a day
marked by an event, like when they'd first boarded a plane together, or had sex by the stacked wooden logs at the farm. She and
Justin and Matt had stacked the wood themselves, brought it
down from Vermont, where they'd bought it cheap, cheaper than
you could get closer to Boston or down the Cape. Lucy learned
how to pile the wood in a beehive shape, the tall cone of logs creating a hollow inside, where the air could continue to dry it for the
next season.

Some days, Lucy looked in her date book to see if she'd kept a
record and could be sure if today was when they'd gone to Petro-
via's for soup before seeing a revival of *Mr. Smith Goes to Washington*
in the square, commenting on their movie-couple likenesses——didn't
all lovers go to black-and-white cinema revivals? Or maybe it was a
Thursday, the day they'd replaced the light fixture in the kitchen,
slipped the dead moths from the old one's curves, and watched their
flat bodies fall into the trash. Other days, Lucy's date book revealed
no details, and Lucy couldn't remember where they'd been, what

they'd discussed, and all day she would find herself edgy—what had she and Matt done on regular days, on days when they'd just been around and with each other?

In the shower sometimes, Lucy will indulge herself and count her life since he'd been gone. How many haircuts has she had since Matt died? What has she done each national holiday since? What clothing does she own that Matt has never seen? Which books? What movies has she watched without him? With panic, it occurs to her, thinking about her hair, that someday, with enough haircuts and growth, there won't be any hairs on her head that Matt has touched.

When Ginny's car stops by the copper beech tree, Lucy looks over and waves, suddenly excited to show her mother all the garden rows, to hold up the small placards she printed with herb names and then laminated. She'd gone to the coffee shop in town, taken more than her share of wooden stirrers, and superglued them to the cards. Heaped by the back door, they were ready to be staked, shoved past the topsoil down deep enough to avoid being relocated by the wind.

"Come see the dress!" Ginny shouts and opens the car door. The breeze has picked up. Past the trees and house are ocean swells topped with whitecaps. From the car window, the plastic garment bag billows out, flag-waving and rustling until Ginny tucks it back in, holds it steady.

"It's beautiful, Mom, really." Lucy nods to the dress. "I don't want to touch it." She shows her dirty hands.

"I have to take it home and put it in my closet until Saturday— I don't want Doctor Jim seeing it!" Ginny says.

"When will you stop calling him Doctor Jim?" Lucy asks.

"Oh, who knows? Maybe never." Ginny smiles like a bride. She'd met Dr. Jim Thorensson first when she was still married to Lucy's father, Mark, who had been admitted for observation after showing up with chest pain in the emergency room. He'd announced himself as Doctor Jim as if he were in pediatrics, but Ginny had been so grateful, so overwhelmed by his knowledge, that she hadn't been bothered. As the papers passed from Mark's lawyers to hers, Ginny had played mixed doubles at the club—usually losing cheerfully, until she was paired with Doctor Jim and they took each set from Aubrey Deltin and Trish Leonard. Since their introduction, even after he'd taken her to St. Bart's and engaged her at the George V in Paris, she still thought of him as Doctor Jim.

Ginny and Mark had eventually divorced, the silence stretching out between them like a sickening moment before a roller coaster reached its pinnacle and began its descent. That same silence was where Lucy felt solace after Matt died—she would retreat to her father's book-filled flat in Huron Village and page through the Signet Classics he'd picked up at the used bookstore but never read. Or she and Mark would sit on his roof deck. The place was small but spare, with two red plastic chairs in the shape of giant palms. Sitting in one of the hands, Lucy would cry until clear mucus coated her mouth, her eyes swelled, her father intermittently sighing empathy or touching her hair. She would open her mouth sometimes to thank him but come out with only "Dad" before crying again.

"Maybe I should keep it here." Ginny gestures the bridal dress at Lucy's house. "Just to make sure Doctor Jim doesn't lay eyes on it."

Lucy imagines the gown swinging, bodiless, in her closet and says, "I hope you don't call him that to his face." Then she laughs. "Doctor Jim."

"Not too often," Ginny says, and then, with her arms spread wide as if she were in a musical set in a garden, she says, "Doctor Jim the cardiologist—he's all heart!"

Lucy rolls her eyes. "Charming, Mother," she says and fixes her mother's scarf so it lies flat against her T-shirt, leaving soil crumbs on her mother's chest. "Sorry—now it looks like you've eaten an Oreo."

"Unlikely." Ginny sighs. She looks at Lucy's bare feet and is about to offer to buy her new shoes, something appropriate for gardening, when she remembers the load in the trunk.

"I brought you something," Ginny says.

They unload the flats, supporting underneath the flimsy plastic until the plants are near Lucy's red clogs.

Ginny holds up a shoe. "Oh, you already have an outdoor sandal. I was going to take you for a pair."

"Yeah, that's okay, these work well," Lucy says, slipping them on.

Ginny, perched above the soil, tries to uncoil the seedlings. Lucy asks, "Are you nervous for the big day?"

"A little, I guess," Ginny says. "I suppose I never really saw myself marrying anyone other than your father. But this is a good thing for me. Don't you think?"

"I do," Lucy says. Then, more dramatically, she says, "I do!"

From her pocket, Ginny takes out the slip of paper that the nursery gave her with the plants.

"I got you these," she says. "They're supposed to be very sweet. Tiny, but really delicious."

"Thanks, you didn't have to." Lucy scoops dirt out and into the holes puts a sprinkling of fertilizer before placing the first plant inside. Ginny, allowing her crouch to topple so the knees of her khakis are dusted with dirt, begins to undo the tomato seedlings from the flat boxes, holding each one a short time before passing it to her daughter.

After the row is complete, the leafy stems watered, Ginny puts her arm around Lucy and says, "Do you know the name of these tomatoes?"

Lucy shakes her head. She is overcome with emotion watching her mother sink in the dirt for her, with her.

"Matt's Wild Cherry," Ginny says. "I thought—I don't know what I thought, really. Just that it was a lovely name, and that you'd like them."

Lucy looks at her mother, the bride to be, and feels quiet tears start. Where will she be in August, when the peas are podded, the eggplants bosom-heavy, the rose potatoes and onions quiet underground?

"Sweetheart." Ginny rubs at Lucy's hair, doesn't try to calm it into order or slip it into an elastic holder.

"I have a date tonight, Mom," Lucy says, crying harder but looking out to the ocean. Ginny nods.

Before the sky lets down its swelling, the wind picks up. Unhinged, the weather vane on the housetop tips up until it points skyward. Lucy takes her mother's hand, thumbing impressions that stay mottled. She traces the hedgerows of Ginny's raised veins the way she'd done as a kid. What is shadow one day, is water the next.

Suburban Solstice, 1977

Next door, Alex's mom has a bag of pot in the kitchen junk drawer, but they don't know that yet. With blond hair that swings hip length, Patti, his mom, is the first grown woman aside from her mother that Lucy will see naked, but she doesn't know that, either. She is twelve years old at the solstice. By autumn, she will turn thirteen, just when the days are hemmed into mucky, unfire-flied evenings that start midafternoon.

Fishing hooks, their prongs splayed like ventricles, loose twine, Halloween candy left too long, chocolate Marathon bar flakes, and M&M's, their edges whitened, bits of dried grout, pencils, hair ribbons, and nails—all of these Alex and Lucy have taken out from the orange Formica-paneled drawer. Lined up, a deformed and ill-combined army, the stuff sits on the counter in a row until they tire of sorting through it and slide it all into the drawer, along with the unsifted items at the back. They take the quarters found at the drawer's bottom and head outside.

Through the sunken living room, with its plush beige carpet, they pause by the Plexiglas coffee table. The see-through, curved chairs are hardly there in the sunlight, more ghostly than furniture should be. Lucy thinks about saying this out loud to Alex, who has stopped to press the backs of his sneakers down so they become flip-flops.

"No blisters this way," he explains.

Alex's hair is as white-blond as his mother's, and it wisps down into his eyes until he tips his head upright, the fringe nearly long enough to tuck behind his ears. Lucy balances in a half-lean against the indoor hammock. Suspended from metal eye hooks on the ceiling, the double hammock is white, a woven mass of silky waxed rope with knots and loops so intricate the whole thing is a widow's web. Lucy is always drawn to it but rarely hoists herself inside. The hammock swings above the step down into the living room, and Alex will climb in and read comics next to Patti, who sometimes lies in it, legs in a widened V for balance while her hair dangles down through the string diamonds that have stretched to parallelograms. Patti's hair would touch the floor beneath the hammock, and she'd drag on a More 100, the soft green pack resting on the rise and sag of her chest. Lucy's parents furnished their house with Early American antiques, Shaker-influenced tables, quilted bedspreads, the blond wood cradle she'd slept in as a baby. Alex's place has an indoor hammock which seems grossly out of place, more evidence of Alex's house being the creepy fun house part of an amusement fair that Lucy both longs for and fears.

Outside, the tarmac's heat is so intense that, if Lucy stands in one place too long, her drugstore sandals begin to adhere to the paving. She jingles the found change in her pocket as they walk the length of the drive and scratches under her arm where the halter cuts into soft, untanned flesh. Alex is already kid-caramel brown, almost fourteen and losing his childhood hips. When they are adults, when she sees him for the only time past adolescence at some graduate school party in town, he will have put the weight back on again, belly and waist will have become one. Here, where the road winds down from his house to hers, they are long-legged, their coltish selves anticipating only mint-chocolate-chip ice cream from the Brigham's in town. It has not occurred to Lucy that she will miss him later, that she will miss anyone.

"I might get peppermint instead," Lucy says when they've turned onto School Street and the town center, spelled "Centre" on all the signs, is in view.

"No, you won't." Alex grins.

He stretches his palm out, and she hands him the money. Alex's hands are doughy, his cuticles ripped, nails squared and uneven from biting. Lucy's mother, Ginny, swats her daughter's hands if Lucy puts her fingernails in her mouth to chew, or if Ginny is across the room and can't reach for her, she'll raise one eyebrow and curl her lips until Lucy's hands are back, lap-resting where they belong. At the end of the drive, in the maple shade, Alex holds Lucy's shoulder back from the traffic. Above, the larks career from a soon-to-be-landscaped rhododendron, and she wonders if Alex has ever thought to kiss her.

Years before, when their parents still socialized, Alex's father would drive her, just for the thrill, unhelmeted on his motorcycle on the black tongue of driveway that separated Alex's house from Lucy's. She would like to say that she remembers the kind of bike it was, or how she felt up high, but she doesn't. The cigar reek on his father's suede jacket stays with her, the prickle of hairs on her arms from the exhaust heat, and how with each sway and turn she was sure she would reel off, fall and skid on the gravel, leaving her parents and brothers lemonade-sipping in the sprinkler spray on their front lawn, without her.

In town, Alex orders Lucy's ice cream, and it never occurs to her to mind. Kelly Hanson, the mean girl in Lucy's grade, slings by on her banana-seated bicycle while they eat their cones. Kelly's ponytails and handle streamers sweep back in the breeze, and even the way she pedals—body up, legs straight—seems cruel. Lucy's shoulders curl forward, her torso slumping. Kelly ignores her, and Lucy isn't sure whether it's relief she feels or like she missed out.

Alex watches Lucy watch Kelly and says, "I heard her dad's an alcoholic," as if that will explain everything.

The sun glints off the car roof in front of them, and Lucy makes her hand into a visor to watch Kelly ride away with one of the free lollipops dispensed at the dry cleaner sticking out of her mouth like a thin cigarette.

"I wish my bike had streamers like that," she says and licks the last of the green ice cream from where it runs onto her wrist.

"Let's look at home," Alex says and arcs his cone wrapper into the trash barrel.

They head for his house, splitting a Dr Pepper on the way back. Each turn, before sipping, they make sure the other has sucked clean the saliva from where it gathers on the soda can edge. Up by Meadowbrook, where the pines thicken, Lucy's mother drives by and tells Lucy it's time for her annual physical. Lucy has to leave Alex there, kicking up the dust on the roadside, while she goes to be weighed and measured.

Next year, she will switch to a female doctor at a hospital-based practice with magazines and pamphlets in the waiting room. Ginny has reassured Lucy that "it is time" to see a woman and that Lucy will feel more comfortable; Lucy suspects already that this has more to do with Ginny's comfort than her own. That her pediatrician is male hadn't registered with Lucy until her mother pointed it out. Lucy watches the physician make a note on her chart and wonders what information is contained in its papers, what they would reveal: not so much if she is of normal stature and well-seeming appearance but rather if he—this knowledge-able person—could somehow predict where she might fall on the happiness chart, the curve of life satisfaction.

Today, Lucy is oversized and dangling from the pediatric

vinyl-covered exam table. Stacked and closed up in glass canisters are sterile swabs, hypodermic needles in varying sizes, and tongue depressors. On the doctor's desk is a white plastic pelvis, the bones splayed like butterfly wings.

Afterward, Lucy and her mother sit parked in her car outside the doctor's office. A downed oak limb, a storm remain, blocks part of the sidewalk. They had lost power several days before, and had listened together in the candle-lighted room, she and her brother young enough somehow not to mind her father reading aloud. Her mother had changed into pajamas early—her nightgown billowed out and made her appear both larger and softer than she really was—and she'd let Lucy lean back onto her chest, her daughter's hands on hers. Lucy had felt the rise of her mother's veins, how they swelled in the heat. The rain had come, soaking the ground and driving the earthworms out onto the bluestone walkway, and they'd found them, withering, in the morning sunlight the day after.

"Well, you're growing, that's for sure," her mother says, clipping her hair back so it's fixed to her neck.

"I guess."

"You know, you could always ask me something. A question, I mean. If you have one," she says and is about to touch Lucy's face when she stops. In front of the car, a bag from the Shoe Barn swinging like a purse from his shoulder, Alex pretends to direct traffic. Ginny laughs, and Lucy feels the blush rise to her cheeks. Alex motions for Lucy to join him on the sidewalk.

"Do you want to go?" Ginny asks.

Lucy nods, despite feeling guilty about skipping out on their mother-daughter trip to the salon. A couple of times a year, her mother went to have her hair straightened and took Lucy along for a manicure. Lucy spent ages choosing from the wine reds and chestnut hues of nail polish, only to scrape it off at bedtime that night. Lucy went with her mother because Ginny wanted her to, because Lucy felt it was what girls did with their mothers—watch in silence as, under the cones of the dryers, mothers fell out of listening range and into the distance.

"Look over there." Alex points to a long cabinet in his pantry in which there might be bike streamers.

Lucy shakes her head and holds up leftover plywood planks from two summers before, when the carpenter Lou, who had only three fingers on his right hand and four on his left, had come to expand the deck and left scraps.

Alex drinks chocolate milk from a recess-small carton, and when he's done he puts it on the floor, stamps on it once, hard, and it pops. Spits of milk, the sappy, dark stuff from the bottom of the carton that never fully mixes in, are all over the floor. Lucy snags the sponge and wipes up what she can see, but Alex takes the sponge from her and slicks her legs with it, scrubs at a spatter on her ankle.

Back at the junk drawer, Alex takes the whole thing off its hinges and puts it down on the terra-cotta-tiled floor, where they can reexamine the contents. Lucy tries on Halloween waxed lips and is wearing them still when Alex pulls out metallic pink bike streamers in their plastic packaging. Lucy wonders why Alex would have pink ones, or if the color dictated their placement in the drawer, unused. He hands them to Lucy, and she fingers the shiny threads. He rifles through the drawer, plucking out Dum Dum lollipops with uncurled wrappers, an army knife neither can open, and then a tinfoil-covered bag.

Lucy removes the fake lips and puts them on the floor, where they grin up. Grotesque and swollen, they resemble her brother's when he had been stung by a bee and gone into anaphylactic shock, eyes puffed shut, throat closing up, lips rubbery and bloated. Alex unrolls the bag from the tinfoil.

"What is that?" Lucy asks, staring at the crumble of leaves and what looks like dirt. Alex doesn't answer but walks out, leaving the bag where it is, junked in the drawer, open.

Moments later, Alex's father, sweatbanded in his tennis whites, stomps into the kitchen to stare briefly at the stuff on the floor.

"Fuck," he says, right in front of Lucy, and then exits.

From her position, she can see him lighting logs and newspaper balls in the living room fireplace. Flames started, he runs for the kitchen, grabs the bag, and throws the whole thing in, plastic and all. Alex watches from the stairwell as the smoke billows out, then slinks upstairs.

"This isn't the first time," Alex's dad says to Lucy. Lucy wants to understand what this all means but doesn't until late in high school, when Riley Tiverton, her crush of senior year, faded flannel shirt and skinny brown corduroys, leaves in her car a similar bag of weed, which Lucy's mother finds and blames on her brother, Jacob, then in medical school, who takes the blame for his sister (and smokes the contents of the Baggie himself).

A week later, after Lucy, her parents, Mark and Ginny, Jacob, and Alex have grilled burgers and eaten them hot with melted cheddar on English muffins, Alex plays Frisbee with Lucy's brother. Shirtless on summer's longest day, the boys run barefooted and briar-scratched into the woods or way back onto the gravel to make their catch, unflinching as the stones jut into their arches.

Arms up into the darkening sky, Alex cheers for himself, his own exaggerated sports fan. Jacob, back from college until the Independence Day parade parties have passed, pretends to be a sportscaster, and Lucy slouches back into her chair to slap at the bugs, arms draped over her new breasts.

Salted from sweat, Alex asks Lucy if she wants to play pool at his house. Her father overhears and looks at his watch as if that will determine his answer. Inside, Ginny flaps open a garbage bag for all the paper plates and melon rinds that lie, arched and bitten empty, on the patio.

When they get back to the stable behind Alex's house, his mother, Patti, puts the brush to Diamond, her horse, and grooms him in the unlighted stable.

"Want the light on, Mom?" Alex asks.

"No," she says, quiet.

While Alex gets milk from the fridge, Lucy watches Patti from the back porch as she stops brushing and lights a cigarette. Smoking, Patti traces the outline of white on Diamond's brow and leans her lips onto his nose. Once, she'd showed Lucy how to feed a horse, palm flat and open, carrot or sugar cubes pressed up. Lucy remembers Diamond's muzzle, soft-haired like fruit. Staring at Patti, Lucy finds her somewhat out of focus, as though draped in gauze, her whole being beautiful, boneless like a flower. Then she thinks of her own mother's facial features, the corrected nose, the jut of jaw, the pressed hair, Ginny's perfectly shaped ears.

"Strawberry?" Alex asks, gesturing with the tin of Nestlé's Quik.

Lucy nods. She can see Patti drop the unfinished cigarette near the blooming rhododendron bush as she heads inside. Alex and Lucy can hear Patti's clogs on the stairs and then the rush of water in the walled pipes as she readies for her postgrooming shower.

Alex makes the milk too sweet, but Lucy drinks the pink of it anyway, too shy to say he's fixed it incorrectly, and puts the glass in the sink before going to the living room. The hammock sags, empty, and she goes to it to figure out how best to get in without flipping herself upside down. She thinks about lying in here with Alex, of the tangle of arms and rope, of lips.

Crying, holding a shiny black box, Alex holds it out half-open for Lucy to see before he goes upstairs. The contents—spoon, needle, purple drugstore lighter, vial—seem thrown together. Lucy follows him, but his door is closed. From the hall, she hears the click and tock of his cat clock and pictures the way the cat's eyes roll one way and back with each second. Open, the master bedroom door reveals the king-sized bed, unpeopled, tropical print sheets that mesh with the wall-sized fish tank behind until Lucy is surrounded by water and palms.

When Lucy turns back to the door, Patti is there, naked and wet, except for the sweep of white-blond hair. It's all one length save the rough chop of thick fringe at the front, and she twists it up and coils it back onto itself until it's knotted. Her pubic hair is just as light, the patch of it bright against her sun-browned skin.

"You're getting really tall, Luciana," Patti says in a hush that makes Lucy feel as if Patti has reached over and touched her. She uses the full name when everyone else calls her Lucy. "Really lovely."

That year, Lucy would try to change her nickname to Luce at school, and the swap would be successful, though neither Alex nor Patti would know that. In the first turn of leaves, Lucy would move suddenly, away from the changing suburban landscape into Beacon Hill, where the sloped bricks and set window boxes of tasteful lamb's ear and hydrangea seemed the same regardless of decade or year. Alex would board at that school in New Hampshire, where he'd be known as the Party Iguana, his father would develop malls in the suburbs, and, when Lucy was a junior in high school, Patti would overdose in Mustique.

"She was always the most beautiful girl in any room," Lucy's mother would say to her as they read the photoless obituary together. "You know, she and I had been friends since we were kids."

Lucy would try to imagine her mother, girl-sized next to Patti, but the image would seem impossibly remote, a black-and-white haze of braids and ankle socks. She could think of summer, though, of the sun-pull of afternoons, the stick of melted things, the hiss and spit of July Fourth sparklers just before they burst.

Animal Logic

After winning the Hortence Tuttle third-grade spelling bee by spelling *portentous*, Andrea and Gabrielle—the first-place team—scraped the top of the Italian ice prize and slid the shavings into their mouths with tiny wooden spoons shaped like paddles. The ice wasn't so much Italian, the girls knew, since it came from Jay-Tee's processing plant near San Antonio, but they felt lucky just the same. As they ate it, Andrea's mouth was green and Gabrielle's bright as a broken strawberry. They pressed their cheeks together and damage-checked in Andrea's pocket mirror. In the reflection, Andrea made her tongue pointed as a lizard's, darting it out and back, searching for something.

"Did you know iguanas actually breathe through their eyes?" Andrea said and let her lids close halfway as if she could hear a noise Gabrielle couldn't. "Or maybe they just taste through their noses or something, I can't remember."

Gabrielle felt her lips with her fingertips, expecting to find them swollen or chapped from the ice, but instead they were just sticky. Then she peeked again into the mirror and licked her mouth

while Andrea took a wide-toothed comb from her back jeans pocket
and put it through her brown waves. Folding in the sides of the
Italian ice container so that the whole thing became a spout, Gabrielle put her tongue to the beak of it and sipped the melted ooze.

Where the tarmac changed to dirt, the girls took off their sandals and held them over their shoulders, dangling them onto their
backs like caught pheasants or laundry. Set back from the road,
Andrea's house was mailboxless, so twice a week she went with her
mother to the post office in town to rifle through the mail marked
"General Delivery." Half-deaf, Andrea's mother speak-signed
everything. She had a provisional driver's license that allowed her
to travel to church or Mahoney's Garden Center, where she bought
discounted bulbs. Each week after Andrea had looked through the
bulb bins and chosen the ones with the fewest shoots already poking through, she and her mother went into town and looked for
letters and packages. Sometimes Andrea asked Gabrielle to write
her a card and post it, just so there'd be something to pick up in
town. Gabrielle used old scalloped-edged cards she found at the
Saturday jumble sales she went to with her grandpa on the town
green for a nickel, pictures of resorts that had closed decades ago,
taut-lawned schools she'd never heard of, dining cars photographed
the long way so they seemed to nose into the other sides of the
cards. Andrea Blu-Tacked the most recent postcard onto her desk
and kept the others tied up as a parcel with a blue hair ribbon.

"Careful not to step in the hole by the garage," Andrea warned as
they approached the wooden tumble of house, toolshed, and roof-
less silo that contained machinery parts and scrap metal instead
of grain. The garage was a carport midway through its remodel-
ing into a recreation room. To the left, near two baled stacks of
drywall, there was a large hole that hadn't been there the week
before.

A freestanding wet bar, an unused kitchen sectional, and a folding card table outfitted with a stereo were pushed up to the back wall, as if the space were in preparation for a dance party. Lining the tarp-walled side were metal lunch boxes and stray boots left by the construction crews that seemed to be there regularly, rebuilding something. Andrea turned to face Gabrielle, slipped her bare foot into a work boot, and pulled her sundress up, exposing her knees like an old-fashioned pinup girl.

"Look, I'm like one of those ladies in a war ad," Andrea said and brought her hands up to the back of her head so that her arms and elbows spread out like bat wings.

"Now all you need is a kerchief," Gabrielle said and hefted her book bag onto her right shoulder so she could spin Andrea around ballroom style.

"Is your dance card full?" she asked in a high-pitched voice. Since Gabrielle wasn't sure what a dance card was, she shook her head and feigned blushing, using her fingers like a fan over Gabrielle's grin.

Each Friday post–spelling bee was the same that spring and early summer. Whether the girls won for *arrangement* or *persnickety* or *resemblance,* and whether the reward was Italian ice or Charleston Chews, or a flaccid mustard-colored ribbon, they'd come back to Andrea's house to find a wall knocked through or string tacked into the ground to outline where a new study would be built.

There'd be a crew of construction guys, smoking Winstons, Pabst ring-tops discarded and stepped on, pressed into the exposed earth like seeds waiting to root. Or, with his tumbler of gin, Andrea's dad would take to the outside wiring with pliers, grounding himself in a plastic bucket. Later he'd pull Gabrielle and Andrea by their hands and lead them around each new project as if they'd never been there before.

"See here? The aluminum siding'll be gone by week's end. Shingles—that's the way to go."

Sometimes the girls would get to the house to find it and the yard empty, and they'd bring Andrea's yellow-and-orange crocheted blanket out onto the pebbly grass and lie flat, thinking how from above they might look like insects on a marigold, collecting pollen. Once, as they'd turned over to lie on their bellies, heels kicking skyward, they'd seen something wriggling by the chain fence and gone over to investigate. Tiny new rabbits curled in the shade. After they imagined keeping one as a pet, they saw that only one of the babies was alive—it lay there flanked on all sides by its fist-small, maggot-specked, and partly hollowed siblings. The mother, Gabrielle understood, wasn't there. Andrea had reasoned that she could have hopped away, looking for food or help, but Gabrielle knew better. "I think she just took off." Andrea and Gabrielle covered the dead bunnies with overgrown maple leaves, but the fanned greenery shifted in the wind when they'd left and gone inside.

After Andrea shed the work boots, she and Gabrielle walked around to the other side of the house, into the shadeless yard where a radio sat on the lower of two diving boards near the in-ground pool. Ten feet up, one of Andrea's brothers jackknifed into the water from the curved slide and surfaced holding a split flip-flop. He whipped it out of the pool so it hit another brother in the side of his head.

"You're fuckin' dead, loser," the thwacked one said and dove in, still shirted, for a water wrestle.

There were four brothers total, but Gabrielle couldn't tell one from the next long enough to have it matter. Each had a name that began with an *A* and seemed more suited to machinery or medicine than humans—Anderson, Alpern, Agrin, Arnoth. Loping across the lawn or emerging from the dark dank of the cellar doorway, one brother loomed taller than the next. Thick-armed from the free weights displayed like wine in the living room, they walked as if they held toddlers on both hips, wide-stepping and slightly out of breath.

All the members of Andrea's family had *A* names except her mother, Carin. Near their homeroom cubbies, Andrea had taught Gabrielle the sign language alphabet Carin had passed on and explained how sometimes you could use just the first letters of people's names to refer to them. After she'd spent the day at Andrea's, Gabrielle would leave in the wide quiet of her father's Impala with images of the closed fist of the sign-language *A* being thrust in the air over and over, as Carin called out to her husband, Allan, or to the boys. On her bare legs, Gabrielle would make the empty arch of the *C*—the sign looked exactly like the letter it represented, and then put it to the window and look through it as Andrea's house faded out of view.

"Let's go." Andrea gestured to the pool and was already lifting her T-shirt up to slide her arms out when they reached the semi-privacy of her room. Between the dining room and den, there was a triangle of space that Carin had sealed into a room by hinging particleboard so that the front wall itself was one giant door. From the inside, you had to slide your fingers underneath the plank's edge to close it, and even still, there were gaps that seeped pool light at night, and sometimes there'd be unidentifiable eyes on the other side that Andrea hardly noticed but that kept Gabrielle from changing in there.

Gabrielle wore her bathing suit underneath her clothes on Fridays, knowing they'd end up in Andrea's room, and as she stood up to spell words at the bee, she'd feel the rise of material under her shorts or shrug her shoulders, trying to ease the cut of the straps in the soft pocks of flesh between underarms and across her new breasts.

"Oh, here she is everyone, Miss Tex-ass, Andrea Arginello," one brother mock-announced from the top of the slide.

Andrea ignored him, just as she paid no attention to the girls at school who called her Ag-jello, and took Gabrielle's hand to lead her over to the shallow end, where they collected damp blue kickboards. In the water they tried to balance on them, sitting first and then attempting to kneel until the foam would suddenly burst from under them and pop right out of the pool. The brothers stayed mainly past the four-foot mark, diving and fountain-spraying chlorinated water from their mouths. Or they'd link their arms backward onto the rungs of the sun-hot ladder and do pull-ups half-submerged.

Sometimes, Gabrielle would make the mistake of looking too long at one of them, and they'd take it as an invitation to come and dunk her. If she got to a corner in time, she could keep hold of the sides as she went under, but without anything to hold, she'd go right to the bottom. She'd feel the slots of the drain with her toes, and look for thrown change to keep from panicking. In the silent glint beneath the surface, Gabrielle could easily envision not coming up, just allowing the fluid to overtake her until she bloated there.

Andrea often would intervene and sacrifice herself, knowing how much being held under the water scared her friend. Andrea played the game and came up sputtering and laughing as Anderson or Agrin palmed her small head, pretending to dribble her like a basketball. Gabrielle would press her back into the cragged pool edge, letting the jet spray go into her thighs as Andrea plummeted and resurfaced, never finding the right time to thank her.

After the brothers and whatever friends they had over had emptied a case of Schlitz, they'd want to see the girls swim naked in the pool in the bug-cluttered dusk of late June. Sometimes Andrea agreed to it, or Mara, their friend who put tampons in before she'd ever gotten her period. From the kitchen window, Carin would watch, and if she thought the boys had gone too far, she'd use her voice to call them in for a made-up errand, sounding like someone caught underwater.

In the late-afternoon sun, the brothers hosed the slide so their legs wouldn't stick on the way down. The lubricating mechanism had failed years before, and no one had been successful in fixing it. The girls watched one cannonball off, and when he came up bleeding from his head, no one said anything. He pressed a towel to it, tilted his half-drained beer back, and later came inside to where they sat having Cokes and eating smoked oysters from a tin on the table. The salted oil coated Gabrielle's mouth and slicked Andrea's lips so they looked glossed. She fake-pouted at Gabrielle, who mimed taking her friend's photograph.

Andrea's mother alternated wiping the counter and turning the pages of her accountancy text with a licked finger.

"Ma," the bleeding brother said.

He had to tap his mother on the shoulder so she could see he wanted her attention. When she spoke, her mouth wrapped around the words, making it sound as if her tongue was folded back on itself. Gabrielle had tried, in the privacy of her bedroom at home, to mimic the voice until she shamed herself into sleep. Carin looked at the cut and made the sign for stitches and hospital visits. Andrea looked at Gabrielle, knowing she'd have an opinion. Gabrielle's father moonlighted the eight-to-eight shift in the Chestertown emergency room on Fridays, and she had a vague idea about what needed sutures and what gash might heal on its own.

Andrea stood up and pulled on the brother's arm so they could get a better view. He leaned onto the table as if he was about to do a push-up and lifted the bloodied towel off until Andrea nodded at him. Outside, the other brothers and their friends rolled out long blue sheets of plastic tarp and sliced them free with X-Acto knives. They squeezed dishwashing soap from a bottle shaped like a legless woman, their hands cupping the hip part, then sprayed water over the length of it and took turns running full tilt until they slipped and sped to the grassy end. The whole house seemed to Gabrielle on the verge of disaster.

"I think you need stitches," she said, careful not to touch the brother.

"Yeah, well, I think you need a rope burn!" He took her forearm into his hands and twisted the skin one way and back until she kicked him in the shin with her sandal side. Gabrielle's arm pulsed, a bruise already beginning to seep up from underneath. Carin tapped her son on the shoulder and scolded him with signs and words Gabrielle couldn't make out.

Andrea's father appeared at the top of the stairs holding an iced drink, glanced at his son, and took his *Want-Ads* over to the side porch to sweat and circle things in the sun.

From one of the kitchen drawers, Carin pulled out a tube of that glue from the advertisement on television where the man's hard hat was glued to a steel beam and was strong enough to keep him suspended there for as long as he gripped his hat. There were only two chairs in the kitchen, so Andrea got up and offered hers to her brother as Carin snipped the end of the glue tube and went to her son's forehead. In a careful line, she squeezed the clear sealant onto the boy's skin and then pressed the edges of the cut together, blowing on it, until the sides adhered.

Gabrielle thought about the words she would use later to tell her father and pictured him looking back at her in the rearview mirror with his eyebrows raised, then how he might ask her to spell the word *adhesion*, and she would, the letters fluttering into place like sparrows.

* * *

Carin shooed the girls out of the kitchen so she could study. In her room, Andrea unfolded a bulky foam chair until it lay flat and long enough for both of them to sit.

"Here," she said and handed Gabrielle a Choose Your Own Adventure book and took one for herself. At the bottom of each page, the reader was left with a choice as to how to proceed— choose to go in the hot-air balloon over the Sahara and maybe you'd wind up lost over the blank expanse of ocean, or trek through the desert and maybe you'd find a cave filled with gold coins and ruby-pointed crowns. Andrea read hers the way the author intended, making her decision and going to the corresponding page until her journey had ended. Gabrielle tried to do the same but found herself marking pages with her fingers, reserving, revising possible outcomes in case the one she'd chosen ended in shark-infested waters or locked in an abandoned castle.

Gabrielle's way took longer, so Andrea stood behind her, braiding her hair, then undoing her work. She twisted it up and examined her from the front to see if she liked the style. Fish-bone braids took the longest and looked the most complicated, even though they were simple to do, and Gabrielle liked the feel of her hair being sectioned and then tightened, the trace of Andrea's fingers on her neck. With guilt, Gabrielle wondered if Andrea knew this was one of the reasons for the repeat visits; Gabrielle had no one else to braid her hair, and it felt so gentle, like the moments right before sleep. She tried all the braids she learned from Andrea on the spider plants her father keeps in the kitchen, their green tufts forever sprouting new baby plants.

"Can you try a side ponytail?" Gabrielle said and didn't look up in case Andrea decided to stop brushing altogether.

"You don't know about hair the way I do," Andrea said and

increased her grip. As Gabrielle flipped the pages of the book, Andrea nudged her to read out loud, and they stayed like that until Andrea's father called up.

"Andrea, your friend's ride is here," Allan yelled from underneath the floorboards, where he stood at the wet bar dog-earing pages in a tool catalog. Maybe Allan still didn't know to call her Gabrielle, even after months of the same routine. Andrea told Gabrielle to wait for her down there while she helped her mother chop red onion for the hamburger meat that sat cooling in a metal bowl in the fridge.

Down the freestanding stairs that connected the den to the garage, Gabrielle saw Allan looking out past the end of his driveway. Her father's car wasn't there. "Guess it was someone else," Allan said, pointing to the wafting dust on the road. "I'm sure he'll be here in a minute or so."

Gabrielle watched her friend's dad, wondered what he thought about then, if the melon light above the neighboring houses made him miss someone, if the ice in his drink had melted and seeped into the alcohol the way it did in root beer, if he minded the wood filings dispersed into tiny coils that nestled near his toes.

Without turning to her, he said, "Carin and I dance in here."

He didn't gesture, but Gabrielle figured he meant in the open garage space and not in his head. She went and stood next to him, closer than she ever had, and she could hear him breathe in between drink sips. He hummed then, a song she knew from a recording her grandfather had played when he'd dealt round after round of king's corner in the one-room apartment he decorated with her spelling bee ribbons. Allan looked at Gabrielle and, tipping his glass, said, "I'd offer you some, but you probably wouldn't like it."

He kept humming until she felt herself about to sway. Midges flitted into the garage, and Allan redirected the black specks away from them as he led the girl in a waltz. The generator buzzed, and Gabrielle noticed the fine dew-sweat that clung to the hairs on Allan's arm. He wasn't holding her tightly, but she felt he could lift her up at any minute and she would be put to flight like some wind-ripped blossom. Allan's drink was gone, but he kept the glass pressed to her back. They turned once more and spun, and Gabrielle noticed he'd stopped humming and looked at her the way her father had when he'd collected the cat from under the Impala's tire.

"You're a good dancer," Allan said as he let her go.

Andrea appeared in front of them, her face registering nothing of what she'd seen, and pulled Gabrielle to the edge of the driveway, where Gabrielle's father sat, the car idling, waiting to take her home. They could see the curls of barbecue smoke from the backyard. Andrea put the back of one of her hands to Gabrielle's nose so she could smell the sharp onions on her friend's skin. "Smell," Andrea commanded. "My mom taught me to cut them under cold running water. You know, so you don't cry?" Gabrielle wondered what else Carin had taught, the moments missing from her own motherless life, if there were a checklist somewhere that might explain all the practicalities she lacked. Only when she is an adult will it register as significant to Gabrielle that she had so many feelings toward a woman who—literally—could not hear the need for her, one who communicated in near silence—not to mention the odd sadness of dancing with someone else's father while her own father rushed through his ER patients to come collect her.

Gabrielle liked when her dad arrived late and she joined the tumble that was Andrea's family cookout. The girls would be offered rare burgers, sometimes so rare they were cold inside, sometimes cut in two, the half circles put into hot dog rolls and relished, whether she wanted it or not. She and Andrea would take their

dinners away from the rest and go to the side of the house, where
a doorless fridge sat turned on its length. They were still just
small enough to fit in it, and they'd fold their legs to their chests,
watching the sun sink behind the juts of pine and leaf-swollen
oaks in the neighbor's yard. From her pocket, Andrea would take
a lollipop and they'd share it—each taking a lick or two until the
center was revealed and they gnawed the last of the sugar crust
from the white stick.

The back end of the sea green Impala might be visible then,
and Gabrielle's father would give a short lean on the horn until
Allan yelled from the backyard that it was time to go. Slinging
Gabrielle's book bag over her shoulder, Andrea would walk her to
the car, where her father sat wearing his stained hospital scrubs.
Pointing to a smear of yellow or the splotches of dried blood on
his shirt, Andrea would make a face at her friend as they moved in
to hug good-bye.

Buckled into the backseat, where Randall, her father, felt she
was safer, Gabrielle would wave to Andrea and then undo the
straps of her bathing suit and let the ends dangle under her shirt.
After she'd been wearing the thing all day, her skin would keep
the string's mark as if unaware it had been undone. Out the side
window, Andrea would shrink to cutout size, and Randall would
ask how Carin's accountancy studying was going. Gabrielle would
shrug and feel her tongue roll in her mouth, forming words and
then spelling them as if she had only half her hearing.

In bed that night, after her father had smoothed her hair away
from her face and kissed her forehead, Gabrielle took his hand and
showed him how to trace letters in his palm. It was something she
did at the spelling bees as she waited her turn, and it was something Andrea did with her mother late at night if they were both
unable to sleep and wanted to sit together in the dark kitchen
without waking anyone.

June was almost over, so Gabrielle wrote *summer* in her father's open hand, and he wrote *sky, cloud,* and *sun,* until she told him he was being too easy and he wrote *honeysuckle, cocoon,* and *marigold.* Summer would pass, and in the fall Andrea and Gabrielle would be placed in their own Language and Learning group. They would read about a fox so fantastic it slipped into another animal's skin, and never came out.

Voler

Heather's smoking the pot Celia's boyfriend, Vaughn, gave her as a graduation present in June. She'd kept the stuff secreted away in an empty Sucrets box in her top desk drawer since June and took it out only an hour or so ago, when she and Jenna came back from Harvard Square. They—really Heather—want to change before going to a party at the dorm of someone they went to high school with and haven't spoken to since graduation, when their class erupted and seeped out into the world.

"Here," Heather offers Jenna in the sucked-in smoker's voice.

"Not right now, thank you," Jenna says and thinks how funny it would be if she could tell her parents how polite she is, even when it comes to drugs.

Jenna doesn't want to be high. Drunk, maybe, since what else is there to do during Head of the Charles weekend except row a boat or stand sidelined while someone else oars to victory or wander around feeling nostalgic for high school days, which are still too close to feel anything but relief that they are gone? Jenna thinks about her first semester at Dartmouth, about the brick and creeping vines that live even in winter. Just like in the hand-book photographs, students sprawled on the quad and hiked themselves breathless with weighty packs up the White Moun-tains, then returned to the dorms to drink until they threw up. Or they'd write papers due the next morning, the football players keeping wads of Skoal in the pouch between lower lip and gum, spitting into empty soda cans, while Jenna watched through her room's open door. The tin smell the radiator emitted in her dorm room came with nightly dull tapping sounds, as if some small creature lost in the looping pipes clinked along trying to get out. Those noises were different from the sighs and sheet shuffles her roommate made the first couple of weeks before she settled on some junior named Mark, who spent enough time in the room that he had his own drawer in the roommate's school-issued dresser.

Jenna suspected already that, while she would make it through the four years until graduation, she wouldn't much use her degree. She worked ten hours a week at the Bagel Basement, even though she didn't need the extra cash, just wanted the company of the bakers and the rank, yeasty scent from the bagel dough. The floating rings that would become sesame or poppy seeded gained their high-gloss exteriors from the hot-water bath Jenna ran. Like inner tubes, the bagels bobbed and danced down the length of the boiling stream until they were ready for the oven. Part of sopho-more year you could spend a semester working, and Jenna had visions of going somewhere to learn how to bake. Something about the science of it appealed: the exact temperatures necessary to make dough behave the way you wanted—to ensure its rise or crust, to make it fly up and swell.

"My parents would hate it if I didn't do something really good with a degree from an Ivy League school," Jenna says suddenly into the blank air. Each word comes out as a gray-white gasp. She hasn't admitted the thought before, but since Heather is focusing on getting high and staying that way, Jenna figures she can say anything without having it resurface later.

"Isn't it funny how I thought we'd go to college together? But there you are, in the snow, while I'm— What was I going to say? Not in the snow?" Heather laughs at herself. When Heather— wide-mouthed, tall, perpetually tanned—laughs at herself, Jenna feels drawn to her, magnetized toward her friend's disheveled beauty.

Somehow, Heather claimed she'd missed the college application and interview process altogether and was taking the year off, supposedly to become a campus peer educator at Harvard—warning students about alcohol abuse or stress-related anxiety, keeping piles of pamphlets stocked in the office, each one detailing a sexually transmitted disease or gynecological issue. Heather had mailed one pamphlet to Jenna, highlighting how many times the word *labia* appeared, insisting that it could be a new expression. Jenna never commented that Heather seemed to spend as much time sleeping as she did peer-educating and so far hadn't begun looking at schools for the next year, either. If she'd gone to a local college, Jenna thinks, she would have spent more time with Heather, and maybe pressed her for reasons, but from up north, away, it didn't seem fair.

Across from where the girls are standing, the Charles River seems solid, sheened by the streetlights. Groups of guys in college-name sweatshirts hustle by while Jenna and Heather remain unseen, tucked to one side of a Gothic-style apartment building. Jenna is on her third beer; only four would fit in her pockets, and she feels lighter since having had a couple, either due to the disposed of cans or the beer buzz, she's not sure which.

"Look up!" Heather instructs, tilting her head back so her face is nearly parallel with the ground, her nose its own mountain for the miniature; a whole breed of people Jenna imagines marching up and tent-pitching before eating tiny s'mores. Above, the apartment turrets seem to sway together, linking, then undoing themselves to reveal the shaving of moon slunk in the sky behind.

Jenna follows Heather's lead, but only for a second before saying, "I think it looks cooler to you."

"I think you're right!" Heather laughs and then drags hard on her cigarette joint. She'd spent time hollowing the Camel Light of its tobacco and refilling it with pot while Jenna sat on the bathroom counter trying to catch a glimpse of herself from the back by angling the door mirror at the one over the sink. Heather had tucked the cigarette into a hard pack, and then they'd gone out together to watch the races.

Oars flecked the water, the sculls slipped along, moving to the yells of "Stroke! Stroke!" until some team won and the people lining the bridges shifted to watch another race, happening along some other part of the river. Heather waved wildly from where she stood on the reed-banked swell of land just past the boathouse.

"Who are you waving at?" Jenna asked.

"No one!" Heather laughed, swinging her flannel shirt above her head the way she had once before, when the smoke alarm had gone off in the midst of baking hash brownies in her parents' kitchen. "That's the point—everyone thinks I'm rooting for them, but really, I don't know who the hell they are!" Heather seemed so cool, Jenna thought, so relaxed and sure of herself in ways that continually elude Jenna. Not that Jenna wouldn't think to wave, she would, only she would feel sad if no one—even people she didn't know—waved back.

They stayed like that awhile and then had burgers and salted pumpkin seeds some students were selling from a barrel. Dipping a measuring cup into the pile, they poured some seeds into a brown paper coffee filter. Jenna held the thing like an ice cream as they walked around Harvard Square, hoping to see people they

knew, mainly boys they'd had crushes on who had graduated before them and gone away to places like Wesleyan and UVM and
come back playing guitar, looking to let some girl borrow their
school shirts for the weekend. When Heather took a couple seeds
into her mouth, she swirled them around, only to suck the salt off,
then spit the wet remains onto the pavement.

Now Heather says, "I love pot. Really." She pauses and puts her
hand in front of her face as if she's dodging paparazzi. "I'm blocking the moon out—all by myself!"

"Good for you," Jenna says and does the same thing with her
beer can.

"But I do so love the weed. I wish that sounded as profound as
I feel it, you know? I bet Vaughn knew that. Probably, he thought
I'd sleep with him or something just because he gave me some.
And I wouldn't—no way would I lose my virginity to him."

Heather hadn't slept with anyone, ever, and talked about it
more often than Jenna thought necessary. When their friend Celia
had been around, she'd rolled her eyes and said, "We know, we
know, you're incredibly virginal. We get it."

But Jenna just listened and chalked the drama up to Heather's
early days, when she was the child, then teenage lead in a couple
movies. When her costars went on to be part of that notorious teen
actor crowd in the eighties, Heather had reconnected with them
long enough to make out with the hot, preppy guy but had stormed
out of his hotel room in New York shouting, "I'm still a virgin for
fuck's sake!" when he'd tried to video her in the shower. There'd
been a shot of Heather in some celebrity gossip rag, which caused
brief but exciting school scandal. At school, Jenna had felt lucky
when Heather chose her for a scene partner in Drama and invited
her over that weekend, just to cement the friendship.

Opening the last pocketed beer, Jenna says, "So, whatever happened with you and Vaughn, anyway?"

Heather gathers her hair into a heap and then lets it go, saying, "You know, who the hell knows? I mean, we saw each other a couple of times during the summer. Then, that night I didn't go with you and Celia to dinner before leaving for college, I almost let him— Well, I don't know. I didn't see him after that." Heather swallows air like a shepherd nosing out a car window, gulping. "Vaughn. Vaughn. It's weird. In my head he is still *vawn*, even though I know he's not."

Vaughn had worn a shiny Celtics jacket the first time Celia had brought him to a party and pronounced his name with a Chelsea or Southie accent so it sounded like *vawn*. Big-shouldered and muscled enough so the senior boys hadn't made fun of him, he'd dropped his accent the next time, becoming Von. Celia had bought him a button-down shirt from Brooks Brothers to wear open and baggy over a T-shirt, but the sizing was off, so it looked lent instead of owned, as if he'd found it in a cousin's closet.

"But so, you never told Celia? Or, I mean, she never found out?" Jenna asks. She pulls Heather down onto the brick-rimmed walkway and wraps her jacket tightly around her, thinking about the townie Vaughn—his beer runs, his undone sneaker laces, the way he touched Heather on the ass when Celia had her head turned toward the keg. At that first party, Heather had gone off with Vaughn, supposedly to buy more Rolling Rock, but they'd come back an hour later with no beer.

In French class the next afternoon Heather had mouthed her confession to Jenna. When Jenna shrugged her shoulders and held up her hands, miming she didn't understand what Heather was trying to say, Heather had taken an empty page of her notebook and written in block letters "I made out with Vaughn," then turned the paper so it faced outward, bold like an exit sign.

Right when Jenna would have reacted, she was called on to read aloud from Baudelaire's "La Mort des Amants," so all the lines came out surprised instead of lusty or sad, as the poem intended. She had memorized it and liked the words; Jenna had copied the poem with a fountain pen into the front of her journal alongside a recipe she'd clipped from a gardening magazine. She left her mother's *Gourmet* and *Bon Appétit* magazines filled with window-shaped holes and bits of paper that fluttered aimless to the ground. One canning and preserving magazine Jenna had taken in its entirety and brought to school to show Heather, who feigned interest outside the girls' gym before tennis.

"How come you like food so much?" Heather asked while Jenna poked her fingers through the squares of the racket strings.

"How come you're fooling around with your friend's boy-friend?" Jenna shot back, thinking that would be the end of the questions and she could go to the bathroom to page through the quince jams and jellies in the quiet stall.

"She's your friend, too," Heather said, then rolled her eyes at herself. "I'm not sure, really. Maybe I don't think people belong to people. Do you?"

"You mean like marriage?"

"I mean," Heather said, "our bodies are just these things that we float around in. It's not like they belong to anyone. It's like I'm just borrowing Vaughn—what can I say?"

Heather rubbed the sole of her tennis shoe against the brick wall, tracing a rectangle, and then tried not to cry. Sometimes Jenna couldn't tell if Heather was acting for an unseen film crew or if she really was upset. Jenna put her arm across Heather's shoulder, thinking at the very least she'd have a walk-on role in the scene Heather had made.

"Are you okay?" Jenna asked.

Heather didn't say anything, and she didn't have a long, sobbing speech the way she'd had at Flynn's party sophomore year, when she'd actually attracted a crowd. She took the magazine from Jenna's hand and looked at a couple of pages before folding a corner down and saying, "This looks good. You should make this."

From the bleachers Jenna watched Heather play doubles with two other varsity teammates. She looked down at the recipe her friend had marked. Persimmon Eggplant Relish called for only forty minutes in the kitchen, but Jenna couldn't decide whether it sounded unusual or just disgusting. On the next page was a recipe for Peach Preserves. Jenna spoke the name out loud with an accent, as if she was saying "Jesus Saves," and told Heather when she came off the court sweating.

"Peach preserves!" Heather said to anyone who came by. Then, when Jenna turned to face her, Heather put her hand to Jenna's forehead, pushing her away, pretending to heal her. "Peach preserves!"

Of course it turned out that Vaughn was tonguing half the girls in Boston, not to mention Chelsea, so Celia broke up with him, still unknowing of his involvement with Heather. Celia was going to Stanford anyway, so Jenna and Heather knew they wouldn't see much of her after the summer. Jenna went back and forth, wondering if the physical distance made it okay that Heather had never confessed to what she'd done, or if Heather had somehow saved Celia's feelings by never letting her know that Celia was Vaughn's second choice.

At graduation, Celia tossed her long, red hair over one shoulder, undid the clasp on the chain Vaughn had given her, and let it slip into his open hand before taking her place in the horseshoe of chairs by the podium. After the headmaster called Heather's name and she returned to her seat with her rolled up diploma, Vaughn had come over, crouched next to her, and slipped a thin bag of pot into the tied scroll before slinking off to his car.

In Jenna's yearbook, Heather had written in French one of the stanzas from the poem they'd studied in class, the one about two spirits mirroring each other. Jenna had pictured speaking to Heather every week once she was up in New Hampshire, but they'd spoken only once since college had started, and that was when Jenna was home already for the long weekend.

"I was going to tell Celia," Heather says. "But then I figured it didn't really matter. I mean, it's all in the past, right?"

Jenna remembers something. "How come you never called me back when I left my number at school?" Sitting on the ground, both girls are flicking pebbles onto the walkway. Heather touches the flaking edges of a maple leaf, then puts it in her hair.

Letting out one last puff of heavy smoke, she says, "Didn't I? Maybe I thought I did." And then, "I have to lie down."

A van pulling rowing sculls stops near where the girls are sitting, and Jenna half-considers asking for a ride back to Heather's house. Heather's parents live in one of the university houses past the square, at least a mile away. Heather lies on her back, her legs splayed and loose; her hair covers part of her face. Jenna reaches over to push it away and says, "Heather, if I ever have a boyfriend, don't borrow him, okay?"

But Heather doesn't answer, not even when Jenna shakes her, kneeling by her face as if she's about to do mouth-to-mouth.

"Hey, Juliet, cut the crap," Jenna says, trying not to sound worried.

Just before Jenna lowers her cheek to check if Heather's breathing, Heather grabs the back of Jenna's head and pushes her down so the girls are kissing.

Jenna pulls away and stands up, looking down at Heather as if she's a cutout cookie, all limbs outstretched.

"I am so much more Ophelia than Juliet," Heather says, and then, "Help me up, Jen."

"Sure. Of course," Jenna says and sounds as if she's trying gracefully to pass a casserole dish down the table instead of taking care of Heather, whose whole body seems to bend and then right itself with the wind. They begin to walk toward the square, heading to Heather's house.

"I think I'm too high," Heather says, and it comes out soft, as if she's given up on something.

"Definitely," Jenna says.

"Talk to me so I don't pass out. Please, Jenny, please," Heather says, but since she's slurring, the *please*s sound like *peas, peas*.

Jenna talks fast, trying to hold Heather's attention. "Well, back to what I was saying. Personally, I wouldn't want you to—you know—take my boyfriend for a test run while I was driving him—or whatever crappy analogy you want to make. You're like my best friend, but still. I just think people should be nicer, that's all. And not think about themselves so much, you know?"

"All you think about is yourself." Heather laughs, stepping off the sidewalk into the jetsam-littered street. "And what your parents think. You don't know how the rest of the world works."

"That's so not true," Jenna says and steers them both away from a group of rowers, still outfitted in their crew shirts. But she knows it is true, that she cares more about what her parents think of her life than about what she does, that the adult world still hovers at arm's length. When will she know how mortgages work, or term insurance, use phrases like *fiscal year* or *tax burden*, or—forget those—just the word *boyfriend*? An Andean band plays on the corner near the newsstand, and outside Au Bon Pain people sit chewing on late-dinner sandwiches, watching a guy throw fire up into the air from his mouth, only to have it explode and instantly disappear.

"Why can't you just do what you want? Go open a restaurant, go to Paris, go bake bread," Heather says and points to the clouds in the fall sky. "They're moving so fast, aren't they?"

"Yeah, they are." Jenna hefts Heather's weight onto her side, grabbing under her arm to support her.

In the middle of the flute music and swaying fire watchers, Heather turns to Jenna and pokes her cheek, feeling the give of the skin before saying, "Who am I to talk, really, right?"

Jenna looks at Heather and wants to tell her how beautiful she looks with her unwashed hair and ruddy cheeks, how fluid her friend's movements are when she's inebriated. Jenna says, "You have the right to your opinion, O drugged one."

Heather tilts inward so her forehead and Jenna's temple touch. Gauzy, the long-skirted girls nearby twirl to the sidewalk guitarist who plays a too-slow cover of a Blind Faith song. Like moths, they flit and bend, unaware of Heather and Jenna standing in their midst.

"Jenna, do you know what I am? Do you know?"

"Let me guess," Jenna says, caught between amusement and annoyance. "You're very very very very high?" She thinks of other words she could put in: *wild, funny, extreme, lovely.* Then Jenna thinks the word *ruined*, but can't think why.

"Yup," Heather says, and when the song ends and there's a moment of quiet on the street, she adds, "And I am also a girl who got—who— Did you know my stepbrother raped me?"

Jenna chases Heather down the street through the red tint of taillights on the fallen maple leaves and follows her into the house entrance of the dorm where Heather's parents are the university-assigned parents. Upstairs, there's no light coming from the parents' room, and Jenna thinks about who she could call to help while Heather strips herself of her jacket and shoes and drinks whiskey from the cut-glass decanter in her stepfather's study.

"Heather, what can I do?" Jenna asks and tries to get the bottle away.

"You can just fuck off," Heather says. "Or drink."

Jenna swigs some just to hold Heather off from having more. Already, Heather is about to fall over, and when she does, she sits cross-legged on the kilim rug and starts to undress herself. Jenna thinks how orderly Heather is with her clothing for someone who is so wasted. Each article is folded and piled up until, naked, Heather stands up and goes into the crawl space under the oak

desk where the housemaster is meant to sit while signing university papers or disciplining undergrads.

Jenna knows now she has to get Heather's thin and shrill-voiced
mother from bed, where she lies, eyes covered with a sleep mask
like the ones they issue on overnight flights. She tries to form in her
head the words she'll use before saying them out loud. Jenna catches
herself in the hallway mirror and blushes even though she's alone,
embarrassed that she cares about Heather's mother assuming that
they both smoked pot, that maybe Jenna is responsible for her too-
high daughter. The parents' room is curtained gray, the mother's
body undistinguishable under the feather duvet. Jenna touches the
side of the bed, and when the mother's eyes are open, she spills
everything out and leads her downstairs to where Heather can't
stop rocking, balled up and still under the desk.

When Heather's mother can't get her to come out, she manages somehow to get in there with Heather and holds her, saying,
"I know, I know. Oh, Heather, honey, I know." Heather's mother is
softer than Jenna has ever seen her, yellow-nightgowned and big-
chested, like a woman on a syrup bottle.

Later, Heather's mother explains that the nineteen-year-old
stepbrother accompanied Heather on the movie shoots long ago,
that Heather hadn't remembered what happened until her first
gynecological exam at seventeen. In the shock lights of the exam
room, the doctor suggested that Heather had been sexually active
at least once despite Heather's shaking head and handed out several pamphlets detailing date rape and incest while Heather, detached somehow from her blue-gowned body, watched the scene
as if she was the offstage actor waiting for her cue—only she kept
thinking, What comes next? Jenna listens and can't believe she
hadn't known about this, wonders how Heather kept it all so quiet,
even when Mandy Jenkins had been assaulted sophomore year
and everyone at school knew, except that had been by a stranger.

Jenna stands watching Heather and her mother until she is motioned upstairs, leaving them together in the darkened room. Jenna
is struck by the idea of family betraying itself, of those boundaries
being crossed. In the hallway, she picks up Heather's coat and
hangs it on the rack near the kitchen. Since the kitchen serves the
entire dorm, it's huge, industrial. The enlarged ladles and colan-
ders lure Jenna inside, where she lets her fingertips graze the stove
knobs, the stainless-steel countertops, and a wooden spoon the
length of a yardstick, which she turns like a baton. In the high-
ceilinged room, with its black-and-white marble floor, Jenna feels
tiny, shrunken under the hanging metal bowls, stacked platters,
and enlarged appliances. But then, when she sees the giant mixer
in the corner—its bowl large enough to climb into—she thinks
about how well it does its job. Jenna understands its functions, how
to work it, what the levers do, and to let the yeasty dough rest after
it has been turned with the mixing hook. She feels good about that,
as if she has a talent nobody else knows. She imagines loaves rising, bulking in the night kitchen, readying.

Upstairs in bed, Jenna tries to sleep, first under the covers and
then lying on top, wondering if Heather had something happen to
her in this very room on this very mattress, and if she did, what
they could do with the mattress and frame just to purge the room.
They could burn it or sling it in a Dumpster somewhere so no one
would touch the remnants.

As the shouts from party revelers passing under the windows
drift upward, Jenna thinks of Vaughn, of red-haired Celia and her
780 math SATs, of friends she will never see again who clutter
her school-themed dreams. Jenna considers whether she could
picture sharing a man with someone and decides she might be
able to—if that someone were really close, like Heather. Then the
guy would sort of serve his purpose but not get in the way. Even
though she can't imagine the faces, she thinks of three people
holding hands, lying head to stomach on spring grass, the tickle

and itch of insects. But just as the image begins to appeal, and Jenna's thinking how close everyone could be, it dawns on her that someone would have to break away and go cook the dinner, and who would decide?

From downstairs, Jenna can hear noises echoing in the kitchen—Heather's mother still pawing at her daughter's hair, both of them sobbing. Remembering Baudelaire's poem from French class, she wonders about the lovers he wrote about, who also cry out, and she can't remember the exact context—if the tears are due to farewells or falsities. Then Jenna thinks maybe that's what this sobbing is about also, figuring what is past and what is now, stoned solid in the present.

Jenna remembers the way Heather used to exaggerate kisses on the back of her hand when they were kids, and then Heather's lips tonight, outside, how they'd felt like pouchy fruit, a plum or an overripe nectarine. The pillow Jenna lies on smells like honey or vanilla, traces from the shampoo in the bathroom. Maybe it's the scent or maybe it's the beer Jenna had earlier, or the thought of a smaller Heather being touched and scarred, but she heads to the bathroom to be sick.

While she throws up, she conjugates French verbs to distract herself from the unease of sitting on someone else's tiled floor and heaving food bits and frothy beer. *Aller, attendre, couper*; then she moves to cooking verbs: *assaisonner*—to season, *chauffer*—to heat, *bouillir*—to boil, *consommer*—to consume. Then she remembers how some verbs have two meanings. When she's back in bed, she conjugates *voler*, reminding herself to explain to Heather in English what she has already learned at college; *voler* is to steal, it is to fly.

Residency

*G*abrielle receives Andrea's phone call at the apartment house after a day spent looking at the vaginas of twenty-three Ecuadorian women. The phone's double rings are louder and longer than rings back in the States, and when she picks up, Gabrielle knows right away it has to be long distance since there's a delay and an echo. She says hello after setting her bag down and slips off her shoes. Padding in her socks to the tiny refrigerator that opens from the top like a camp trunk, she pulls out a Thirsty Boy!—the local equivalent to an orange Crush—and uses her hospital scrub top like a glove to twist off the cap.

With the first sip, she and Andrea are past their overlapping hellos. Andrea's voice is the same as in fifth grade—deep, raspy as if she's been smoking, jagged from a cry. Since Andrea is quiet or the delay is longer on Gabrielle's side, Gabrielle goes on with a description of her flight to Quito from Bogotá. There were miniature tins of smoked fish that she'd picked at with a spear-tipped toothpick, and the swell of mountains she'd seen when she woke up thirsty and hot a half hour before landing, the disorganized sway of customs lines. She'd taken her duffel to the guesthouse and slept again until dinner that first night. Strings of plastic limes and bright beads hung up around the doorway. When Gabrielle had gone out that first night by herself, she'd walked through them thinking that if they'd been lit from inside, the place would have the feel of a themed frat party.

In Old Town, she sat having coffee in the Plaza de Santo Domingo trying to read the Quito newspaper. Bright-robed pedestrians, women in suits, and shoeshine boys holding footstools all listened to a band playing curbside while behind them a church bell rang. The paper listed movie times, and Gabrielle was wishing she had someone who would join her at the Cinema Esperanzado when a white-haired woman carrying an enormous basket of long beans came close enough so that Gabrielle could smell the green shoots and heaped loose seeds.

"You want?" the woman asked. Gabrielle opened her mouth to speak but was suddenly very aware of her poorly accented Spanish so instead shook her head. In the windless dark, the old woman loomed large. Gabrielle wondered if she had children or grandchildren, if she'd hefted them to her two at a time and let them play with the folds of empty skin on her arms, if one had fallen asleep on her lap as the woman shucked the plump green beans of their pods. She thought about being held to the woman's chest, and lying there hair-smoothed and quiet until she felt she'd found home.

"Hmm," Andrea responds. Gabrielle can hear her lick her lips, imagines Andrea gnawing on dried lip skin. "And where are you now? Where am I calling?"

It's a relief to speak English, and Gabrielle feels the words slide out fast, detailing her life from Quito to Manta, where she'd arrived four days later with time enough to bring her pack and carrying case to her new apartment and change into her scrubs before heading out to the sanded pavement and walking to the

Centro Médico de Manta, the local hospital. The flight had been only forty-five minutes, and Gabrielle found that she enjoyed walking out to the small plane. On a postcard to Andrea, Gabrielle wrote that walking up the steep steps after being out on the windy runway made her feel like a president or a Beatle, and she'd waved even though no one was watching.

"Did you send it?" Andrea wants to know, then clarifies. "The postcard."

Gabrielle shakes her head even though the gesture goes unseen by her friend. "No." Then she sees herself in the mirror and watches her mouth move as she adds, "Not yet, I mean. Do you still want me to?"

"I guess so—even though, I don't know, maybe you don't have to? Since you told me what's on it already." Gabrielle remembers the corkboard in Andrea's old bedroom, the postcards from over state lines, the Irish pen pal who wrote once and then stopped, Gabrielle's school photo tacked to the corner under the yellow of a pushpin. "Send it anyway. So I can see the stamps. Is there a post office at the hospital?"

"No. Not even close." Gabrielle goes on with her descriptions, tracing the past weeks in her mind as she speaks. Above the hospital's front desk, the clock's time was wrong. Gabrielle stood waiting for the clerk to bring her a name tag and read the letter Dr. Sandoval had left for her explaining the new initiatives—fewer cesareans, a bigger emphasis on family planning, a push for maternal prenatal vitamins. With the name tag pinned to her blue top, Gabrielle was given doctor status that denied her fourth-year medical school reality. A nurse took her arm and lead her toward the first curtained exam area; Gabrielle tried not to focus on the tiny white caps the nurses kept pinned to their bunned hair or the grainy kick of sand under her shoes.

Gabrielle takes a pause, waiting for Andrea to butt in, but she doesn't. Andrea takes a sip of something—Gabrielle can hear her swallow—and says, "Then what?" like Gabrielle is reading a kid's book with pictures, or sharing in grade school circle time.

Most of the hospital lights were dimmed or off for conservation, chips of paint flaked from the walls and lay in clusters on the linoleum floors. All the doctors and nurses wore white shirts and slim trousers that seemed even brighter against the walls and barely lit stockrooms. The supply rooms themselves were nearly empty of bulb syringes, suture kits, and Betadine swabs, and Gabrielle spent her second day hauling the stuff her medical school back in New York had donated to the hospital, which Gabrielle had shipped before her arrival.

Gabrielle tells Andrea about how she and her fellow fourth-years had raided the medical stock at Bronx Memorial first, before getting approval from the trustees and head of staff. Soft piles of gauze sponges, 3 cc syringes, needles, and sterile gloves all tucked in tight, an immigrant medical supply heading off to warmer climates.

"I'm going to miss Match Day," Gabrielle says. Then, before she explains the match system to Andrea, she adds, "But there wasn't another chance for me to do this."

"How come?"

"It's complicated," Gabrielle says. She'd arranged the extended rotation in Ecuador knowing that she wouldn't be there for the mid-March ceremony when all the fourth-years found out where they'd be going for their residencies. Gabrielle was fairly certain she'd get her first or second choice and stay on the East Coast, maybe at Hopkins, in Baltimore, where her father lived now with his new wife, Diane.

On Match Day, everyone gathered in the banquet hall near the president's office and, at precisely the same time, opened white envelopes that revealed where they'd be for the next three, four, even seven years, depending on their specialty. Instead of this, the bagel breakfast, and the mad rush for the phones, Gabrielle would place a call back to New York the day after and have the secretary read her placement from a list. It seemed a bit anticlimactic, the lack of ceremony, but then, what was residency after all? Another four years of working sleepless nights, dreaming of cancerous ovaries and pregnant women with high blood pressure while pretending that she really lived in whatever city she was stationed.

Each segment of her life so far had been an extended visit in a particular state, so despite the name, Gabrielle felt residency would be another stop like that, a settling in to the point of familiarity and then going on to practice somewhere else.

Andrea listens while Gabrielle talks on and on into the phone.

"It's so good to talk to you," Gabrielle says. Andrea musters up a small *hmm,* as if she's chewing on bread. Gabrielle wants to say she's grateful for an English ear to hear her take on this country where she confused being a temporary resident, *temporal residente* with a *temporal implantación* in which the fertilized egg implants in the uterine lining. Gabrielle had thought about herself literally implanting somewhere, in something, but then realized she'd been incorrect. The doctors and nurses had laughed as she blushed behind her coffee-filled travel mug brought all the way from Manhattan. But all she says next to Andrea is how the smells are potent, how one reminds her of Andrea's basement, some combination of alcohol and dankness the girls used to pinch their noses against.

In Manta, Wednesday nights had late vending hours. Unlike the weekend market, which smelled of fish parts and bags of roasted *canahuate* seeds, the extended hours in the cafés and open-air stalls meant smelling chicory coffee and mint liquor all the way up on her balcony. Gabrielle watched from above as the townspeople danced oceanside or sat eating bowls of soup while old men played guitar. The aluminum lights swung on wires connecting one shop to the next, splaying odd shadows onto the dancers, and when she'd ventured down, Gabrielle had leaned on the concrete wall that edged the beach, facing into the action as if it were a film reel until she'd been spotted by Gloria, one of the younger nurses at the hospital. Gloria was desperate for children and had told Gabrielle, in the first week, how many times they had tried to conceive, only to find she either couldn't get pregnant or couldn't hold the embryo once it implanted inside her.

In the stockroom, while Gabrielle had organized and stacked, Gloria had cried and pointed to her empty belly, wanting to know why. Gabrielle had tried to console her, giving a pat on her shoulders and telling her to try to relax, but it was her fifth day there, and the thought of attempting to translate Clomid or *in vitro* seemed impossible. Besides, there wasn't much point in talking about drugs and procedures that weren't possibilities in Manta, since they might make Gloria even sadder.

Gabrielle touched a pulpous bag of saline solution that lay like a beached jellyfish on a metal cart and wondered if she'd ever carry a child, not so much if she could conceive but if she could find the time amid all the training to meet, maybe marry, and produce. She tried to picture herself full-waisted with her bladder space infringed upon but couldn't.

"Hold on," Gabrielle says into the receiver. She pulls the phone back from her ear and wipes at the sweat that's accumulated on the earpiece. As she had in New York, where a thirty-six-hour shift left her achy and nauseated, Gabrielle existed full-time in a nauseated but pleasant haze of fatigue. In Manta, she dreamed of needle sticks and preeclamptic women, the bloat of their bodies looming like clots. There was no one to talk to in English, and Gabrielle tried to force herself to think in Spanish, just so she'd sound more natural with the patients. Dr. Sandoval commended

Gabrielle's kindness, her ease with the worried women and speculum-invaded teenagers.

"I've had four babies named after me," she says to Andrea.

"Oh, yeah?" Andrea says. "I could see that."

"Two C-sectioned ones, a vaginal, one VBAC," Gabrielle says.

"VBAC?" Andrea spells it out.

"Vaginal birth after cesarean. Sorry." Gabrielle wonders what she is apologizing for and then covers up. "I've given out so many prescriptions for the morning-after pill I've lost count."

"I took that once," Andrea says. She is eating something, Gabrielle can tell from the crunching noises, the gulping.

"It can be a good thing," Gabrielle says. Then she reconsiders her word choice. "A good option, I mean."

Friday mornings Gabrielle assisted in the scheduled abortions. At the *clínica terminación* Dr. Sandoval had supervised a twenty-two-week abortion, first showing how to insert the prostaglandin rods, then, after the dilation, how to use the forceps. In a gloved hand, Dr. Sandoval had held a tiny gray organ and asked Gabrielle to identify it.

"A lung?" she'd said, looking closer.

"*Pulmón?* Are you sure? Right or left?"

"The right has three lobes and the left has two, so—I'm not sure, the right?" Gabrielle felt hot in her gown and mask. She meant heart, the chambers of the heart, and felt foolish for her mistake. From the tented rise of the patient's stirruped feet, she could envision falling, knocking herself out on the hard floor.

"*Realmente,* this is the heart, *el corazón,* of a nearly twenty-three-week fetus," Dr. Sandoval said and turned it gently with her finger to show Gabrielle how it pulsed.

Gabrielle nodded to show she understood and said, "Well, now I know for next time."

Later, in the bare-walled recovery room, Gabrielle had put her hand on the woman's shoulder and asked how she was feeling, if she had any questions. The woman shook her head and then asked how long the bleeding would last; the large obstetric pad was uncomfortable, held in place by disposable mesh underpants. Gabrielle assured her the flow would ease up in a few days and watched the woman as she covered her eyes either to rest or to cry, you could never be sure.

The white curtains billowed in the afternoon beach breeze, and it occurred to Gabrielle that, had she not known what the women were recovering from, the room could have been a spa, a post-herbal-wrap meeting place like some day spa somewhere on the Upper East Side. Gabrielle is proud of her detachment, her ability to comfort without being involved. She watched the *conserjes*, caretakers, the hospital employed just to tend to the emotional needs of the posttermination patients, and wondered at their grace, their casual kindness, felt she would benefit from more connectedness but she cannot think how to have it without changing her whole self.

Some of the patients had had elective procedures, others had been induced for stillborn deliveries at twenty-five weeks. The *conserjes* were the only hospital workers not outfitted in white. The murky blue of their drawstringed dresses made them appear fluid, gentle bodies of water seeping into the recovery rooms and over the emptied patients.

After the Friday outpatient clinics, Gabrielle went home to change before meeting Dr. Sandoval at her house on the western side of town, up where the mountains came into view behind the odd glow of dispersing light. The shuttle bus ended its route there, and sometimes, if she were the only passenger, the driver wouldn't bother to poke a hole in her paper ticket and she'd save the thirty cents each ride cost. Once she'd started a letter to Andrea, imagining her paging through the skin-thin airmail sheets all the way back in Austin, but she'd gotten only as far as "Dear

Andrea, I am on a bus," before she'd been distracted by the purple
margin of newly tarred roadway ahead.

Gabrielle liked to sit in the very front of the bus, facing forward as if she were a driver without a steering wheel. The front
windshield was so large and flat, and the bus seats came up so
close that you could see the sandy tarmac slipping underneath the
rounded front, and if you looked too long, it seemed like you
might go under there, too. Along the Río Tarquí beach, small,
bright blue fishing boats bobbed unpeopled, various mesh traps
and crates belted down with heavy cords.

When the fishermen returned from five days at sea with their
catches onboard, hundreds of frigate birds wheeled overhead,
waiting for a chance to swoop down and grab a meal left un-
guarded for even a few seconds. In the early mornings after her
weekend shifts, Gabrielle brought hard cheese and a roll to the
beach and watched the men unpack the boats, careful not to flaunt
her snack as she had the first time, when the large birds dipped
right to her, trying for a peck at her bread. Some of the birds were
Tarquí residents, others flew in with the fishing boats and stayed
until the sun slipped down and the sky went dark.

On the way to Dr. Sandoval's house, the shuttle bus passed the
ferry terminal where some of the Galápagos boats docked. Gabrielle tried to imagine her father and his wife on one of them as he'd
described it to her: the diesel smell, the bottle-nosed dolphins
cresting, the armies of marine iguanas that lined the shore as
they'd disembarked, the continuous fuss his wife had made over
her frizzing hair. Gabrielle hadn't made the time to go out there,
but, at Dr. Sandoval's suggestion, she'd gone during her four-day
vacation to the Parque Nacional Machalilla. A small group of lo-
cals had included her in a day hike, and then she'd joined a Spanish-
language school for a program in the coastal province of Manabí,
south of Manta.

Each morning Gabrielle sat in a hut roofed by tagua palm

leaves and practiced her verbs, her accent, the idiomatic expressions that came only after living somewhere long enough. The hotel where she stayed was the Alándaluz, the "winged city of light," which prided itself on being an ecologically minded place, self-sustaining with replenishable building materials and organic gardens. Gabrielle's arch-shaped cabin was made from bamboo and located near the outdoor eating area.

She'd been taking Larium still, an antimalarial drug, and it gave her odd dreams in the national park. In one, she and Andrea had kissed, her friend's tongue purple and long, darting. Sometimes people complained of nightmares from the medication, or depressive episodes, but Gabrielle enjoyed the bizarre flits and jolts of her sleep, especially in the jungle, where she fell asleep to the scent of babaco fruits cooking.

The fruits were served at breakfast. Heart-shaped and heavy, the five-sided babacos were about a foot long and yellow. Gabrielle thought they tasted some like a papaya and a bit like a strawberry, and like something else she couldn't think of, and she loved how all of the fruit—the flesh, the juice, the thin outer skin—was edible.

Away from labor pains, the maternity rooms where the women clicked their tongues to the roofs of their mouths more often than moaned, separate from the white-gowned staff and dingy hospital walls, Gabrielle felt like a part of the jungle, some plant grown from a discarded fruit dropped by a tourist—a flower or tree that wouldn't so much change the ecological system as blend into it. By boat, she'd gone from the hotel to the Isla de la Plata, the Silver Island, which contained some of the same bird and marine species found on the Galápagos. Blue-footed and red-footed boobies, masked boobies, and frigate birds all hunkered down in the headland cliffs, then launched themselves airbound. From the sunny boat where Gabrielle ate her lunch, she thought about who she wished were with her and couldn't say. With her medical school friends, the talk inevitably returned to studies or tales of the sad or dim-witted patients; with college friends, they past-delved and then came up with nothing. A childhood friend like Andrea was best, Gabrielle decided, since there was no middle to the relationship, no context—just Popsicles and flat chests and then suddenly adulthood.

When they'd met in Austin on Gabrielle's way down to Ecuador, Andrea had talked about the job she had at Grant's Books and Beans, the coffee place in town where used books nosed up to the mug racks. Andrea's world seemed small and relaxing, and Gabrielle wondered what it would be like to move back to Texas—to move back to anywhere, really, since she preferred to move somewhere new. Andrea asked about medicine, about the procedures, wanting the details of Gabrielle's everyday life, if she wanted to have her own practice, if she saw herself having kids of her own or just delivering them.

In Andrea's red Ford Fairmont, they'd driven to the miniature golf place they'd gone to as kids. Putting into a windmill, a waterfall, a maze of hedges, and an enormous plastic hot dog, they hadn't written on the scorecards.

"I can't write with these things." Andrea had laughed as she showed Gabrielle the abbreviated pencil that came with the clubs and balls. By the shaved ice stand inside the golf club return area, Andrea had tied some toddler's shoelace. "That's Ginger Lawson's kid, do you remember her from fourth-grade social studies?"

Gabrielle shook her head. In the car on the way to the airport, she'd thought about how Andrea had patted the kid's shoe when she'd finished tying it, quiet praise for standing still, the way Gabrielle did with her patients after an internal exam or when she'd given test results.

Gabrielle unloaded her bags from the car, putting her hiking pack on but not fastening the waist belt, and slipped her daypack on backward so it rested against her chest. Andrea held Gabrielle's

plane tickets, and as she handed them over she said, "I hope you
have fun in Quit-o."

"Actually, it's pronounced *key-toe*," Gabrielle said and then
wished she could suck it back.

Andrea nodded and chewed at her top lip. "Either way," she
said, and as if that constituted a good-bye, she tried to hug Gabrielle around the waist but couldn't arm the girth of bags, so she
leaned in and kissed her cheek near the ear.

Leaning on the bus window on the way to her Friday dinner at
Dr. Sandoval's, Gabrielle would think of Andrea, who'd never left
the South, and of her father, who loved to travel, to forget his city
of origin and live like a local for weeks at a time. As the bus
slowed at the newsstand, Gabrielle would get out, buy a couple
caramel pops wrapped in pink cellophane, and walk the quarter
mile out to the Sandovals.

Dr. Sandoval was married with two children. Holding Martina,
the infant, Gabrielle would listen to the boats docking, their gut-
tural horns seeping into the night. In the kitchen, Dr. Sandoval
and her husband roasted vegetables and potted them into water
and ketchup. The resulting soup, which the entire family ate, was
so dark it looked menstrual. Gabrielle watched how she was supposed to drop popcorn kernels in her bowl and push them into the
liquid until they saturated and nearly sank.

The husband played guitar while Dr. Sandoval cleared the table.
Martina was put to sleep in a bassinet, and the toddler, Enton,
spun himself dizzy in the living room holding a half-sucked lolly
that Gabrielle had given him.

The evenings at the Sandovals made her flushed and lonely.
Gabrielle would get a ride home on Mr. Sandoval's scooter. With
no helmet, her hair lashed at her face, and she tried to hold it out
of her eyes while still clutching Mr. Sandoval's waist. He wore
thin, cream-colored shirts with pockets on the hips and curled

stitching on the lapels. Through the cloth, even in the dark, Gabrielle could see his chest hair. His arms were hairy, too, and he
sometimes would tell her in Spanish to grip tighter on the sandy
stretches of road. Once, Gabrielle had thought about kissing him
as he helped her off the bike and steadied her feet by palming low
on her back, but she hadn't.

Back at the apartment complex, she walked the six flights of
stairs and hoped that somehow she might have a late-night visi-
tor: maybe her father had come down to surprise her, or a medical
school friend might have left a message for her, asking for a place
to stay before a trip to the Galápagos, or an old boyfriend could
have resurfaced, wanting a shower and simple accommodations
until he had to move on.

Weekends, Gabrielle worked Saturday mornings, five until noon,
then again on Sunday nights. During her break, she drank milky
coffee poured from the street vendors' galvanized tubs and sat on
the beach until the sand flies pecked at her thighs and she went
toward the market to buy supper. One of the nurses had given her
a recipe for fried squid with a sour cherry sauce, and Gabrielle
made that quite a lot, since it tasted good warm or cold. The food
at the hospital, even what the patients brought for her, was mainly
meat, and she ate it while writing notes, trying not to place the
animal that the flesh might have belonged to.

Animal lungs, tripe, and esophagi were all customary in stews.
Guinea pigs were a popular food source, and when offered some,
Gabrielle could only think of Miss Penny, Andrea's copper-furred
pet, which grew too fat to fit on its running wheel and eventually
suffocated itself.

As girls they'd found the unmoving mound in the cage, and
Andrea had reached in and picked it up. Tiny black beads fell from
her hand as she moved it to her desktop.

"Gross," Andrea had said to Gabrielle. "Miss Penny poops even when she's dead."

Gabrielle had put a finger near the rodent's mouth, trying to feel for a pulse or breath, the way she'd learned in Water Safety class at the Y that fifth-grade summer, but all she could feel was fur.

"We should get rid of it," she'd said to Andrea. Andrea had nodded, and they'd carried the pet to the toilet but soon realized it was too large to flush. Gabrielle had wanted to call a zoo or pet store to see if they could feed Miss Penny to some deserving animal, but Andrea wrapped the guinea pig in a wad of paper towels and threw the ball of it into the Dumpster behind Stetson's Drug Emporium, where they went afterward for slushies that turned their mouths blue.

Later, Andrea had moved on to a ferret, which lost itself a couple of weeks into its stay, and then Petunia, a ceramic pig that sat on her bedside table, holding first loose change and then, when Andrea had started dating some guy from San Antonio, cubes of dark, sticky hash. Gabrielle had found the stash in high school, and though she hadn't said anything to Andrea, they both knew. Junior year was almost over then, and Gabrielle took SAT-prep classes at her father's urging, then was accepted early decision to Yale. She wrote to Andrea from New Haven, long letters describing her classes and how she raised her dorm bed on concrete blocks so that underneath was a tapestry-curtained fort. Only once Gabrielle got a postcard back that Andrea had sent from Twitty City, where she'd gone with some girlfriends after seeing Dollywood. Andrea had written "New Haven" as "New Heaven," but the card had reached Gabrielle just the same. Gabrielle laughed about Andrea's misspelling to herself but felt too embarrassed about it to show it to her friends.

Since her father and his wife had moved to Baltimore, Gabrielle had had no reason to go to Texas, but she'd called information and found Andrea listed as Rebecca-Anne Summers; the surname was her mother's. Andrea told her that she was tired of always spelling Arginello, that Summers sounded cheerful. When they'd spoken, Andrea had offered to pick Gabrielle up at the airport terminal and took her to Little Lila's, the twenty-four-hour diner out on the motorway. Spooning rice pudding and cheese grits, Gabrielle told Andrea about postcollege life, about the autopsy she'd done as part of her pathology rotation. Andrea picked at her Belgian waffles, splitting the strawberries into thirds while Gabrielle talked about how heavy the man's brain had been, how dark the lungs, how the person responsible for sewing up the bodies afterward had sat off to the side doing a crossword. As she and Andrea finished breakfast, Gabrielle ate in silence, remembering how, from under her eye protection and mask, she grew woozy and sweat-lined while trying to help the necrologist think of a four-letter word for "shuttle site." She'd finally managed to say, "Loom," before passing out.

"Just so you know, I talked to your dad," Andrea explains, exhaling something into the phone. "It was bizarre to hear his voice after so long. I asked when would be the best time to call. I'm not sure he knew who I was."

"Maybe he's just tired," Gabrielle says. She wipes a rim of sweat from her chin, where the receiver has pressed for so long there's a mark.

"Could be," Andrea agrees.

"He has prostate cancer."

"Oh," Andrea says. "I'm sorry. I didn't know that."

"It's the early stages, anyway"—Gabrielle passes it off—"so, he'll be fine."

From the balcony Gabrielle listens to the slow night waves fall to the sand and seabirds rasp, scouring the jetty rocks for rotting crab or mussel remains. She'd tried it herself one night, chucking a bloated snail coil up into the air and seeing if it cracked open when it landed on a slab by the waterline.

"Gabby?" Andrea says. She hasn't used the nickname in years, since grade school, when they'd been Gabandrea, one name, one word for both.

"Yeah," Gabrielle says.

"I need money for an abortion."

Cradling the phone between shoulder and cheek, Gabrielle puts her soda bottle on the cement deck and crouches down, looking at the ocean through the slats of the guardrail. She asks the expected questions: how far along, how much it will cost.

Pulling her gestational wheel from her pocket, Gabrielle calculates a due date, keeps it silent while she tries to imagine Andrea ready to deliver, wide as a bell, in April. She remembers the way they had shoved bolster cushions in their T-shirts once and turned sideways to look in the mirror, pretend pregnant, before yanking the pillow babies out and marveling at their empty, stretched-out shirts.

"It's really hot here," Andrea says. "And I feel pretty sick."

"It's hot here, too," Gabrielle says.

She could mention alternatives, or tricks for fighting the nausea, describe the dilation and curettage Andrea will have in ten days' time, but she doesn't. She thinks of their fifth-grade summer, how they'd held hands underwater and fingered the pool drain, pressing into the grate so each palm showed the indents and bulges. Towel-dried, they'd turned the lawn chairs on their sides, slinking behind them, shut off and invisible to Andrea's mother, Carin, who drank rum and Coke inside.

"I bumped into Sheldon Marks," Andrea says while she's waiting for Gabrielle to say something, to decide.

"Where?"

"At the Big Burger Barn." Andrea laughs. "He's married now. Looks like he did in eighth grade, though, when you went out with him—you know, same hair, same tilty mouth. Wasn't he the first boy you kissed?"

In her mind, Gabrielle can see the class photo from then, the argyle sweaters and dark denim, the braced teeth and thin arms as everyone faced forward and smiled until the flash went, then let their faces go lax. Inevitably, one of the boys would fake-fart, and Jill Weston would close her eyes the way she did each year, even in her prom portrait, and Andrea would give Gabrielle a kick.

"Yeah, he was. Then again before we moved." Gabrielle suddenly feels ancient, as if time has sped up to where she can't keep anything still. "Do you want me to come back?" she asks. She takes off her socks and rubs at the spots above her little toes where blisters are beginning.

"No—you don't have to do that," Andrea says. Gabrielle wishes she'd demanded it, needed her, wanted her there to hold her hand and explain everything as it happened. But Andrea just wants get past it all and move on.

In the last photograph Gabrielle has of them together, Andrea is in her old driveway. Hair clipped at the nape of her neck, Andrea uses her hand as a visor. It's difficult to tell if she is leaving or being left, if it is a temporary state or a permanent removal.

Textbook-style, Gabrielle can draw the cell cluster splitting inside Andrea, can give a list of symptoms and warn of the milk-cold stirrups. It will be done. Gabrielle will wire the money from the office downtown, and Andrea will call once to say that everything is fine. In the exam-room quiet on the phone, Gabrielle will listen for clues in Andrea's story, wonder about her wounds and how they clamp themselves quiet, twist the mouths of both of them until they are empty and closed.

Who's Got the Monkey?

At Amanda Lyons's Halloween party, Amanda's not even there, rather she is holed up in the downstairs coat closet, kissing Jimmy Dearborn between the heavy navy peacoat and the embarrassingly red parka Gabrielle has just shoved in there. The coat, a last-minute purchase by Gabrielle's father, Randall, has convinced Gabrielle that there is no way she could move this far north; even with its wool lining, she is freezing, her long fingers gray and sore. Gabrielle's cousin Jenna has—at her mother's insistence—invited her out-of-town cousin to this party while Randall dines at L'Escargot, a restaurant downtown where the Boston Medical Group hopes to lure him with a job offer and—presumably—snails.

"Come on." Jenna, already halfway up the stairway, tilts herself over the banister and calls to Gabrielle, who has recoiled from the closet and her glaringly new winter apparel. Tonight is Jenna's third boy-girl party, Gabrielle's second, and neither girl knows what to expect; they, as of yet, have no party routine. Jenna wears a loose-knit purple cotton sweater—it's a V-neck, but she has turned it around so that the v dips down her back; her hair—the color of a fawn—is parted far to one side, bobbed at the nape. Upon finding out that her mainly unseen cousin would accompany her, Jenna tried to dress Gabrielle.

"You look too southern," Jenna said in her bedroom, her mouth rumpled.

Gabrielle stood side by side with Jenna, staring at her southern reflection and asked why, how. Jenna sighed, her voice softer, wistful. "I'm not sure what it is, really. Just something different."

Called by her mother to demonstrate her piano playing for Randall, Jenna had left Gabrielle to change clothes. Gabrielle chose a white turtleneck with hearts on it from the back of Jenna's drawer, dark jeans with tapered legs, and big, bunchy blue socks that heaped over the sides of her Keds.

"That's from sixth grade," Jenna told her, touching the turtleneck's tight elastic wrist cuff as they sat in the car's cold backseat.

"I thought it would be really northern," Gabrielle said, and she and her cousin laughed.

"Except you've got Keds." Jenna tapped the bright white of Gabrielle's shoes with her own roughed up Tretorns. "Oh—we're here!" Jenna gave a squeeze to Gabrielle's cold hand, letting her know just how excited she was to be going to a coed party.

"So what's your point?" Gabrielle asked her as they walked up the brick path to the arched front door of the house.

"Nothing." Jenna shook her head and pulled at her shirt hem, then readied her hair the way Amanda Lyons did: half a toss followed by a quick smooth-down. "You look fine," Jenna said and thought it was something her mother might say, which really meant "You are lacking somehow," but hoped her cousin wouldn't hear this.

Gabrielle wishes she could whisk herself away from the front door and join her father at his medical dinner. She would fit in better there, amid the fine flatware, the *amuse-bouches*, the adult conversation, than here, where Amanda Lyons is rustling around with some boy at the back of the closet.

"Gabrielle," Jenna says, her voice stern. "Come upstairs now!"

Bowls of salty chips, caramel popcorn, and an ice chest filled with soda cans line the buffet table. Kids sit in clumps, boys stretched out the length of the twill-covered couch, girls clustered around Dina Montello, the go-to girl with Amanda Lyons temporarily out of the picture. Jenna slings her lavender leather purse over her right shoulder and motions to Gabrielle to come meet everyone. Gabrielle has a purse, too, one of Jenna's mother's castoffs, wrinkled and brown, the pouch of it deflated like a withered old person's cheek. Gabrielle has never carried a purse before and has nothing to put inside it, but Jenna has insisted she have one with her. In the car ride and before hanging her coat up, Gabrielle undid the clasp and looked inside the purse but, of course, found nothing.

"This is my cousin Gabrielle," Jenna says and then points to each girl, naming their names, and when she reaches Dina Montello, she adds, "Dina's in eighth grade." Gabrielle watches as Jenna perches on the side of Dina's chair, causing Dina's tiny tote bag to drop onto the floor. Jenna listens for a way into the conversation. As far as Gabrielle can tell, the girls are comparing notes on who likes which bag and which boy. Finally, Jenna breaks—she cannot understand why she is one of those girls whose secrets no one asks. Daringly, she throws in the name of her crush, Peter Devlinson. Gabrielle is sure, upon hearing this, that Dina and another girl wince, but she feels powerless to do anything.

"Which leads me to my next point of interest," says Dina, conversational tour guide for the evening. "How to get a boy to notice you." Dina is so smooth, so able to weather the gusts of judgment and jealousy. Gabrielle pictures herself at this same party but in Texas and knows that the Dina role would be played by Melinda Sayles, and she is—despite considering herself an aware person— surprised to find that it is all the same. Everywhere you go, nothing changes; you are the social second in command or fringed forever, in any place.

Gabrielle wonders why Jenna can't see Dina Montello plotting her demise by the Chee-tos and diet 7UP. Dina licks an orange finger and whispers something to her cronies that make them shudder with laughter. The giggles, Gabrielle thinks, have more to do with relief than with true humor.

"Jenna," Gabrielle says. "It's almost nine." She checks her watch to prove to her cousin that they can leave soon, that they've been in a room with boys for nearly two hours and have nothing to show but mouths ringed with fake barbecue sauce from the chips. Gabrielle clasps and unclasps the brass fastener on her borrowed purse. Then she realizes that she is nearly head-to-toe covered in borrowed goods and feels itchy, caught in some fraud. Without her cousin, she would be wearing only her underwear, bra, and Keds.

Jenna suddenly bursts into action. "Oh, I almost totally forgot." She dips into her purse and pulls out a handful of colored hair elastics, each one thick and ropy, topped with a tropical flower. Like hounds to the scent, the cluster of girls shifts from the snacks to Jenna, who, momentarily in command, doles out one per girl.

"These are awesome," Amanda Lyons says, stretching her red one from thumb to forefinger. Jenna does not say that her mother bought them for her to give out.

"I love it—thanks, Jen," Dina Montello says and holds hers like a bunch of flowers and sniffs. Amanda's elastic rockets through the den, landing near Peter Devlinson's head. Jenna immediately blushes, remembering she's admitted he is her current crush.

"What the hell?" he asks, emphasizing the *hell* since no parents are around to hear.

Dina offers, "Jenna did it!"

Which is how Jenna finds herself downstairs, heading toward the closet with Peter, leaving Gabrielle upstairs alone in her heart-covered turtleneck playing games with the rest of the partygoers.

"So," Peter starts, his voice three coats away, distant enough for Jenna to feel even more dreamlike than she already does.

"Yeah," Jenna says. Her lips feel perfect, not too wet, not flaked. She checks her mouth for residual cheese and thinks about leaving a note for herself in her purse not to eat cheesy snacks, just in case she might get kissed.

She can feel Peter's knee tipping toward hers. They have their backs against the closet wall, flanked by wooden tennis rackets, stacked board games, and with a rush of worry, Jenna suddenly understands that she will always look for boys like Peter, who don't talk, or who can reach for her hand only in the protected darkness of the coat closet. But then, Peter is reaching for her hand, is shifting closer to her, and touches her hair just the way a boy ought to, tangling his fingers near the back and nearly elbowing her cheek.

"I heard you like me," Peter says.

Jenna feels each cell inside her racing to find the correct path, is aware of her blood, her heart, and—the way she has imagined so many times before—waits for Peter to kiss her. She is dimly aware of Gabrielle stuck upstairs, of the fact that the closet door could open at any time, ruining her moment and her chance of being kissed, maybe even dashing any hope of being Peter's new girlfriend.

"I do," she says and then feels ridiculous, as if she's trying to be in a wedding, so she adds, "like you, I mean." In the dangle of coat arms and windbreaker sleeves, Peter puts his hands on Jenna's shoulders and kisses her.

* * *

Upstairs, Amanda Lyons displays a turquoise plastic monkey. Sitting cross-legged on the taupe carpet, the girls have demanded integration, sliding themselves between the boys. The baggy purse sits next to Gabrielle, leaning against her leg like a toddler. As she listens to Amanda, Gabrielle wonders if maybe her father wishes he'd thought to buy her a purse along with her bright red parka. Thinking about her father trying to do right by her, outfit her in the way a mother might, makes her slouch. Then, remembering her dad didn't actually offer a bag she rejected makes her proud—he knows she is not the sort of girl to want to carry a purse. Simultaneous to this thought is Gabrielle's acknowledgment that she is, however, the kind of girl who might carry a bag to make her often unseen cousin happy.

"So, whoever ends up having it," Amanda reiterates, "chooses who they kiss."

"Whom," Seth corrects, and he is handsome enough to get away with the remark.

"Shut up!" Amanda smiles at him. Gabrielle imagines Amanda in the closet with Seth and then tugs at the neck of her shirt; not used to wearing turtlenecks, she feels constricted and bored, but not only that—bored and nervous.

To prepare for the game, Amanda asks Gabrielle to help her. Gabrielle senses she is showing the other girls how to be a hostess, how to be nice to the stranger they can later pick apart, but she is grateful enough that she complies. Together, they empty the contents of the Scrabble bag.

"Don't bother cleaning up the letters now," Amanda says when the tiny squares of *s, u, e, g*, and ten-point *z* fall to the floor. "I'll do it later."

Gabrielle places a pile of red, green, and yellow monkeys into the sack, and Amanda smiles at her. "Jenna said you might move here?"

Gabrielle nods. "Maybe."

"Cool," Amanda says and holds the turquoise monkey in her hand.

"It would be," Gabrielle says, even though she hasn't thought it through. "But it's not up to me." She thinks of her father eating French bread, how right now he could be spreading the butter or eating soup or deciding where she will live next.

"Everyone ready?" Amanda asks but doesn't wait for an answer. The turquoise monkey is added to the sack of plastic monkeys, and the sack is passed from one kid to the next. Hands reach in, pull out a green or a yellow, and collective sighs exhale. When Seth holds the bag, he does a dramatic swish of his right hand, waving his fingers in calisthenic form. He pulls out a red monkey.

"This is lame," Greg says and slides out of the circle to get a snack.

"It's down to two monkeys!" Dina Montello says, her hand already in the sack. She closes her eyes, and when she looks at what her hand has found, she frowns. Then she reconsiders, flips her hair, and says to Gabrielle, "Looks like you've got the monkey."

Even though she knows the color of it, Gabrielle goes through the ritual of extracting the turquoise monkey from the bag. Dangling it by its curled tail from her pointer finger, she taps it so it swings slightly. Then, as quickly as she revealed it, she closes it in her palm, and only the question mark of the tail sticks out.

Jenna wants to ask what, if anything, this means, if the fact that Peter's lips have been on hers, that for a few minutes he was allowed to hug her really tightly means they are going out. Then she thinks of the advice her mother gave her about boys, how going to them is a surefire way to scare them off.

"We should go," Jenna says. "My cousin's upstairs." She feels proud, coy, like she's supposed to.

"Yeah," Peter agrees. "So's my girlfriend." When Jenna doesn't respond, he softens his voice and asks, "You know that, right? Dina Montello asked me out, like, ten minutes before you got to the party."

Jenna can feel that she's going to cry and presses the one nail she hasn't bitten into her palm so she doesn't. "I didn't . . . So then how come . . ." She stands up, bumping into something furry, and remembers that Amanda Lyons's mom wears a mink.

"Dina told me to bring you down here," he says. They are both standing up halfway, jangling the hangers.

Jenna puts her hands on her cheeks, willing them to stop blushing before Peter opens the door. "I'm so embarrassed," she says.

"Oh." Peter says and tries to hug Jenna. "Look, she told me to bring you in here, but she didn't tell me what to do. I did that . . ." They both think back to the kiss that already feels miles—grades— behind. "I kissed you because I liked you, too."

"Liked, as in the past?" Jenna slides her fingers through the square holes on a tennis racket. The thought of being in a such a big closet jammed with old sporting goods, out-of-date athletic gear, and unworn jackets makes her feel impossibly small, and lonely.

"I guess so, yeah." Even as he says this, Jenna thinks that she still has a chance with him, that he might reconsider until, in the half-cocked door, light shocks them. Peter is saying, "Just tell everyone that nothing happened," as Dina Montello opens the door.

She stands with her hands on her hips. "You guys are missing everything!"

Dina locks hands with Peter, and they head up the stairs two by two in front of Jenna, who lags slightly behind. In the middle of the circle, Gabrielle is having a full-fledged kiss with Seth. They are on their knees, with the boys cheering and a couple of the girls agog, wondering why they didn't get the turquoise monkey.

"Hey." Dina kicks Amanda with her socked foot and pulls Peter down so he's practically on her lap. "Gabrielle, you staged this!"

This forces Gabrielle and Seth to break their kiss and instantly reminds Gabrielle of who she is: namely, not the girl who gets to kiss the smartest, best-looking boy at the party without ramifications.

"Just admit it," Dina says and nudges Amanda.

Seth whispers to Gabrielle in a Russian accent, "Tell them nothing."

Amanda shrugs and then, fearing Dina's wrath, adds, "She did put the monkeys in the bag."

Outside, a car horn beeps. Parents have begun to arrive, and Jenna looks at the strewn snacks, the scattered letters, trying to spell words so she can avoid staring at Peter and Dina, who are dancing in the corner, even though there's no music.

"Can we go?" Gabrielle asks Jenna.

"Where were you the whole time, anyway?" Jenna asks when the girls are back at the closet, reclaiming their jackets.

"I was here, where were you?" Gabrielle slips into the red parka, relaxing into the foreignness of it.

"Here." Jenna thumbs to the closet as if she half-expects it to refute.

"Oh." Gabrielle watches Jenna flip her hair and then smooth it. "Are you okay?"

"Yeah—fine." Jenna looks as if she will break any moment. "What about you?"

"Same." Gabrielle nods. She takes a last look in the purse and finds she has unknowingly filled it with something; the turquoise monkey sits quiet inside the folds of faded brown cloth, its curved tail caught on the coin pocket. She thinks about showing the illicit contents of her bag to Jenna, whose zipper is stuck, but doesn't.

With one hand, Gabrielle fixes Jenna's zipper, and with the other, she tucks the monkey into her new coat pocket so she won't forget him when she gives back the jeans, the turtleneck, the purse. Outside, the yard smells like burned leaves, and Gabrielle can still taste cranberry on her tongue. The sharpness of that flavor will always remind her of this party, pull her back to one of those nights, the ones between childhood and the adult world in which nothing really happened.

The Shortest Night

The first thing Lucy's mother told her about dressing for a date was this: if you can't get your hands into the pockets of your jeans, then they are simply too tight. Ginny said this to her the summer she turned fourteen as she packed a trunk for overnight camp. The camp was Camp Lenox, in the Berkshires, and they'd picked it out of the pile of brochures that arrived during the course of the long winter. The lake gleamed on the cover, and inside, the Lincoln Logs–style main lodge promised Ping-Pong and indoor games when it rained. This appealed to Ginny, who hoped Lucy would be high scorer on the soccer team, as she was at school, or win the blue ribbon for diving. Neither happened because Lucy tore the ligaments in the bottom of her right foot. But that was midway through the summer.

"Ping-Pong"—her mother smiled as she read aloud—"pottery shed, archery range. You've always been good at archery, haven't you?"

Ginny often asked questions that required nothing but a nod, and Lucy nodded as she glanced at the pictures on the back cover of the

brochure in her hand. Ginny might have liked the shooting range
and the potential for basket-weaving sessions, but Lucy's interests
differed. The photographs on the back were the same as all the
rest—sporty, filled with wide grins, cookouts, and watermelons—
but they stood out to Lucy in one way. While all the other camps
had girls around the fireside singing songs and cheers, girls playing all the roles in *The Sound of Music* and *Peter Pan*, Lenox had the
real boys to fill those roles. Camp Lenox for Girls was really Camp
Lenox for Boys, and had been since the 1920s, but the parents had
complained, so the owners built Camp Lenox for Girls.

Camp Lenox had only one cabin for girls the summer Lucy
went, and for all her memories of that June through August, she
can't remember the name of her bunk. They all had placards far
above their decor and structural soundness: Shangri-la, Bluebell
Ridge, Pine, and Spruce. Maybe Lucy's cabin had a name like this,
perhaps it was just a number.

Ginny looked at Lucy with her eyebrows raised to ask if she
would like to spend eight weeks tucked into the woods and hills of
the Berkshires. And while Ginny pictured her daughter growing
into more athletic prowess, Lucy envisioned being asked to dance,
an event that in what she thought of as her real life, her life at
school, had not occurred.

Looking back at that moment, Lucy sees that, even then, she
fancied herself as part of a breed of girls who got asked to dance,
who enjoyed the first time makeup snuck into camp without parental knowledge, who liked the sturdy, shiny boys called Jake or
Dan. Usually these girls came from Connecticut or New York
maybe, even California, and it was with great pity that they saw
Lucy—no eyeliner, long, unstyled hair, and actually wearing the
camp uniform.

She doesn't remember being dropped at Camp Lenox, cannot picture the spillage of girls and their trunks; it seemed as if they all

just appeared there, sitting on the edges of their bunks, putting cassettes, pictures, and candy into the small shelves at the bases of the bunks. Actually, Lucy hadn't brought anything to put into these spaces, but she realized the shelves fit a week's worth of rolled up socks perfectly, and left just enough room to house her journal.

It amazes her now to think of the names of the girls; Gabrielle, two Kims, Beatrice, Heidi, Bethany. Those are the ones she remembers. Gabrielle approached her first.

"Do you have any pads?" she asked.

"Sure," Lucy said, glad she'd brought them, even happier that she'd started her period the year before with the Jewish tradition of being slapped in the face by mother or grandmother as a "welcome to the world of being a woman." Ginny had done it, hard, then recoiled and hugged Lucy in a panic, whispering "Sorry, sorry" until Lucy had kissed her. Lucy handed Gabrielle a box of maxipads and looked at the woman on the front of the box, her gauzy dress flowing around her as she walked on the dunes of some beach.

"Lucy, right?" Gabrielle said.

"Yeah." She nodded.

"I already memorized everyone in here; it was pretty easy with the name tags and all. You don't have a name tag, but you're on the address list, so you must be Lucy." Gabrielle stood with her hands on her hips, a stance Ginny flatly despised as indicating what she perceived to be insolence. Later, Lucy found out that Gabrielle had only a father, no mother, and she wondered if that made the difference in gestures.

Lucy smiled. The two Kims came over and sat on her bed. They looked at each other, and then one nudged the other. One was thin, wiry, and with a permanent toothy grin; the other full-faced, also smiling, and with a figure people would deem "large-boned"

even though everyone knew what that really meant. The whole
camp called them Doublemint when they were together and split
the name when they were apart: with Thin Kim as Minty, her side-
kick, Double.

That first night, the girls had an orientation meeting on the floor
of the cabin. Their counselor, Pam, sat them down and asked a
series of ridiculous questions meant to open up what she called
their "secret selves" and make them closer.

"Now, a couple more questions," said Pam, who had worked at
Lenox the summer before and was now back as a senior counselor
after a year at Brown.

"Pam, do you have a boyfriend?" asked Bethany, the tall, pretty
girl from Greenwich who had been soccer captain for her high
school as only a freshman.

"Girls," said Pam in a tone that let the campers know she did,
"let's get back to the point. Heidi, if you had to be a hammer or a
nail, which would you be? Let's go around in a circle."

"A hammer."

"No doubt," Minty said, serious as she popped her gum.

"Me, too," agreed Double.

It was Lucy's turn. She was looking out the cabin screen at
main camp where there were lights and noise, one last party before the boys arrived tomorrow.

"Lucy?" The group looked at her. She knew any comment except a straight answer would be seen as a rebellion, an attack on
Pam, since everyone seemed eager for her to ask the next question.

Lucy started to laugh midsentence. "Ah . . . I guess I'd be a—a
Simon and Garfunkel song," she said and thought how, if her
friend Kyla were there, she'd be laughing, too, and they'd leave the
circle to skip rocks into the late light of the flat lake.

"Very funny, Lucy," said Pam. No one laughed.

That was the moment. In every one of Lucy's stories she felt there was a single moment that, had it been paused or altered just slightly, would have changed the entire outcome. That was her moment; she'd been the cool, name-tagless girl but had gone to the other side, no longer a joiner. At fourteen, loners are seen only two ways—cool or weird—and no girl strives for either; all want just the low-flying haze of not being singled out. At that point, Lucy became both, treading water somewhere in the middle.

After a loose-egged breakfast the following morning, they had swim tests. Bethany and Lucy tested out of required swimming. Both girls had both grown up swimming and sailing, so while the others swam their laps and did the dead man's float, Bethany and Lucy went to the boathouse to rig one of the small sloops.

James, the English boating instructor, set them up, then called them into the Sail Shack, one of the few buildings that actually suited its name. James was tall, sandy-haired, with a full mouth. He bit the side of his cheek and marked something on the paper in front of him.

"So, Bethany," James said, looking through a file. "You seem like you know your way around boats." Lucy wondered for a minute if that meant she knew her way around more than just the jib sheets and Turk's head knots. She looked at the scar James had on the third knuckle of his left hand and wished he'd explain it. The smoke from his cigarette looped up into the buggy air and hung there. He suddenly realized his error and put the cigarette and his soft pack away, tucking it inside an upturned brass bell on the desk.

"Boats are cool." Bethany shrugged, leaning her lanky frame on his desk. Lucy waited for James to ask her something, if she liked the ocean or lakes better, if she even knew how to sail. He said nothing.

Bethany kept looking at him. He glanced up at her and smiled. Lucy grabbed a towel from the rack in the corner and headed for the boats. She clipped the small sail into place and lowered the rudder. Bethany ran up the dock.

"Don't untie it yet. James wants to see you in the shack. He says I can take out my own boat."

Lucy climbed out and walked the length of the dock, her wet footprints leaving a trail behind.

"Hey," she said to James, who was smoking another illicit cigarette and jumped when he saw her standing in the doorway.

"I didn't expect you now," he said. "I thought you'd go sailing first and then stop by."

"Bethany said you wanted me to talk to you right away." She paused and then said, "Don't worry about the smoking thing, it's really not that big a deal."

"You're the business, Lucy, the absolute business," James said, taking a drag from his freshly lighted Camel, and she laughed for the first time since arriving at Lenox. She watched James smoke his cigarette. He noticed her doing this, put it out on the edge of the desk, and flicked the butt end into a half-filled bucket of sand by his bare feet.

"What'd you want, James? Am I in trouble, or did you just want permission to smoke?" Lucy asked.

"Your counselor Pam says you're not cooperative. And that kind of stuff doesn't go down too well in a boatyard."

"Okay." Lucy undid her life preserver and placed it back with the other ones, which hung from an old oar suspended from the ceiling by wires.

"Just okay? C'mon, I thought you'd have a better answer than that."

"Okay," Lucy said again, drawing the word out as a space between them. "Did Pam explain *why* she thinks I'm difficult? Pam thinks I'm not going along with camp spirit because I didn't answer her lame hypothetical questions last night: Would you rather be a country road or a city street? A hand-knit shawl or a designer scarf? Do you know what it's like to be put on the spot like that?"

James laughed. "Jesus, I didn't know it'd be that bad." He studied Lucy's face for relief and, finding none, stood up and stretched. Lucy stood still.

And then suddenly from James, "You want to go into town? Billy from the main house can take over here, keep watch on Bethany and whatnot."

"Sure," Lucy said. She thought of the others trying to pass out of advanced beginner swimming and Bethany waiting for a sailing partner, and felt her pocket for her wallet.

She and James walked the dock in silence, then cut through the grassy circle of lawn by the lodge and headed in back to the counselors' area, where campers had already been told not to go. James went inside his cabin and picked up his backpack while Lucy sat on the steps looking at the view of the other cabins from his porch.

"Ready?" he asked, walking to the staff parking area and not looking back. Lucy kept up pace and then suddenly sprinted to his truck. She had seen him in the yellow pickup the day before, driving and then unloading box after box of dry goods into the mess hall's delivery entrance, and she recognized the truck right away.

"You're a fast sprinter," he said, out of breath.

"But I suck at long distance, so it's okay," Lucy said, laughing, about to open the door to the truck. For a second, she thought of her mother, and how Ginny hated the word *suck*. Lucy knew her mother's reaction had less to do with the implication of anything sexual than with the word's connotations of class, or lack thereof; it was the same reason Ginny preferred *dollars* over *bucks, perspiration* over *sweat*. Lucy realized she was, in fact, sweating, the slight trickle running from between her breasts down to her stomach. She tried to mat the dampness with her T-shirt while opening the door to the truck.

"Actually, we're taking the camp van," James said, heading to the stout brown van emblazoned with the camp's shield on its sides.

James drove down the dirt road to the camp's entrance and onto the semipaved road toward town, looking at Lucy as he took a tape from his backpack. Lucy's mouth felt sticky with the kind of saliva it produced in the heat. James steered with his knee and turned up the volume of the tape deck, then Lucy sang along with the music. James raised his eyebrows.

"What are you doing knowing the words to English Beat songs?" he asked, amused and annoyed at the same time. Lucy almost made some comment about his being an English boy and wanting to be all special with his different music and different words, but she didn't, because of the night before. She didn't want to appear too witty for her own good.

"My older brother," she said. "He's into them and we listen . . ." Her voice trailed off. She had set up an unfortunate parallel between James and her brother—older, platonic—and hoped he didn't notice.

"Well, now, there you go," James said and lit up. He drove with the window down and his arm all the way outside. The only time she saw his left hand was when he took a drag.

"You know," Lucy said, "just because you keep the butt out the window doesn't mean it doesn't exist. We both know it's there. It really doesn't bother me."

"I don't want your clothes to reek when we get back, Lucy." There was a no-smoking policy at Lenox, although later, in July, Beatrice and Double would get caught behind the cabin with a pack of Salems, one of them lit. The rest of the girls would joke at first; get busted for real, at least, with Camels or Marlboros.

In the town of Marshville, which consisted of a bar, a post office, a bank, and a country store, James and Lucy got two Cokes from the machine by the closed-down gas station and sat on the roof of the van. The buildings looked like facades, the kind she'd seen in Hollywood—whole fake Western villages with swinging saloon doors and empty, horseless carriages. She wished for a minute she and James were there—inhabiting the general store, she in a hoopskirt and bonnet, James with a holster and a horse that could lead them anywhere.

In Marshville, nobody was around, so they blasted music and James let bits of information about himself leak out as they watched their Coke bottles sweat in the sun. He was from London, the son of academics, one of three kids, his sisters were older. He had taken his gap year between school and university to travel and work his way around the world, and landed the job at Lenox through a friend in New York who had been the nanny for the camp owner's kids. All of these details he told her laughing, as if he couldn't believe he was really in America, sitting on a van with someone called Lucy, some girl he might never had met.

James looked at her and brushed something off her shoulder. "Just a bug," he said. Later, in August, they would sit on the roof of the main lodge, looking down at the lake where an all-camp barbecue smoked and music played, and James would offer Lucy a cigarette and, again, brush some insect from its perch on her arm.

By the time they drove through the camp gates, it was rest period. The boys had arrived earlier, and Lucy had missed it. James and Lucy walked to the main lodge.

"See you at cookout," he said.

"Yup." She nodded and walked through the staggered pines and thick green back to the girls' cabin. Inside, she kicked off her shoes by the door and went to her bunk. Beatrice and Bethany were sleeping. Heidi was writing a letter. Doublemint came over and sat next to Lucy.

"Where were you?" they asked at the same time.

"I had to go into town," she said and reached for her journal.

From her bed, Bethany, not moving from lying with her hands behind her head, loudly said, "Lucy and Boat Counselor are *so close.*"

"His name's James," Lucy said and wished for a retraction.

Heidi put her pen down and looked at Lucy. "Are you gonna do it with him?" This would be the first question Heidi asked of anyone during the course of the summer, staff or camper, even on parents' weekend.

Before Lucy could think up a reply, Pam came in with a stack of mail. Instead of handing letters and packages out quietly, she stood in the doorway and read the names aloud, calling attention to whoever was the unlucky person not receiving anything. Pam took pride in her mail delivery role, the power that being messenger brought. That day, Beatrice got a package of crystallized ginger and a letter from her aunt in Maine, who was a ceramics teacher and didn't believe in candy.

Beatrice and Lucy sat on the edge of Lucy's bed, eating the ginger.

"My parents are abroad for the whole summer," she said. "Would you let me read the letter from your parents?" Lucy puzzled at the thought of this providing comfort since Beatrice had never met or seen her mother and father, but Lucy agreed.

"Okay, everyone," Pam shouted. "Get up, get ready, it's time for camp meeting and then the cookout." Lucy looked at the girls. They scurried around, trying on miniskirts and sundresses. She and Gabrielle were dressed first. Lucy slid into her jeans and T-shirt, and went to brush her hair. Gabrielle was putting on blue eye shadow and curling her lashes.

"Looks like an implement of torture," Lucy said as Gabrielle squeezed the metal-hinged tool in front of her eye.

"But it works great. See the difference? You should try it," Gabrielle said and then, "You want to borrow a top? I mean, not that the T-shirt's bad, but maybe my green one?"

Lucy let Gabrielle lead her by the hand to her cubbyhole, where her folded shirts and jeans were stacked in perfect piles. Gabrielle pulled out a soft cotton shirt the color of moss and handed it to Lucy.

"Thanks," Lucy said, taking off her T-shirt and slipping into Gabrielle's shirt.

"There." Gabrielle studied her. Doublemint, Heidi, and Bethany walked by and paused to wait for them, watching in approval as Gabrielle adjusted Lucy's hair.

Inside the lodge, it was hot and windless. The boys had already filed in and taken seats on the floor. The small sets of bleachers to the side of the room were empty except for a few counselors, so Pam sat the girls there. Some speeches were made about fun and expectations for the summer, trips to the beach, and the camp musical, which would be *Guys and Dolls*, and it was announced that each Friday night, after sports, there would be a dance. Gabrielle and Heidi nudged each other. Doublemint giggled. Lucy surveyed the boys for a potential partner. She noticed one boy, dark-haired and tall, who motioned to his friend when he saw her looking in their direction. They looked at the girls, and the girls looked back; Bethany whispered to Minty, and they laughed loudly. Pam turned around to quiet them. The boys talked and then shoved each other until Big Henry, the wood-working instructor, came and led them outside for a lecture.

Through the screen windows that lined the walls of the lodge, Lucy had a view of the lake. She could see a figure walking the sandy grass toward the docks. As the speeches ended, she looked again. Out on the water, the white sails of one of the boats curved into the wind, and she pictured James steering the boat, wishing herself there.

On Thursday night before bed, Pam called the girls into her nighttime circle.

"Girls," she said, "the social is tomorrow. I know you're excited, but remember, they're only boys, and it's only one night." That first Friday dance fell on the summer solstice. When Lucy thought of not being asked to dance, she would remind herself of two things: she wouldn't be the only one, and, she didn't really like to dance anyway.

With some surprise, she found herself one of the first being asked to dance. Only the senior boys were there, which still provided a ratio in favor of the girls, but it was thrilling. Brian walked over and said something like congratulations on the part in the play. She had tried out by singing the main song, even though it's meant to be sung by a guy. Lucy knew only the men's vocals because her brother, Jacob, had once played Nathan Detroit and she'd helped him learn the words. Brian and Lucy danced two songs, and then she walked back to talk to Double, who wasn't dancing with anyone.

"I think Brian likes you, Lucy," Double said, smiling.

"Really?"

"Look," she said. "Heidi's already glued to Cory. I bet she likes him 'cause he's the best basketball player."

"Maybe," Lucy said and leaned against the wall. Across the room was the boy she had seen at the camp meeting.

"That's Flip," explained Double. "He's been going here since he was six. Cute, huh?"

Flip and his shoving partner, Eddie, walked over to the girls, and Lucy and Double took their cue to dance the slow song. Flip linked his hands around Lucy's back, and she rested her hands on his shoulders.

"Lucy, you play soccer, right? I bet you and that Bethany girl are gonna fight over who gets captain."

"We both play," Lucy said, wondering why he couldn't have asked anything more romantic. "We'll have to see who gets it."

Lucy danced with Flip the rest of the night. Bethany and

Brian had gone outside and were led back in by Pam, who found them making out by the pottery shed, shirts untucked. Flip walked Lucy back to the cabin, and they stood outside in the dark for a half hour talking. The whole night seemed too long.

As Flip finally turned to go, he paused. "You're pretty cool. I mean, to talk to," he said. And then, Lucy imagined because he knew he could, Flip stood closer to her. When they kissed, she felt as if she was standing next to herself watching it happen. It occurred to her then that kissing and being kissed were two different things. And being kissed by someone you've really wanted to is something else again.

Lucy was never asked to dance for the rest of the time at Camp Lenox, but for the next couple of weeks, Flip would meet her after the *Guys and Dolls* rehearsals and they'd walk to the mess hall for dinner, sometimes with his arm draped over her shoulder like a damp towel. Lucy went to his baseball games, and he watched her archery competition against Camp Windmere, after which Lucy sent her blue ribbon home in hopes her mother would feel satisfied and her father proud.

During free time Lucy would go to the Sail Shack and talk with James before taking out a Sunfish or helping clean the undersides on the sloops that were up for repairs. One afternoon, as she was walking to the dock, Heidi and Bethany called to her from the lodge. They were playing Ping-Pong with Cory and Brian while Doublemint watched.

"Come on up," Heidi said. Cory and Brian shouted in agreement.

"Hey, Lucy," Bethany called, using her hands like a megaphone, "Flip's inside, you better come up." Lucy debated. Flip emerged from the lodge and came halfway down the steps.

"You going sailing again?" he asked.

"I'm supposed to," she said.

"Supposed to? It's free time, you can do what you want. Do you want to go sailing or do you want to hang out here?"

She wanted to go sailing; wanted to rig the boat, cast off lines, and find her way to the middle of the lake and swim. She walked over to Flip. He took her hand. Then Lucy kicked her heels against the chipped pointing on the lodge wall while she watched Flip beat Cory five games in a row, and then it was time for dinner.

As the campers ate red pineapple cubes encased in red Jell-O, Lucy looked for James. He was laughing with the other counselors and had his face turned to Susie, the head of the lower camp. Lucy looked away.

That night, Lucy lay in bed listening to the distant bug-zapping machine near the infirmary and counting Beatrice's snores, waiting to leave. In shorts and a T-shirt, Lucy crept out the screen door and walked in the dark down the path to the lake. The light of the Sail Shack was on, and she looked inside the window to where James sat shirtless, reading by the light of an old brass lantern. She knocked on the window. He flinched and got up to open the door.

"Why on earth are you out of bed-bed?" he asked. Lucy didn't know if *bed-bed* was an English term or an exaggerated reference to her age.

"No possibility of sleeping," she explained. James grabbed his book, turned the light down, and came outside. They sat on the edge of the dock with their feet in the water as he smoked.

"I thought maybe you'd send me back to the cabin," she said.

"If you'd really thought that, you'd have gone somewhere else."

"I guess that's true," she said. Lucy reached for James's cigarette, and he didn't stop her from taking it.

After a couple of drags she handed it back. "So." She exhaled. "You like Susie?"

"Sure, she's nice." He laughed. James hoisted himself up from the dock and went into the water. Lucy watched him swim a couple of strides. "You coming in?" he asked.

"How much do you like her?" she asked and stood up. Then she dove in and surfaced.

"I like her a bit," he said. They floated on their backs and looked up at the cloudy sky.

"It's going to rain tomorrow," Lucy said.

"I know." James paused. His held his palms so they barely touched the water's surface. "You know, Lucy, you are a lot younger than I am."

"You were barely five years old when I was born." Lucy didn't look at him.

"And that's a lot. I see you with Flip. Do you like him?"

Lucy lay still, floating on her back, and felt a tear go down her face into the water. "A bit."

When they got out of the water, James went inside the Sail Shack, took his rolled up T-shirt from the desktop, and threw it at Lucy.

"You can get changed behind the life raft," he said.

After Fourth of July carnival, Beatrice and Double got caught smoking in back of the cabin while the rest of the girls were taking off their sweat-slicked shin pads and cleats on the field. Double had to call her parents and tell them herself, then wait to be picked up. Minty cried harder than anyone.

"Kimberly," Pam said, and Double followed her out the door. They had forgotten her real name, so having it be the last thing she was called startled the girls into silence. Beatrice's parents couldn't be reached, so Beatrice got to stay, but she couldn't go on any trips with her bunkmates and had to miss the midsummer party on the baseball field.

When the crack of the fireworks started, Lucy was in the dugout, watching people.

Flip sat down next to her. "Hey," he said.

"Hi."

"I think," he said, not looking at her, "we'd be better off being friends."

"Why?" she asked. Lucy wasn't surprised. She knew Brian had broken up with Bethany, and Bethany wanted Flip. Lucy didn't feel particularly sad about it, except when she realized Flip wouldn't kiss her anymore. She'd gotten used to his kisses, his long fingers getting tangled in her hair, and Lucy kissed him one more time so he would remember it.

"Well," he said. Lucy knew she could have kept kissing him, held him there, but she backed away, trying to show enough hurt to make him feel important.

"I gotta go," he said.

The noise of the fireworks filled the space of the field. Groups of campers sat on blankets and watched the lights and drips of color as they ate melting Hoodsies ice-cream cups and orange Creamsicles. Lucy walked past them and toward the cabin. In the woods were two people pressed up against a tree. Lucy recognized James's red shorts before she saw the other person, but once the laughter was audible, she knew it was Susie. Lucy watched them for a moment and then went inside.

The next day held nominations for soccer captain and a dive meet in the afternoon. That evening, the senior camp was going to a town nearby to go roller skating. In the morning, Lucy took out a canoe and stopped in the thick patch of water lilies by the side of the lake. Before she had the canoe dragged from the lake edge, the breakfast bell rang and she ran toward the mess hall, tripped, and fell over a tree root by the flagpole. Bethany and Flip saw her, laughed, and kept walking.

From the lodge, James came down to help. He pulled her up from the ground. Lucy tried to walk to the infirmary without him. He put his arm over her shoulder and secured her around the waist.

"I'm fine," she said, trying to shake him off.

"No, you're not," he said.

The day's activities went on without her as James drove Lucy to the clinic in town.

"Let's take my truck," he said, "that way you can stretch your leg out."

Bandaged and with crutches, Lucy was quiet. James turned onto a paved road labeled Route 105. She didn't ask where they were going. Twenty minutes later, they reached a dusty roadside restaurant called The Place. James parked and helped her out of the truck and inside, where the room was empty except for one young waitress and a gray-haired cook they could see in the back.

James guided Lucy to a booth, where she slid in backward so she could keep her foot up.

"You know what I love?" he asked.

"What?"

"A good grilled cheese. Toasted cheese sandwiches we call them back at home. Always make you feel better."

"I don't feel bad now, so why would I want to feel better?" Lucy smiled. Her mother would say Lucy was "in difficult mode," and she said this to James, who agreed.

"Okay, then. We can order something else."

"Grilled cheese is fine." Lucy pressed her fingers to the grimy plastic menu cover, listening to the stick of her skin when she pulled them off.

They ate and talked for an hour and then played pinball at the back. The shiny silver balls raced over spaceships; flashing bells and noise echoed out into the dank back room. Lucy felt James watching her score points on a multiball round, hoping he was looking at her and not the cartoon heroine's breasts bulging from the rocket's side. When they ran out of quarters, they leaned against the machine, wondered who named The Place, and took turns suggesting alternatives.

"The Dive?" Lucy offered.

"Sandwiches and More." James raised his eyebrows. "Don't you think that sounds a bit naughty?"

"How about Fat, Sugar, and Coffee?" Lucy smiled. James nodded.

"Fat Millie's?" James asked, and when Lucy made a face he explained, "She's the cook."

"You've been here before?"

James shook his head. "No, it said her name on her apron when she served us, remember?"

Late that afternoon, while the campers and counselors were still away, James came to check on Lucy in the cabin. He saw the decorated bunks of the other girls and then commented on how bare hers was—no pictures, just a journal.

"And socks," she said defensively.

"And socks. How understated." James surveyed the rest of the cabin and then said, "So this is where you live." She didn't respond.

"Lucy," James said flatly.

"Yes?"

"It wasn't a question," James said. He looked at her once more before standing up and walking to the door.

The next week was the production of *Guys and Dolls*. The director hadn't counted on Lucy's version of Sarah having a limp, but he worked it into the story. After the bow, the actors went backstage. Pam and Gabrielle came back first to hug Lucy. Billy, who played Sky Masterson, hugged her, too.

"Hey, you're a good kisser," he joked, because he'd tried to make it a real kiss rather than a stage one.

"You wish you knew," she said. There was the rush of performing, then the sudden slink of air from her chest when she looked at the garish rouge on her cheeks, the ill-fitting brocade Salvation Army jacket she wore, desperate to win Sky over to sainthood.

With ten days left of camp, Bethany called the girls into the bathroom. "I'm going to do it with Flip," she announced. Heidi seemed more excited about it than Bethany and kept telling her what it was like.

Bethany turned to Lucy the next day in the pottery shed. "You know, Lucy, it could have been you," she said as she worked her clay into a vase.

Lucy dipped her hands in the muddy water bucket and wet the beginnings of a clay bowl that sat on the wheel in front of her. She wondered what had become of the floppy clay ashtrays she'd sculpted and given to her mother, even though Ginny had never smoked.

"Me with Flip?" Lucy asked.

"Yeah," Bethany said. "If you really wanted, it still could be."

Lucy didn't know what to say. "Look, Bethany, if you don't want to be with Flip, you don't have to be."

"Thanks, Mom." Bethany whipped around and stared at her. "I was just giving you one last shot, trying to be nice, since I got captain and all."

"It's okay," Lucy said, and then slowly, "You deserve it."

That night all the girls except Beatrice ignored Lucy, and they ate hamburgers by the lake as the final party began. The Friday Social was an all-camp event, with music and food, and candles floating on the surface of the lake. Pam had each of the girls write a wish on a piece of paper, roll the wish up, and stick it into a piece of birch. The tiny candle and wish boats bobbed in the dusk, sailing off on the lake's surface. Lucy hadn't known what to write. The other girls gave knowing glances, wrote hastily, and grew tearful watching the wood and paper drift. Lucy gripped her miniature pencil and paper but pocketed them without sending what Pam called her "innermost desires" into nature.

When the dancing started, Billy came over and asked Beatrice to dance. He smiled at Lucy, and she was thankful as he took Beatrice's hand. Lucy walked to the main lodge and played the piano alone inside the cavernous dark of the empty room.

"That was lovely," James said when she'd finished playing. He was sitting on the edge of the stage looking out at her.

Years later, as Lucy unpacked boxes from storage with her mother, she found the T-shirt James had given her, his name still written inside. Lucy had moved to England to study, and the boxes had arrived by ship. There was no correspondence in with the shirt, just the clear, steady letters of black ink on the inside neckline. Lucy imagined she could happen upon James in one of the coffeehouses she frequented in London, how they would greet each other, the smell of his English Cusson's soap coming to her in a wave.

Ginny sat next to Lucy, cross-legged on the concrete of the ship's storage warehouse. She said nothing as she watched her daughter fold the shirt. With one hand, she brushed Lucy's hair from her eyes, and with the other hand, she touched the shirt, taking the fabric between her thumb and fingers. She looked at Lucy.

"It's very soft," she said.

James and Lucy climbed up the back of the main lodge via the drainage pipe and broken trellis. James got there first and pulled her up the way you're supposed to pull someone up from a man-overboard drill, hands linked around the forearms. From the roof, they could see the expanse of water, and the rest of camp, the voices muted by the strains of the brass band that played in the gazebo. They lay back onto the upward slope of the shingled eve.

"It's almost over," James said. In the inked sky the night larks flew low and landed by their bare feet. Lucy thought of winter, of the softness of the underside of the foot when summer goes. James turned to face her, their knees touching.

"Want a smoke?" he asked, already having drawn a cigarette from his pack.

"Sure," she said, and it came out softer than she'd intended.

"I'll light it." James passed her the cigarette, and she inhaled. In the air around them, the tiny lights of fireflies switched on and off in thirty-second intervals.

"What the hell are those things?" asked James, pointing to the flicks of light.

"Fireflies, Jamie," she said and laughed. He let her nickname him even though she'd heard him scold others for calling him that.

"What, we don't have them in England, you know. They're beautiful."

The fireflies came closer, slowly. As James and Lucy took drags from their cigarettes, the coral glow of the tips attracted the bugs.

"Look," she said, "they're calling to us."

"Yes," James said as he sat up with his knees to his chest, "the poor sods think we're mating material."

He turned to face her. They were still for a moment, and she thought about touching his hair. He stretched his legs out around hers and draped her own over his.

"I feel as though I ought to ask you something terribly important," James suggested.

"Well, go for it," Lucy said and wondered what it could be, what the question could be, if maybe she'd know the answer right as he spoke. James leaned in, talking in a confidential voice, and let his hand lightly touch the side of her face.

"Would you rather be a city street or a country road?" he asked, and before Lucy could be disappointed, they both began laughing until James started to cough, which made her laugh more.

Just as they were steadying themselves, James looked out at

the glimmer of lights again and kissed her. He leaned in close and put his hand flat on her collarbone, his eyes half-closed. In a fluid motion he pulled her to his chest, and Lucy let herself lean into the warmth of his shirt, his strong arms, wide hands.

"I'm already missing you," he whispered.

When they climbed down from the roof, James went first, lifted Lucy by the hips from the trellis, and set her down in front of him. They held each other, rooted to the spot, against the pine needles underfoot, the fading heat of the end of summer.

✱

starting from seed

And She Was

The car in front of them has a 100% JESUS decal on its back window.

"What about ninety-eight percent?" Jenna asks.

"I'll take skim," Alice says, which is particularly funny to the girls because Alice is well into her second round of *anorexia-bulimia-etc* (her phrasing, not Jenna's), so they both laugh at her nonfat version of the Lord. Doctors at the hospital where Alice goes twice a week for weigh-ins refer to Alice's relapse as her "second bout" of anorexia, as if she'd caught a germ from a dirty bathroom doorknob or someone's unwashed hand and come down with a cold.

"Achoo," Alice would fake sneeze. "I have a bout of anorexia-bulimia-etc." She pronounces *etc* as if it is a full word, not *e-t-c*, and is beautiful and funny enough to get away with it. All the girls on their hockey team watched how Alice laced her skates and tried to imitate the crisscross pattern she'd woven, securing the skate tongue so it didn't rub against her foot.

For some reason Jenna still doesn't understand, Alice has chosen her to be her friend this summer before they start their last year of high school. True, they'd been randomly paired for matchup, covering someone on the opposing team, and Jenna had blushed when the coach linked her name and Alice's. Their parents had sent them to a summer hockey camp composed of girls who either were natural players who needed to stay fit during the off-season or whose parents didn't want them working at the local Subway, but didn't want them sitting at home in the leafy months with the neighborhood boys, either.

Alice would have been in the first category, despite the note from her physician. She'd been a state-ranked player, a forward with a fast wrist flip, the girl who wound up on everyone's shoulders in postgame cheers. Jenna's parents had signed her up for a three-week session without consulting her, saving her (their words, not hers) from a summer of sifting flour for fresh bread at the local bakery. Jenna had gone out with her mother the day before hockey camp started to be outfitted.

"Aren't these a bit bulky?" Her mother touched the shoulder pads and frowned to the salesperson. Jenna stood in the air-conditioning looking out to the street, where two kids sat licking fallen ice-cream streams from their wrists and hands. The body armor weighted her, making her feel as if she'd somehow been given strength.

"They're for protection, Mom, not fashion," she said. Jenna looked at her mother through the bars of the helmet, pretending her brain was in its own tiny prison. "So I don't get a concussion."

"Oh, right." Her mother nodded and studied a tennis outfit— white pleated skirt and fitted top. Jenna knew her mother was wishing she had signed her up for doubles camp or at least some sport that would make her look more prim, less like a girl in a beer ad.

"Anyway, this fits," Jenna said and walked to the cash register in full hockey pads, pants, and helmet. The camp would give her a shirt upon registration.

That's where she met Alice, who was checking names off a clipboarded list, handing out team insignia tops, and constantly licking her dry lips. She had her blond hair pulled back from her face, but broken bits, wisps, fanned out above her forehead, hovering like a hair halo.

"Isn't she adorable?" Jenna's mother had said of Alice, as if they were in the Guggenheim and Alice were a sculpture or a well-positioned painting. Her mother nodded and gave Jenna a slight push, so she stepped over to where Alice sucked on her pen top.

"You must be Jenna," she said. A nod. "Well, hi, Jenna." Alice looked at her, and they smiled at each other—maybe already understanding each other, or understanding being daughters of someone or just needing some comfort—whichever way, Jenna felt that Alice got her. Alice had seen Jenna's mother peck at her, seen that the girl's skates were new, signaling that Jenna didn't really belong at hockey camp. Jenna had already noticed the red marks on Alice's knuckles and figured they were from gagging.

Alice's teeth were mottled, white and gray with clots of yellow. Picked apart, Alice was already in a state of ruin—her hair, her hands, her teeth, not to mention her flower-stalk body. But when she backed up, looking at the composite, the whole Alice was amazing. "Everyone," Alice said and made a sweeping gesture with her hands to the cluster of girls that stood near the rink, "this is Jenna. She's a starting forward, too, and she's my friend."

Just like that, Alice had handed off her clipboard and led Jenna to the locker room, where they'd tried to guess combinations by putting their ears to the knobs and listening for tiny clicks, which supposedly made a click at the correct number. Alice leaned into one of the metal slatted doors and giggled as if the locker had told her something outrageous.

Then they hoisted themselves up onto the wide window ledge and watched the rest of the girls register. Alice hummed, and when Jenna asked what the tune was, she said, "That Talking Heads song. You know it?" Jenna shook her head, and Alice went on, "It's called 'And She Was'—it's cool, kind of odd, but I like it."

Jenna told Alice about how she used songs to transport her back to certain times, and Alice agreed.

"Sometimes," Jenna said softly, as if what she was about to say was an admission, "it's like I try to make a song fit—you know, search for one until I have a tune that sort of sums up where I am, or where I have been." She looked out at the leafy green, at the sway of full-limbed trees. "Now 'And She Was' can be the song of this summer, or of this." She meant hockey camp but realized maybe Alice would think she was referring to them.

Alice tucked her bony knees under her T-shirt. She seemed collapsible, foldable like a stepladder. "I'm glad to give you that song, then," she said. "You know, like a reminder of when we met."

Jenna watched Alice fidget with her earrings and wished she'd known her before she was so thin—not to have seen her demise but to have a vision of who she'd been before she started attacking herself.

"That girl looks like my mom," Alice said. She pointed to a dark-haired pouter who stood in line with her skates draped over her shoulder like a beach towel. "My mother always had her hair like that."

"I've never seen mine with long hair." Jenna sighed. Somehow it was sad that her mother had lopped off her ringlets, that she'd tamed her hair into submission, keeping it short and sprayed flat. When she'd asked about it, her mother had said, without flicking her eyes away from the highway in front of her, "Show me a non-famous woman over forty-five with shoulder-length hair who doesn't look like a tramp." Jenna thought it sounded like a dare but didn't offer up a name. Instead, she thought of her mother's friends, their cropped heads of hair, the terse phone calls, the occasional raw laughs that escaped their taut mouths, sad reminders of the girls they'd been. Then she thought of her mother pleased, when the dahlias bloomed in rows, when she'd taught Jenna how to make jam, their bodies working like machinery, sterilizing, canning, stacking the jars of strawberry-rhubarb preserves.

"I've never even seen my mother at all, so." Alice let out a burp at the same time she revealed this. She looked at Jenna's face. "Oh, my God—that was so after-school special. Sorry." She scraped the gum line of her front teeth with a fingernail. It's no big deal or anything. But we have these pictures in an album—you know, the kind with the sticky pages. Except the pages aren't sticky anymore. My mother's in a long purple dress." Alice gestured to her collarbone to show the dress's style. "It kind of flares out here, and she's so beautiful. Really chiseled, with silver earrings. Very sixties, I guess."

"She sounds pretty," Jenna said and thought about her family albums. They were mostly navy blue and embossed with gold dates or initials; her mother kept them rowed up on the built-ins in the study. They sat there, too high to get down and look at easily, but on display enough so that everyone who came in remarked how many there were, how many photographs and memories must be contained in their pages, how many years had passed since the first gold-embossed spine had been marked.

Jenna looked at Alice's thighs, how her kneecaps exposed themselves through the skin.

"I'm sick," Alice said softly and didn't look at Jenna. It was the only time Jenna heard her say that without making a joke. She didn't say that she'd get better or that she was trying to get help, she just let Jenna know the state of her. Maybe so Jenna could make a decision about spending time with her, so she could keep this knowledge in the back of her brain to refer to when she felt herself getting a best friend.

On the ice, Alice and Jenna could shut out the players, their families, the glint of bright sun outside. They worked on clearing the zone, which is when a defending player sends the puck out of the opponent's attacking zone and all the attacking players have to leave the zone, clearing it in order to avoid being called offside when the puck comes back. Two weeks into hockey camp, Alice and Jenna had nearly perfected their blind pass, both skating fast. Alice would hang back about a yard, then suddenly she would pass the puck to Jenna without looking. Alice was good like that— once she got a feeling about where Jenna was on the ice, she could just let go and shoot to her without worrying about whether the puck would get there.

"It's my own kind of faith," she explained to Jenna. Alice was watching her eat toast with cheese and honey. They sat in the bakery Jenna wanted to work in, the kind that sold fresh apricot muffins and braids of glossy bread, and watched people in their summer modes. Kids dripped fluorescent Popsicles onto their shirts, women in the realm of her mother wore linen outfits that never seemed to wrinkle, and preteens stood like stars—their limbs jutting out like points all around them.

"Can you at least smell it?" Jenna asked Alice and shoved her bread up to her nose. Alice knew Jenna knew about her "food quirks" and was comfortable enough by this point to make jokes.

"Yum," Alice said. "Vanilla."

"Do you—did you—like vanilla?" Jenna asked. Sometimes she felt guilty asking Alice about food, but it was fascinating, like watching surgery on TV—on the one hand, absorbing and, on the other, too remote to cause a reaction—and Alice could shrug it off.

"I used to. It might be too *casual* now."

Jenna loved how Alice used nonfood words to talk about food, which was nonfood to her. Vanilla was casual, blueberries were annoying, caramel was slutty. They'd baked Annoying Slut Muffins earlier in the week to celebrate their win against the Kenttown

Vikings, and Alice had actually eaten an exact quarter of one, declaring them amusing.

"You really love all this stuff, don't you?" Alice said to Jenna and looked behind her at the large oven in the back of the room, the baguettes poking up from their baskets.

"Yeah," Jenna said. "I always liked rolling dough, decorating sugar cookies, that sort of thing. Braiding bread."

"So you're going to be a baker?" Alice smiled. She didn't laugh at Jenna or make a joke; she tilted her head and nodded. "I can totally see that. You're so nourishing. Jenna the Baker. It sounds like a children's story."

Jenna liked the sound of that, enjoyed the image she had of herself piglet-plump with an apron and puffy hat. Alice looked at her hands as if she expected something to be in them. Jenna thought about what she'd said, about the nourishing part, and how that was one of those sentences she'd never forget.

Sometimes, Jenna knew them when they were uttered—the sentences could be meaningful like that one, or just some angry deli lady shouting about how corned beef is the devil's work, or a seventh-grade boy asking her at the 1950s-style sock hop if she wanted to dance but phrasing it as *cut a grug* instead of *cut a rug*. Other times, someone could say something to her and it dissipated quickly, only to resurface at a strange moment. Once, when she'd wanted sneakers, the expensive ones, her father had told her it was a mistake to go through life always feeling entitled. The words slid by unnoticed, then presented themselves again when she was baking a ginger-pear upside-down cake. The top layer of sticky sliced pears kept drooping over the sides, making the cake look as if it had had a pastry stroke, and she found herself saying it was a mistake to go through life entitled. She whisper-chanted the words until she'd fixed the whole thing, secured it on a glass cake stand, and stood looking at her work, making her father's words into a

song. Basically, she had no choice, it seemed, about which words
stuck to her and which left.

"You should come visit me in Connecticut," Alice said. She lived
near a cheese outlet and a huge ice rink, and had an older brother,
Justin, who bought beets for her when she asked. "He's going to
Dartmouth," she said and pointed up, as if New Hampshire were
in the ceiling. "But he'll come home for breaks. Maybe he could
pick you up on the way down sometime."

"That'd be great," Jenna said. There was something pulsing,
daring about riding in a car with someone's older brother. More
so when that someone was as slim a presence as Alice. Alice
showed her a photograph of Justin.

"He's so cute. He looks like . . ." She couldn't think what.

"A Labrador?" Alice said. She put her lips together. Jenna sometimes found herself doing Alice's gestures, clamping her mouth
shut suddenly or twisting just the front lock of hair around her
fingers. Alice knew it, and would tell Jenna she was "being me—
without the gagging part."

And that part always came. Jenna had to wait for Alice to finish in the bathroom, puking silently if anyone else were around,
or running the tap. She never let Jenna come in with her, not that
she would have wanted to, but Jenna wished she could hold her
back, less because she feared for Alice's health than because she
needed her friendship, wanted her to be around for her own benefit. It wasn't like hearing about some senior girl at school and
how her friend held her hair back while she threw up Rolling
Rock or wine coolers. There was distance. Alice wanted Jenna as
close as possible—right up to the bathroom doorframe, nosing
against the wall, even, but not inside.

Alice told Jenna she always ate bright-colored foods first—
Chee-tos or strawberry licorice, yellow peppers. After that she
could move on to mozzarella sticks or bread, bland visions of

starch. Then later, when she threw up, she'd know she'd reached the last of the food, cleared her whole system, when she vomited red or yellow. The shock of color signaled a win of some kind.

Jenna preferred to think of Alice that way—like an art project, colors swirling inside her, rather than of how sick she was. During that summer, Alice ate only on days that had a *t* in them, so Saturday afternoon Jenna could tell Alice was preparing herself for that night's binge. Alice was fun when she was just about to eat—it was the time she was most excited, bouncy, singing Top 40 songs, skating the rim of the rink at full speed, daring her body to collide with the ice.

Then, later, she put on "And She Was," the Talking Heads song. Jenna listened to the lyrics and how they mention the highway breathing. Suddenly it didn't seem cool, the way Alice had said, it felt scary and unsettling—too bizarre to imagine things that weren't meant to feel or have lungs expanding and contracting right at the roadside. When she came out of the ladies' room, Alice wiped her mouth on her hockey jersey. Her eyes were teary and bloodshot, but she looked beautiful, placid. Calm and ease drifted onto her after she'd been in the bathroom, as if she'd solved everything.

All the padded hockey girls skated to the music while they practiced. Jerseys and pads made rectangles of them, and Jenna would think about their geometry as they shucked by one another, passing the puck, dekeing, making a decoy, a fake motion that players do when they have the puck and make the defensive players think they're going to move in a certain direction when they're not. Teammates can shoulder-deke or stick-deke, even head-deke—the kind of shot that made Jenna feel kind of conceited after she'd done it right.

Sometimes she thinks that Alice is dekeing everyone; that maybe she dekes the players and coach, her brother or whoever else is at home, that Alice is this superstar who doesn't even need fuel to make a goal. And maybe Jenna is the one who's been completely deked, thinking she's made a lifelong friend.

This was the year that the overtime loss category, the result for a team that loses in overtime a game that was tied after regulation, worth one point in the standings, was approved for hockey. Their camp team won because of this, and when the girls got their fake gold medals from the coach, who walked in her shoes out onto the ice, Jenna thought about those words. Overtime loss. Would those words stick? The coach looped green and orange ribbons—the team colors—around their heads and then let the weight hit each padded chest. Flush-faced and proud, the girls stood, steadying themselves on their sticks as the other team offered palms of congratulations.

Summer is nearly over. The fanning arc of full trees shade Jenna and Alice as they walk to the car. Jenna is giving her friend a ride to the train station out on Route 128. That night Alice will be in Connecticut and Jenna will go back to her house and put the hockey gear away. They'd all signed each other's pads, graffitiing the shoulders so they looked like tattooed butterfly wings. Jenna imagines shutting them into the cocoon of her closet until the next time she plays hockey—whenever that will be.

At the second traffic light, Jenna stops behind a car with various stickers on its rear—LABEL GENETICALLY ENGINEERED FOOD, NO VICTIMS EVER, and NO NUKES. She thinks about waking Alice to tell her to read them, how she might change NO NUKES to NO PUKES. Before the light switches to green, she watches the slight rise and fall of Alice's chest, breastbone visible through the T-shirt; ribs, clavicles, all juts and eaves—as if her bones were struggling to escape the confines of her body. Jenna wishes that Alice had buckled her seat belt, that something held her down so

Alice would stay with her, but she has the feeling her friend will be gone soon, that she's let herself be deked.

Passengerless later, Jenna knows that what she loved about Alice—part of the thrill of being with her—was the absolute certainty that she wouldn't last. That she would pine for her when Alice eventually flushed herself, her laugh, and her song, right out of this world. Alice would leave Jenna missing her the way Jenna misses the parts of her parents that aren't young anymore, the way she misses the weight of what was on the other side of all her choices—colleges, camps, ice-cream flavors. The way you can miss someone you never met, never even had the chance to—like a sister, like a boy.

Come to Iceland

When Randall drives to Keflavik Airport, he brings with him a small pot of skyr, thick yogurt made from skimmed milk curd, to which he has added a teaspoon of raspberry jam. He stands near the customs exit, keeping back from the turnstiles so Gabrielle won't feel bombarded by her father and his dairy products when she emerges dry-lipped and untucked from the plane.

"Hi, Dad," she says and hugs him from the side so only half of each of them touches. He hands her the skyr, and she folds back the tinfoil top before even moving out of the way of the other grounded passengers. He watches her and wonders at each motion of her fingers, thinking she has doctor hands and digits—he has a daughter who can slice skin, remove tumors, and open yogurt containers! He lets her have a couple of mouthfuls and then leads her over to baggage reclaim, where they stand in the zoom and hush of circling luggage until her knapsack clumps onto the belt.

In the rental car, green fields slide by, tiny farmhouses and pitted rocks surrounded by grassy tufts mark nameless roads, and Randall reaches over to touch Gabrielle's face, patting her cheek, then resting his arm on the headrest as if he's about to back up.

"We need to catch the bus at two this afternoon," he says. "We go right to Landmannalaugar. Did you remember gloves? I think we need them for the glacier."

"For the fifth time, yes." Gabrielle smiles and fiddles with the radio controls on the dash until a local station comes on. She and Randall listen to the Icelandic, which neither one understands.

"It's sort of nice," Randall says, "not to know what they're talking about." He gestures to the radio as if the announcers live inside.

"I know," Gabrielle says. Treeless, the verdant landscape passes outside the car window. So low, the shrubs seem like new growth, and Gabrielle thinks that if she were to step out there, she would feel giant, enlarged.

"It's relaxing, really," Randall says and points to the radio.

"What is?" Gabrielle looks at her father.

"Not knowing what people are saying," he says. "It takes the pressure off responding somehow."

In the center of town, Randall drops the car back at the hotel lot, where they'll pick it up at the end of the hike, when they'll drive the Golden Circle, stopping to swim in the lagoon. He walks to meet Gabrielle at the food stand by the waterfront, where they order lunch. Each hot dog is the size of a toddler finger, some dotted with cut cubes of pickle, others served with sweet sauce. They sit on the seawall and face the harbor, looking at the boats and the silver-domed dairy processing plant before heading to the bus terminal.

"I can't believe how empty it seems here," she says, sweeping her arm back toward the city.

"Not like London?" Randall says.

After the trip, Gabrielle will begin a yearlong fellowship at St. Mary's Hospital in London, and she looks forward to leaving

Baltimore and residency, and moving on. Each place she's lived ripples out in her mind, ringing her from Texas to Maryland to New York, and Ecuador, where she'd lived half a year to learn rural medicine.

"What's the population in London?" Randall asks, nudging her until she smiles. It's an old joke, one from their first trip to Iceland that had resurfaced when they'd met in the leafy quiet of the botanical garden near her medical school in the Bronx, and she knew he'd do the same in London.

During their first trip to Iceland, right before Gabrielle had started her residency at Hopkins, but several months before Randall's further prostate radiation treatments had been announced, they'd met in the north of Iceland, in Akureyri, and hiked the Súlur Mountain. At the top, snacking between two red marking poles, Randall had quizzed Gabrielle about Ecuador—wanting to know average incomes, the details of importing and exporting, names of the local wildlife.

"What was the population in Ecuador?" he had asked.

She had said, "God, Dad, don't know. Why do you have to ask like that?"

"How do you want me to ask?"

"In a simple way," Gabrielle had told him. She picked at a torn flap of rubber on her hiking boot and looked at the fall of her father's mouth. "Just—something like— 'Was it crowded there?' Or maybe 'Did you have a good time?'"

She had wondered then why they both referred to the country in the past tense, as if, since Gabrielle wasn't posted there anymore, it had ceased to exist.

"Fine," Randall had said. He'd folded his finished bag of chips into a triangle and held it at arm's length in front so it lined up with another mountain across the way. "Tell me about how crowded Ecuador was."

She'd told him of walking, arms pinned to her sides, through Old Town in Quito, the half-paved streets, the jumble of it all; how close the waiters there had leaned in when she'd placed an order. Sooty children, ready to shine shoes came right to her ears, first smelling her hair, then whispering in Spanish, asking her for money or gum. Then, in Manta, where she'd lived for six months, the streets were suddenly vacant except at market time, when men spread out sheets of blue tarpaulin and set on display eels and fish caught that morning. Merchants vased the *canahuate* flowers in empty coffee tins. The flowers' large purple stems could be dipped into butter and steamed, or wrung for sour liquid that was mixed with sugar for an after-dinner drink. At the hospital there, when Gabrielle prescribed antibiotics for urinary tract infections or diagnosed pyelonephritis, the attending physician had also recommended the patients drink the *canahuate* pressings.

What Gabrielle loved most were the seeds that were shucked and sprinkled onto salads. Bags of them swung from hooks on the market stalls next to halved guavas or cluttered rows of *borojo* brought in from Colombia and prized for their cure-all qualities. Often, husbands brought containers of the squeezed tonic to their wives as they labored, and no matter how many times Gabrielle asked the women not to drink too much, or took the jars of juice away, they would always find more.

At the end of the market, the ice had melted in the stalls, slicked the tarps, and rings of squid had hardened in the sun as hunks of unsold dark fish were hauled away for chum. Along the dusky beach near her apartment complex, there were often loose tentacles and severed crab legs so pink and dried that Gabrielle had taken a couple inside and set them on a window ledge with some shells like collected flowers.

On their descent, Randall had said, "I wish I'd gotten down there to visit you." This is the closest he can come to apologizing for the secrecy; it escapes him completely that his wife, Diane, with

whom he had had an affair, has turned his daughter into the other
woman.

Diane, a personal decorator who enjoys travel for its shopping
arcades and cheap leather goods, hadn't wanted to repeat what she
considered a wasteful trip to the Galápagos, despite the albatross
photo framed in the entryway, so she'd begged off visiting Gabrielle and asked Randall to do the same. He'd thought about asking
Diane to take a trip to celebrate Gabrielle's new status as a resident, but instead he'd gone ahead and booked the Iceland trip as
business and not mentioned to his wife that his daughter would be
there. Diane hadn't been suspicious, especially after Randall had
sent away for golf brochures that described the most northerly
golf course in the world, where every June the Arctic Open was
played through the night in the midnight sun.

Of course, Randall hadn't watched golf but had instead explored Hrísey, an island populated by two hundred people and an
abundance of birds, with Gabrielle. Ptarmigans, the most common birds on the island, roamed fairly tame, waddling the roads
and gardens of the town in groups. Randall had wanted to sit on
the bench that marked where the island's center bell had stood
and tell his daughter that his prostate-specific antigen test had
come back elevated, that he'd seen a swirl of blood in the toilet one
morning. Instead they'd rested there and he'd described the lu-
pine fields on the western side, the way the domed bell had been
used to announce a catch of herring.

His own bloody urine had made him think about the labs
Gabrielle could interpret now, the way she could suture incisions
with the same deftness she'd had in high school sewing brocade
onto the band uniforms or fitting Sky Masterson's double-breasted
blazer for the camp production of *Guys and Dolls*. As the blood ed-
died to the sewage pipes, he'd thought less about what it might
mean for him and more about Gabrielle. When she had first had

her period, she hadn't said anything but had led him into the bath and hygiene aisle at the grocery store and pointed to a box of Lady Softness pads, saying, "I need these." Randall admires her surety in this memory, what he perceives as her ability to ask for what she needs, feels pride when he remembers that he didn't blush, never wished her mother had been there to handle that side of being female.

On Hrísey, they'd unrolled sleeping bags onto the thin air mats Gabrielle had thought to bring and slept in the echoing dark of the island's elementary school. Other campers stayed there, too, unwrapping cheese and brown bread sandwiches bought at the ferry port and whispering as if they were all disciplined school-children.

"Daddy?" Gabrielle had said as she kicked her feet free from the nylon sack.

"Yes," he'd said, and before he could wait for her to talk he asked, "Is everything okay?" He did not want her to turn the question back to him; he wanted to appear solid, as capable as Gabrielle.

"Yeah, fine," she'd said and watched him turn onto his back, face to the arch of ceiling, and then, when she was sure he was asleep, she'd put her hand on his, watching both palms rise and sink with his breathing.

After Gabrielle was in her third month of residency, Randall had met her at the Hopkins cafeteria and managed to inform her of his treatment. From her white coat pocket she'd produced for him a photograph of the two of them in hiking gear, smiling widely, shoulders pressed together so tightly they appear to be wearing one giant black-and-yellow plaid shirt. Gabrielle had offered him a copy that he'd had to refuse lest Diane know he hadn't been alone in Iceland. Before she was paged away, coat flapping like a loose-winged egret, Gabrielle had sighed and shrugged, as if her father had refused traditional medicine of some kind and was waiting to see if the herbal remedy worked—it was his choice not to tell his wife about Iceland, but she didn't approve.

This time, with his radiation series completed, Randall had intended to tell Diane about Iceland and Gabrielle, but she'd gone away to Golden Horizons, the spa near Santa Barbara famous for skin peels and hydrotherapy weight loss, before he'd had the chance. Looking out over Reykjavík Harbor, he watches gulls flap close to the water, fishing in the early-afternoon murk.

"I'm so glad you're here," he says to Gabrielle. "Maybe this should be an annual pilgrimage."

Gabrielle imagines how a pushpin-marked map would look, blue ends sticking out to show out where she has had her father alone, all to herself, how the pins would cluster on this one floating country.

They walk up the main street toward the hotel to rest before the bus ride out to Landmannalaugar.

"Me, too," she says, then feels she needs to clarify. "To meet here annually."

Randall wonders if passersby see the resemblance, if they look alike enough to be seen as father and daughter or if he is assumed to be a divorced man dating the woman who would have brushed him off in his youth. Before he'd remarried, back when Gabrielle was still in grade school, they'd go out every Friday night to Fox and Hounds, the fancy restaurant in town. With her in patterned tights and new flats, father and daughter would sit at their table for two and try to guess what other tables were talking about, if the people sitting next to them were sisters or friends, if the hostess was in love with the sommelier. He thinks of her as having been grown-up then, housed in a flat-chested body but already a surgeon somehow, cutting away at the debris that lay between people, figuring out what clues might lead to diagnosing someone's condition.

At Gabrielle's fourteenth birthday dinner, when Diane—her

hair newly streaked and sprayed—had first joined them at Fox and Hounds, they'd tried to include her in the guessing game ritual, but she'd wanted to know which pattern the plates were, if Randall had a preference for cut crystal or plain. Gabrielle had kept playing by herself, deciding that the man in the blue shirt loved the sad-mouthed lady in the corner but couldn't tell her. Randall had assumed Gabrielle would comment on Diane, on her invasion into their routines and rituals, and was both guilty and pleased when she didn't. He did not think her muteness on the subject had anything to do with her own guilt, the knowledge that she would—someday—have to leave her father to take care of himself. If she ever sees him with a stain on his shirt, crumbs flecking a cashmere sweater, she is covered by a tremendous wave of nausea, as if somehow her father is a stroke victim unable to dress himself and she is partly responsible.

Gabrielle's hair is coiled into a bun. A couple of twists have escaped and dangle by her ears, so he tucks one back as she looks at the tourist displays in the shop windows. Pulling back out the hair that Randall has just secured, Gabrielle looks at the Icelandic sweaters for sale. Empty of mannequin bodies, the woolens hang on wooden racks, pinned into various positions.

"What's weird is," she says as she points to them, "they're gesturing, even though there's no one in them."

One sweater arm bends at its elbow, another flops onto its neighbor, two are turned toward each other, headless lovers, while a step or two lower, the kid sweaters frolic with arms posed over the neck holes. One even holds an American football, miming a pass or a victory dance.

On the bus to Landmannalaugar, Gabrielle falls asleep and wakes to rain slapping the windshield. She looks at the other passengers and decides she and her father are the only non-Icelanders. One woman sits with her purple-tighted legs apart, Achilles tendons stuck into the spaces on either side of the seat in front, and notices Gabrielle looking at her. The woman stands, turns around, and waves at Gabrielle, offering something from a plastic bag. With Randall asleep on his rolled up Gore-Tex coat, Gabrielle feels she has to accept, so she braces herself on the seatbacks and joins the woman.

"Salted licorice?" the woman in purple tights asks.

"Sure," Gabrielle says and unwraps the hard cube, knowing she will want to spit it out. In every country it seemed there was a bitter candy or unusual condiment that appealed only to natives; candied cod or Marmite spread, jellied passion fruit or baked twists of lime rinds. In Ecuador, the gourd seeds weren't bitter, but they'd been fried in curdled butter. Gabrielle had liked them raw and wanted to bring some back to share with her father, since she knew she couldn't translate their pungency or the way they recalled her whole time in Manta, but of course they'd never let her through customs with them. She had thought that, if Randall had visited, he would have somehow found a way to sneak them onboard—in his shoe, rolled up in his blue T-shirt, or between their hands. The same thing had happened the last time they'd been in Iceland; she'd wanted to take a cup of skyr on the flight back to start her residency, but the flight attendants, with their tiny red fez hats and A-line navy skirts, had smiled warmly as they'd removed her open yogurt from the plane.

"Will you look at that?" Randall says when they've laced their boots and put their packs on. Ahead, sanded cliffs jut from the black lava ground.

"I feel like I'm in a sand castle," Gabrielle says, then feels embarrassed for some reason.

They walk with the rest of the group until pairs and friends clot into groups, some farther back and others, wanting to be first, trekking faster. Miles later, the first hut appears, a Monopoly house set on the side of lake Alftavatn.

Each hiker sets his or her pack by the boot room and then claims a bed. Gabrielle gives her father the bottom bunk of one set so he'll have easy access to the outhouse during the night, even though the sky will be light. She sits near a heater, drying her damp socks while she watches the flat lake water. During the hike they'd passed bubbling sulfur craters murked with sand and silt. Randall had taken to calling the sulfur-smelling land the Lost City of Flatulantis, and Gabrielle had laughed so hard that later, when she thought about it, she felt despondent, as if her father might evaporate into one of the misted clouds.

Bleak volcanic ash and rocks had given way to cookie-crumb-textured dirt. Through the black, tiny pink flowers poked through, showing leaves the color of newborns' skin, mottled and red. Then the lake had appeared, flanked by small, algae-covered hills.

"I'm so glad not to be taking care of anyone right now," Gabrielle says when she and Randall are seated at the communal table for dinner. Slices of salmon, cheese, and hard bread are passed, and Gabrielle bites into a tomato round before adding, "I keep expecting my pager to go off." She has the anxiety and adrenaline built into her now, the constant waiting for alarms and need.

"You work so hard, sweetheart," Randall says. Tomato seeds slip from his lips onto the side of his chin, clinging until Gabrielle collects them in her paper napkin. For a second, she thinks she will cry—it's so easy to imagine her father having a stroke, unable to walk or feed himself, relying on Diane to interpret his slurred speech and invariably losing something in the translation.

"I love you, Dad," Gabrielle says quickly, then reaches for the plate of hard-boiled eggs to cover her words. The slippery eggs wobble and roll like blind creatures bent on suiciding from their platter.

Randall gives Gabrielle a pat on the back. The purple-tights woman from the bus stands and starts singing in Icelandic.

Everyone except Gabrielle and Randall joins in. They sit listening to the indecipherable lyrics as the sun stays high in the sky.

When the light is dim but still there at two in the morning, Gabrielle climbs down from the bunk bed and goes outside. The outhouse door flaps open in the wind. Inside, when she's latched it, she sits on the cutout circle part of a wooden plank and tries not to listen to the sounds of waste slushing beneath.

By the lake, Ragnus, the cabin master, sits with his knees splayed out, each one pointing to a hill. Gabrielle goes over and sits down near him.

"What are you doing awake?" he asks her.

"There's a lot of snoring going on in there," she says.

"The big sisters?" he asks, referring to the kneesocked twins, heavyset and wet-lipped, who'd arrived after dinner and taken the last empty bunks.

Ragnus runs his fingers through the silty, dark sand and looks at Gabrielle. "Are you having fun with your boyfriend?" he asks.

"Oh—no. That's my dad," she says.

"I know," Ragnus says, laughing. "I was just making a joke."

The whole scene is fogged, barely lighted and mellow at the edges in the unsetting sun, and when Gabrielle moves in to kiss Ragnus, it's as if she's watching herself from the other side of the lake, hardly able to make out what's happening. She finds his tranquillity appealing, then wonders if maybe she has taken his lack of language skills for poetic quiet. Ragnus kisses her back and then leans her into the sandy ledge. Gabrielle can feel her undone boots about to come off and wonders what she'd do if one slipped from her foot and into the lake. Above her, Ragnus grins, mouths her neck some, and then he leads her to his small room at the back of the cabin.

Over coffee the next morning, Randall asks Gabrielle how she slept. "The snoring's quite something, isn't it?" he says.

"Tell me about it," she says.

"Maybe tonight we'll be in a different cabin than they are," he says quietly, gesturing with his head to the twins.

Right then, Gabrielle has the urge to stay at the lake, to sleep and laze in the gritty sheets with Ragnus, to eat tinned fish and walk barefooted on the algaed hills. She can see living here, the simplicity of the food, the hikes, the shared cabin, her father available.

"Should we stay another night here?" she asks Randall.

"I don't think that's an option," he says. "We have to stay with the group. Besides, today we're heading to the glacier. You have your gloves, right?"

Gabrielle nods and goes to pack up her things. When she's slung her pack on, she finds Ragnus by the breakfast table.

"You should sign the guest book," he offers. "That's where everyone puts their name and address—to show they've been here."

Gabrielle looks at the comments people have written in other languages. In one column she writes her name. Since she doesn't have an address yet where she'll be in London and doesn't think to give her father and Diane's address in Baltimore, she has to leave that column blank. In the comments section she writes "lovely," then hands the pen back to Ragnus.

"Come back soon," he says to her when the group is out, scattering over the green rises like Gore-Tex ants.

"I'd like to," she says.

When the glacier is in sight, the group stops to reoutfit in snow pants, extra fleece vests, mittens, rainbow-knitted hats. Randall is set.

"You ready?" he says to Gabrielle, who has put a long-sleeved T-shirt and oversized wool sweater on underneath her jacket.

"Yeah," she says. Randall hands her one of his folding ski poles.

"You might want this," he says, looping a strap around her wrist. "Where are your gloves?"

"I guess I don't have them after all," she says.

This annoys Randall more than it should, and he shakes his head at her. "All this time you said you had them. Let's see if someone has an extra pair."

"Dad, I'm fine."

"It's freezing over there. It's a glacier, for God's sake."

"Dad—I will be fine." Gabrielle speaks each word slowly.

Randall looks at her again, then faces the path. The ground is covered in ice so thick and pure it gleams blue, and the group members duck and lean into the ice caves. Randall stands inside one, dwarfed by the cavern's mouth. Gabrielle takes a photo. Her hands are cold, and she puts them against her belly to warm them.

The purple-tights woman lies flat out on the ice, looking up at the blank sky. The hefty twins take identical Polaroids with the white caves as backdrop.

"Fantastic," Randall says, sweeping his pole arm past the ice mounds. "I've never seen anything like it. Isn't it amazing?"

Gabrielle nods. She looks at the unfamiliar landscape, how one sledge of snow slips into another until there aren't any clear lines of which hill or cave is on what surface.

"So, Gabs," Randall says, taking off a glove and giving one to her, "how do you feel about babies?"

"What?" Gabrielle balls her fist up into the too-big palm slot. "I like them, of course. Why?"

"Well, you know I never planned on having children—after you, I mean. But since this"—Randall gestures in the direction of his groin—"the treatment and everything, Diane's been talking about having one." His words are practiced enough that Gabrielle can tell he has thought about when to say this.

She is tempted to ask, "One what?" But she knows. "You're actually considering having a baby?" She immediately flashes forward to Diane puttering through the layette department at Saks, decorating the nursery with a theme. Then, in a much smaller image, she sees her father holding a newborn and wants to shake him—it should be Gabrielle's baby in that image, his grandchild.

Randall leans on his pole. "Probably not a baby—you know Diane. Can't really see her wiping anyone's bottom. Anyway, she's been thinking about adopting."

"She or we?" Gabrielle says, and it comes out tight. She detests herself for being able to cope with blood, feces, cancerous ovaries, and unable to express how she feels about this: the imaginary baby, the secrecy of this trip, the feeling her father is somehow hers only in the barren landscape of this country.

"We, I guess. It will make her happy, and I have to say, it'd be pretty nice to have a little one around again," Randall says and looks around as if he expects to see a toddler bobbing and snow-angeling in the ice. "I did love taking care of you then."

"I know. You did a good job." Gabrielle nods.

"So, you're okay with it?" Randall asks.

"You know, Dad, what can I say?" Gabrielle takes off his glove and hands it back. "I don't need it. Here." Then, when they've stood a moment in the cold quiet, she adds, "There are a lot of people in medicine who go back and forth between ob-gyn and pediatrics—you know, who can't decide which to specialize in."

"Really?"

"Yeah. But eventually, you have to look at a delivery and see where your instincts are—when the kid is born, do you want to go with it to the warming table or do you want to stay with the mother?" Gabrielle adjusts the laces on her boot with her red fingers. "I always want to stay."

They don't talk much more about it. Gabrielle never knew what was a reality for Diane and what was an ephemeral desire, and sometimes she found that if she didn't object to something—say, a kitchen renovation or turning her childhood room into a huge walk-in closet—nothing happened. Soon Gabrielle would be in London, lecturing, examining women on their sides instead of on their backs, using terms like general practitioner instead of primary care provider, and using a postal code when she wrote an unsent postcard to Ragnus back at the lake.

"How often do you need to get checkups, anyway?" Gabrielle asks, as if they've just been talking about his prostate.

"About every three then six months," Randall says. "I have one when I get back."

"Are you going to tell Diane where you've been?" she asks.

Randall sighs as they start walking away from the glaciers. "I'm planning on it," he says, "but I guess it depends."

"We could send her a postcard," Gabrielle offers. Randall shakes his head and smiles. "It could just say 'Come to Iceland.'"

"Just that? No slogan?" he asks.

They take turns coming up with slogan endings.

"Come to Iceland," Gabrielle starts, sniffing the sulfur pools as they walk over them. "Where you can eat beans and no one will ever know."

"Come to Iceland," Randall says. "Where you won't understand a damn word."

"Come to Iceland," Gabrielle adds. "No one else does."

Randall has walked ahead of her a few yards and turns to face her. Suddenly she can see him living forever, remaining ice-fixed and well. Then, just as quickly, her father is only a spot, a red-and-black Gore-Texed figure on the white landscape ahead.

Defining Moments in the
Life of His Father

Off Route 80 in Branford there's a dead dog splayed out near the highway guardrail. Justin's not sure his father saw the golden retriever as they pulled into the Laundry Land lot and headed to Benny's A-Pizza, but Justin looked at the dog's body from the passenger seat and again when he passed by the parked cars and Friday night litter that collected by the curb.

"Justin," his dad said. And then when he didn't respond, "You want eggplant?"

"Sure." Justin nodded.

They always got the same kind in the hope that Justin's sister, Alice, might actually eat something. Eggplant had been her favorite, and they'd taken a large pizza to the hockey rink where she'd played on the girls' league back in high school. Since she'd come back from college after only one semester, she hadn't eaten much of anything and stopped going to the games. The father still played spectator, cheering for Alice's younger teammates, folding his slices and eating them down to the crust, then boomerang-shooting the dried ends into the open trash cans in back of the seats.

Alice stayed home. She liked to needlepoint and ordered kits from a catalog, pillows usually. The patterns were of the home-sweet-home sort, but Alice would change them, twisting the threads into whatever letters she felt like stitching. The living room now hosted rectangles, circular-shaped cushions, even a hexagon with gibberish yarn spellings: "Hip snurf herm," "Whap Goof did Yop," and one into which most of a question mark had been stitched but the bottom never finished and the bare netting scratched if you leaned on it too long. Justin would sit next to Alice, watching her fingers slide the needle up through each tiny square until she'd made an x in blue or gold and moved on to the next.

"It's very satisfying," she would say. On her middle fingers were red-chaffed marks from gagging. She knew Justin knew. She knew everyone knew, but she kept stitching and not eating or eating only popcorn or just licorice cut into pieces and then ridding herself of them.

This time when Justin came home for Thanksgiving break, the house was locked. He pitched some driveway pebbles up at Alice's window, and she came down the stairs to let him in wearing her hockey jersey like a nightgown. Number 17 dwarfed her, her insect legs pressed against him when they hugged, and he tapped her clavicle in a strange brother-sister hello. Their father stood at the top of the stairs. He looked down at them as he gripped both sides of the banister, lifting his feet slightly, an aging gymnast ready to perform.

Justin tried to picture his dad as a kid, as a teenager, as a guy his age attempting to sleep with college girls, who felt impossibly re-mote, and he couldn't. His father still slept in the same striped paja-mas that he'd worn when his kids were in grade school, and this made Justin desperate, lost. He thought about buying his father new ones—maybe from that catalog that arrived every week or so in the mailbox and depicted families chopping trees together or roughhousing with their Labradors, ruddied and snow-cold as they tramped through some field. But Justin knew his father would just continue to wear the ones he had on now. And that was worse for Justin to think about: having to sort through his father's things when he died one day and finding unopened pajamas in a drawer, having to donate them to someplace or get rid of them, although he knew that same catalog place had a lifetime return policy.

None of them said anything then, they just went to bed. The next day was Wednesday, and Justin asked Alice if she'd come watch her old team try to beat the New Haven Hooligans in that afternoon's game. All the girls' teams had ridiculous names, ones that tried to pound into everyone's heads that girls could play hockey, could side-check and take a puck in the teeth just like boys. Alice's team was the Whitby Wolverines, and darting out from each shirt belly was a toothy wolf snout, open as if about to consume the shirt number or the person inside.

"No thanks, Justin," she said. "I have cooking to do besides." She didn't say besides what but showed him a magazine photograph of a bowl filled with stuffing, fake steam rising from the top of the cranberry-littered mound.

"You know," Justin said, pointing to the puff of it, "I saw on a show once that the steam in food pictures is really smoke. They just put it there to make all the stuffing or burgers or whatever seem fresh-baked."

Alice nodded in the way she always had, listening but not affected. "Interesting," she said. "Have fun."

"Go, team!" their dad shouted with a fist raised in the air. "Need anything special while we're out?" he said, poking his head into the living room, where Alice sat with her feet tucked under her bagging sweater.

She shook her head, and Justin stood up. "You guys," she said, as if Justin and their father had done something funny just by being there. Then she went back to her needlepoint, keeping the cooking magazine open in front of her.

Justin's father drove toward Benny's A-Pizza, pointing out construction sites and prime developments his son had only a mild interest in. A new middle school was set for groundbreaking in the spring, the old rectory was being converted into apartments. To keep conversation up, Justin asked about who got the contract, or what kind of materials might be used, and his dad told him. Tapping the wrong beat of the song on the radio, Justin's dad asked about exams, if he liked his classes, if the dorms were well-heated in New Hampshire, and then said maybe he and Alice would take a trip up to visit in the spring.

They parked where there wasn't a real space, half on the yellow line that marked the exit to Route 80 toward New Haven and half on the sanded slope of tarmac. They walked past Laundry Land and the dead dog body, which neither commented on. Inside the Laundromat, high school couples dressed in denim leaned on the dryers for warmth, with the hum and slosh of wet clothing as background noise.

Next door was Benny's A-Pizza. The place was famous for its pies and calzones. After ordering, Justin's father stood looking at the taped advertisements and flyers by the trash can. People put prices for cars, pets, or cleaning services, and medical researchers from the hospital nearby hung posters asking, "Are you an overweight smoker between the ages of 40 and 55?" or "Is your sixth to tenth grader too active? Out of control? Join our ADHD study and earn money while finding out the truth about your child's condition." Local bands pleaded for concertgoers, claiming the night would be "surreal." Girls wanting babysitting positions handwrote their numbers on frayed bits of eight-and-a-half-by-eleven, and Justin's father would sometimes tear one off and say, "Makes it look less pathetic, don't you think?" The tooth gap of torn paper at least made it seem as if someone had read the misspelled ad, or thought about hiring. "People see one torn bit of paper and take one for themselves. Good business strategy—I'm just helping these girls out."

Justin's father paid for the pizza while his son stood looking out through the fogged sheet glass to the roadway, where he could still see the hump of dog lying. He knew that the next time he came here the body would be gone, and that he'd wonder then if some family mourned the loss of Buster or Sparky or whatever the thing's name was or if they never even knew what had happened and just assumed the dog had run away, mating maybe, in the cold night.

Holding the cardboard box flat on his palms, Justin's father opened the door by backing into it. They walked out into the cold night, anticipating pizza and pucks in the chill of the ice rink.

"Jesus!" his father spat out. "Where the hell's the car?" Ahead of them, next to the Dodge where they'd parked, was just a gap that faced the dog body. It occurred to Justin that he'd been watching the whole time from the restaurant but hadn't seen the car move anywhere.

"Who would steal it?" Justin asked. His father loved his car— not like a movie dad in the 1950s, but like a guy in an advertisement. He'd found the Saab convertible in the want ads years back—decent price, only fifteen thousand miles, life-guard-ring red. He'd paid cash and garaged it every night since, even in summer, to protect the paint from the slick of bug bodies, rain, dew, beer can scrapes from when the parties Justin'd thrown back in high school had filtered into the driveway. Two years ago, when she first started looking drawn, her lips chapped, shirts baggy, their father had offered Alice the opportunity of driving the car. She'd balked and then accepted, then passed out while admiring the fall foliage on Pike's Path. Luckily, she'd been doing only twenty miles an hour, and she emerged with scrapes, one large facial laceration, and a

broken toe. The front of the car was crushed, and despite the me-
chanic's rehammering of it, and a touch-up job, the car was forever
flawed. Not that their father registered this. He sucked his cheeks in
when he first saw the damage and then shrugged it off. Justin truly
believed that even now, when his dad went to the car first thing in
the morning, warmed her in the winter and waxed the body in the
spring, he didn't notice her dents. "From the inside," his dad said
more than once, "she's the same as when I first saw her."

"Plenty of people would want to steal my car," his father said in
the parking lot and handed Justin the pizza. He began circling the
lot, pacing with his fists in his pockets.

"It's gone, Dad," Justin said. He wanted to laugh but knew
better.

"Did you see anything?" His father turned. Justin shook his
head. "What were you doing in there then?" His father gestured
back to Benny's with his head. "Weren't you looking right out
here?"

"I guess," Justin said. "But I didn't see what happened to the
car."

They stood there smelling the eggplant pizza and growing
colder as cars pulled in, picked up food or videos, and then left.
Justin moved over to the guardrail and rested there, not putting
all his weight on it just in case it toppled.

Suddenly his father was jumping up and down and waving like
an aircraft director. "Jesus mother of God—will you look at that!"
he fairly shouted and pointed across the double-lane roadway to
the gas station at the intersection. Justin didn't correct his father's
botched attempt at religious cursing. Under the turning gas sign,
nosed up to the side of a building, was the car.

Still carrying the pizza, they crossed the highway to inspect,
Justin unwillingly imitating his father's great loping strides, the
way his neck moved out and back like a pigeon's.

"How could this happen?" His father laughed.

"No idea," Justin said. "Maybe you didn't set the hand brake?"

His father didn't answer. He leaned down and checked the undercarriage, then felt the sides of the car as if it might speak. Justin wondered if he should worry about his father's driving skills, then thought he remembered the squeal of the brake being set and thought maybe he should worry about the safety of the car.

"Amazing," he said. "Not a scratch on her."

Justin didn't mention the other scratches, which were there from Alice's accident; he just watched his father's face as he looked from the car back to the highway, back to the pizza place and where both men stood in the empty air. His father didn't say anything else—he patted the car and kept his hand on the roof for what seemed like a long time.

The Wolverines won that night, but Justin and his father didn't end up going to the game. They got in the car and ate the cooled pizza there, facing the zip of headlights and tail reds that stopped then slurred along the highway. When they finished, they drove home and found Alice rinsing a large turkey in the sink. She explained the process of fast defrosting, how she had to keep changing the cold water in order to avoid giving them salmonella or some other food-borne illness. Justin hefted himself onto the counter and watched her fill, empty, then refill the sink. When their father came in at midnight, Justin thought they might tell Alice what had happened with the car, but they didn't. Their dad kissed her cheek and said he was going to sleep.

Justin heard him up early the next morning, stacking chopped wood on the porch and then helping Alice lay the table for Thanksgiving. Justin showered and shaved even though they weren't having company, and went to the garage, where they kept an extra pantry for storage. In the summer it held fruit or items from the farm stand down the road, but in winter they used it as an ice chest since the garage was unheated. Justin grabbed a quart of eggnog and nosed around the cabinet shelves for dry goods to take back to school. Once he'd found Alice, in a sundress, hair loose around her face, sitting on the floor here, shoving straw-berries into her mouth until she'd finished at least a pound. When she'd chewed the last one and pocketed the green stems, she stood up and headed to the compost heap outside. She'd looked at Justin just before, and he'd been nervous, wondering if maybe she'd wanted him to follow, to watch her or clean up for her, but he'd stayed in the garage counting boxes of Rice-A-Roni and Ham-burger Helper, its cartoon hand suddenly seeming severed and disgusting. Thinking about it now, he wondered if maybe that was the tiny dot of their relationship summed up.

Their father called down to ask for beer. Justin brought up a six-pack of Sam Adams and set it in the counter. Football narra-tion filtered in from the den as Alice and her brother plated and served. Their father joined them at the table, sitting where he could still see the game in the next room.

Later, when Justin was hand-washing the plates, Alice puked up not only the acorn squash and dried fruit stuffing from Thanks-giving lunch but blood from her worn esophagus. Justin turned the faucet off and went to where their dad was standing, looking to where Alice leaned against the pedestal sink in the bathroom. Their father's face had the same look as it had when he'd seen his car safe and moved across the highway—as if God had stepped in and performed the miracle of car preservation only to bestow a daughter who wrecked her own body and slumped, bleeding then, onto the white-tiled bathroom floor. Their father picked her up like a basket of laundry. Arms akimbo, Alice had her ankles crossed, a southern belle whose chin was speckled with blood.

"Jesus, you weighed more than this in fifth grade," her dad said to her. He would have cried then, Justin thought, but some cheer from the television stadium burst out. Their father's fingers went tighter into Alice's ribs, and her sweater lifted just enough so they could see her stomach—or what should have been a stomach but had gone concave, covered with fine, downy hair. "You weighed more than this in grade school," her father said again, and his voice slipped.

"I already weighed seventy pounds when I was ten? Gross." Alice let her head flop to one side. Her father could reach around her lower thigh with his thumb-to-middle-finger grip.

All three went to the car, and Justin secured Alice in the back to make their way to the hospital. Justin tucked his fleece coat around his sister, and their dad handed back his parka, which she put on front to back; the high black collar made her look like a shriveled priest. Justin went to sit in the front seat, but Alice pulled his hand, and he sat back with her.

That spring Justin's father called to tell him hockey season had ended with the Wolverines as regional champs. Justin thought about how Alice had looked way back in high school—bulky in her hockey uniform, ruddy-cheeked and able—goal-scoring for her team. Then he thought about how his father had looked at Alice for the last time: blanketed in her hospital bed, her legs and arms spread slightly, making her whole form look like some thin, star-shaped ornament for the upcoming holiday season.

Justin thinks more about how his father looked then than about his own reaction, how he didn't think about losing his sister until later, in the middle of portioning the funeral lasagna for his father to thaw and eat by himself. Only when Justin has to fill out some sophomore form for Dartmouth that queries about the names and ages of siblings does he realize that he is now an only child. With the tomato sauce ladle in one hand, Justin remembered the night they'd lost and found his father's car. For the first time, he imagined the weight of it rolling across Route 80, headlights off, body silent as it slid into safety without accident. How it had emerged from the whole incident untouched but altered.

Eggs

At Imogen's house the fridge is covered with magnets that say things like "A minute on the lips, forever on the hips," but she and Lucy are allowed to eat nonfat Cool Whip straight from the tub with a spoon. Downstairs in the basement are murals that Lucy figures came with the house—eerie paintings from the 1950s, when the room held socials and sock hops. On the wall, flat men dressed for a hunt smoke pipes and wear green knickers. Wagging knee-height near their masters, flop-eared mutts point their tails toward the bar as if they want a scotch, too.

Imogen and Lucy take the imitation whipped cream, spoons, and a jar of Tang, and sit on the floor surrounded by the partying painted people. Sometimes they give them names and pretend to interact with them, but today the girls just dip their fingers into the orange powder and lick it off. Upstairs, Imogen's mother is Jazzercising. They can hear the rhythmic thud of her ankle-high Reeboks on her floor, their ceiling.

"I wish she'd shut up," Imogen says, tilting her head back so she's staring up at the ceiling.

"It is kind of loud," Lucy agrees, studying the sway of Imogen's hair and wishing hers did the same.

Imogen pulls Lucy over to where the crust-rimmed bottles of Gordon's and bourbon are lined up and pretends she is the barkeep, unscrewing the tops and sniffing the sharp liquor. Like nail polish remover, it stings to inhale for too long, but Imogen tips a bottle just to coat her pinkie and then dabs Lucy's tongue. Lucy swirls the saliva in her mouth and slicks a Tang-covered finger in to get rid of the alcohol. Fiddling with the soda tap her father has rigged up, Imogen manages to fill two tumblers with an uneven mix of cola and fizzy water.

From the slatted windows that rim the large room, stalks of sunlight cast a golden sheen on the plump painted ladies who, arm-linked and haughty because of it, smirk at the men. One woman's hat has a feather that curves up like a question mark. Lucy imagines that the woman's clothing wants to ask something, like why her painted friend's cigarette is unlighted in its holder, or why her high-button boots turn in on themselves in conversation. Imogen stands up suddenly and slams herself against the wall, trying to shadow the smoking woman.

"Who am I?" Imogen asks, holding her fingers in a V by her lips and mock-inhaling. Lucy puts the sticky Cool Whip spoon down and jumps up to rush next to Imogen. They stand flush with the mural and sip cocktails with their eyebrows raised, speak with English accents, and with their arms latched, march out of the basement and up to Imogen's room to decide what they should wear for their first day of high school on Monday.

In class, Mr. Denozzio claps his hands so everyone will be quiet. Imogen, in her argyle sweater plucked from the closet heap several days before, swings her feet out and back as if she's small in her chair until Lucy plucks a piece of string from Imogen's hair and deposits it onto her desk to get her to stop. Next to them, Carl and Mike sing "Love Stinks," while Lissa Macdougal stands in the doorway talking to a sophomore boy, and the rest of the students foot-tap the chairs in front of them or listen to see if Bradley will fake-fart like he did last year.

Huck Yorensen links his pinkie fingers to the corners of his mouth and whistles hard and long. Everyone shuts up, and Mr. Denozzio goes right to the board, where he draws what looks like a balloon that's come untethered—its string trailing in wave-water dips and rises behind.

"What is this?" Mr. Denozzio asks. He takes a seat on a metal stool, then points to Lissa. Before she can speak he says, "And don't say 'a balloon.'"

Hair back in a band, Lissa tugs at the wisps near her temples and writes her name in cursive on her notebook, as if this will help her formulate an answer. When Mr. Denozzio says the word *sperm*, Mike laugh-coughs, but everyone else is still, facing forward, ready.

Next to the lonely single sperm, Mr. Denozzio uses blue chalk to make a disproportionately large egg. He draws it like an edible egg, even though Lucy knows by the page she's turned to in the text that a real egg looks more like an eye, one circle within another. The biology textbook suggests making a dot in the center of a piece of white paper with a pen tip to see how small an actual egg cell would be, and even that point is many times bigger than ones that sit waiting in the girls' ovaries. Lucy feels her abdomen as if she expects to find something firm inside, then rests her fingers near her hips.

Imogen nudges Lucy for no reason and looks on later as Lucy copies the egg shape into her notes. Then Imogen, sucking on a honey cough drop, leans over and draws an arrow to the balloon-sperm, writing above it, "Don't pop it!"

From a shelf near the chalkboard, Mr. Denozzio produces an egg carton. He cradles the bumpy thing, rocking the entire box back and forth, singing to it until the students all laugh.

"You can laugh all you want," he says, "but these little eggs are your babies for the week."

He goes on to explain the experiment, how everyone will partner up and parent a blown-out egg, keep it safe and never unwatched until class on Friday, when he'll inspect the eggs one last time and give a final score.

"The bad news," Imogen says when she and Lucy choose each other as egg parents, "is that if you want to try out for JV soccer this week, I'll have to watch this thing by myself."

"I'll take the baby to your play auditions," Lucy offers in return. She tries to imagine taking the egg to the movies, or even to the bathroom, and wonders whether she could hold it and wipe herself at the same time or if the egg would be okay just resting in the soap slot on the sink.

Mr. Denozzio interrupts the chatter to announce, "Your egg babies may be decorated or given whatever accessories you feel necessary to make them more real."

The next day, with signed permission slips from the egg grandparents at home, Mr. Denozzio does the first check. Mike's egg is already damaged.

"May I remind you," Mr. Denozzio says after he's put Mike's egg back into the egg crate, which sits flapping open on the microscope cart, "the purpose of this project is to allow you to experience some of the responsibilities that are involved in the care of human babies. Would you toss your human infant into the air on the bus ride home as Mike did? You cannot underestimate how quickly cracks and breaks can occur. Keep this in mind at all times."

By Wednesday, Lucy is used to cupping her egg baby as she walks, book bag slung over her left shoulder, from the science building all the way to the dining hall. At lunch the day before, Imogen had nearly thrown the egg out as she cleared her tray, but at the last minute Lucy had run to a pile of mayonnaise- and crumb-coated dishes to retrieve it.

"I think I should take her—Egg—home tonight," Lucy had said when Imogen said she was overreacting.

"It was an accident, Lucy," Imogen said as she bent down to highlight Hermia's opening lines.

The auditions for *A Midsummer Night's Dream* were being held on Thursday, and Imogen knew she wanted Hermia—especially if Jake, the boy who was gorgeous enough to wear overalls without ridicule as a junior and who made it into every school play, was cast as Lysander. At night, when she'd held the egg, Imogen had pictured stage-kissing with Jake, how they'd press their lips together in the fairy-dusted forest set, and no matter what occurred during the show, they'd wind up kissing again at the end.

Imogen mouthed her audition lines one more time before standing up. "Fine. You can have it tonight, but I want it to see me try out tomorrow, okay?"

Lucy nodded and let Imogen straighten the tiny hat Imogen had made from an old doll's outfit.

"It makes Egg look like a sailor," Lucy had complained when Imogen had brought the cap into school.

"It looks stylish," Imogen had said. "Plus, it'll keep the sun off its face."

At home, Lucy had taken the hat off and let the egg be naked on the bed she had constructed in the bottom part of her mother's body powder box. Before getting into bed herself, Lucy had tucked the egg under the puff, wiped what she could of the gardenia-scented powder off Egg's face, and kissed it.

The next day, Lissa unfolds her palm to reveal the only pieces that remain of her baby.

"The rest are in my dog's stomach," she says and sits down with her mouth twisted up, sorry. Mr. Denozzio makes a mark in his grade book and checks the condition of the rest of the babies. Only three are left, and Imogen sits up straight and proud, kicking Lucy to attention. Lucy is too busy running a finger over Egg's head, smoothing the part that would be the cheek, if eggs had cheeks.

After the audition, Lucy and Imogen put their baby into the egg day care their friend Carl started when he realized the best way to keep his egg safe was to keep himself and it motionless on the grass near the library. For twenty cents an hour, he watches and makes sure no one touches or moves the eggs.

Cleated up, Lucy runs her two required laps around the field and then takes practice shots at the net while Imogen, on the side-lines, talks with a fellow would-be actor about line-memorization skills and how Jake never does an empty stage kiss but instead inserts his tongue to make the whole scene seem real. Later, when Carl has to leave and hands Egg back to Imogen, she sticks the thing in someone's empty sneaker nearby so she has her hands free to gesture.

The next morning, Lucy gets to the posted cast list before Imogen.

"Hi, Hermia!" Lucy yells up the corridor to her friend.

"Oh, my God, really?" Imogen drops her books and rushes to find her name on the wall. She reaches for Lucy's hand, but Lucy steps back, protecting Egg, still hammock-swung in her cupped hand. Imogen waits for Lucy to hug her, or say something else, but Lucy just smiles small and raises Egg up so Imogen can see.

"She made it," Lucy says as they walk to class.

"So did I," Imogen says. At the doorway, Imogen is still an-noyed and asks, "How do you even know that Egg is a girl?"

"Sometimes you can just tell," Lucy says and thinks about how her mother, Ginny, tells that story about eating cherries straight from the grocer's display and suddenly knowing she was pregnant with a daughter.

When Lucy takes a seat, Imogen leaves a space between them. As Mr. Denozzio enters the room, Lucy can feel her chest swell; it's all she can do not to stand up and run to him to show him how well her egg girl has done. Lucy looks at the carton Mr. Denozzio has placed in front of him, which holds the remains of all the babies who cracked or shattered during the week, and realizes that her whole baby will be alone unless Carl's has managed to survive overnight.

Before the final points are added up, each student has to write an in-class essay titled "Egg Baby—What Did I Learn from Caring for Mine?" worth ten points of the total score for the project. Imogen watches Lucy say good-bye to the egg, placing it into an end space in the carton. Carl does the same. Lucy turns the face side of her egg girl toward Carl's, and the two brown shells stand there among the ruins of the others. She wants to write something funny, like the other kids, who are guffawing over their egg puns and jokes, but instead finds herself writing a poem for her egg girl, and how she loved her, and worried for her, and wishes she could have her back. She thinks maybe Mr. Denozzio will get it, understand her connection to this project, but after fifth period, when she runs back to ask him if she can keep the egg, she finds the whole carton chucked into the industrial-sized trash can in the science lab. She picks through the debris but doesn't find her egg, just shell remains and trash.

After the whole year has nearly passed and Mr. Denozzio takes the class outside to sit in a circle on the lawn, Lucy looks across at Imogen, who wears a jacket that is obviously not hers. With the cuffs pulled over her hands, Imogen looks small, and she puts a sleeve to her mouth so it looks like an elephant trunk. Lucy wonders if the jacket is Jake's, and if Imogen has shown him the murals in her basement, if they've kissed surrounded by a painted audience. She misses that part, the basement part of Imogen, but not the rest. She will miss only that snapshot memory of her when Imogen moves to New York City a month later and doesn't return.

Mr. Denozzio stands up in the sun so the students use their hands like visors to see him and explains the next project, in which teams will try to construct a cushion so that, when they drop an uncooked egg from the top of the science building, it won't break. He tells how they can use cotton balls, Popsicle sticks glued together, or a balled up wool sweater—any means necessary to keep the yolk and white from seeping out onto the asphalt.

"It's a bit like the egg parenting you did before," Mr. Denozzio explains with his palms flat, as if he's holding something up for show. "Except those babies were hollow. With these, it's more than just the shell. You'll have to protect what's inside."

Things We Talked About Smoking

Cordelia, Beatrice, and Imogen were still wearing their coats when one of them—they later couldn't remember who—told the rest of them they couldn't smoke Marlboros anymore. Rumor had it that the design on the hard-pack box symbolized the KKK and, much as they liked the gold and white of the Lights, they'd have to switch to Camels and the hard pack, with its pyramid and distant palm trees.

Cordelia liked Silk Cuts best. She'd come from the Latimer School in London and sometimes called cigarettes "fags," just to remind everyone she wasn't from Manhattan, as if what she did there didn't count. Beatrice and Imogen had met in Earth Science the year before, when they paired up just to bemoan their Shakespearean names.

"At least yours sounds normal," Beatrice had said, lighting the Bunsen burner under the test tube. They were distilling bits of wood that looked like skinny tongue depressors.

"Imogen is not normal," Imogen said, looking at Beatrice

through the protective eyewear they'd been issued to avoid possible lawsuits by litigious school parents.

"I guess not. But at least you can go by Jen, which is fine," Beatrice said.

"But too common," Imogen said, taking notes on the liquid pooling at the bottom of the test tube.

The two adopted Cordelia as soon as they saw her name on the admitted students' board. One side of her hair was longer than the other and covered her left eye. Cordelia wore jeans patched with a U.K. flag bandanna and a Psychedelic Furs T-shirt that had some concert dates printed on the back as well as the name of the current hit single, "The Ghost in You."

"Great band," Beatrice said to Cordelia on the first day of school while the headmistress detailed the new dress code rules.

Cordelia flung the long side of her hair back and looked at both of them. "Who are you two?"

After they'd exchanged names, Cordelia smirked and nodded. That afternoon, the three met out in front of the lions that flanked the school's main door and walked to Kelter's Deli four blocks down to sit and smoke.

I. Imogen

That was the year Imogen's father was diagnosed with terminal lung cancer and decided to order all the Christmas presents from TV. Her brother, Brian, got a clock radio shaped like a football. The receiver had white plastic ladder marks, as if it was the part of the football you're supposed to grip, and when Brian talked to the girl he liked, he'd line his fingers up on the fake laces as if he were about to spiral-throw. Her mom opened her box and pulled out what looked like a red gun—something from a cartoon.

"It's the Labeler," their dad explained. He was propped in the yellow chair by the window so when they were all in other rooms he could look out and watch the specks of people on the sidewalk, the stop and go of the cabs, the distant flick of lights strung from the traffic poles in the shape of wreaths.

"Fantastic!" her mom said and slipped the tape coil inside so she could start using it right away. She typed out LABEL GUN and stuck it on the thing. Then she wrote HARRISON, and slicked it onto the dad's foot, then went into the kitchen to start on the confectioners' sugar and flour-filled canisters.

"Open yours," her dad said to Imogen when Brian had gone to his room to try the phone jack there.

They used a large spider fern as a Christmas tree, one third due to laziness, another to Imogen's father being Jewish and his guilt regarding traditional fir trees. Another third, Imogen figured, was so no one would be stuck with the dénouement, the task of cleaning the fallen needles at the end of the holiday season. Offshoots from the spider fern's main stems perched on the pot's rim, dangled nearly to the rug, and burst like fireworks above, bobbing until the cat pawed at them. Imogen pulled her gift out from the few that were left. On the tag her father had written, "To Imo—May this help with the final frontier." An unspoken rule for all their birthday and Christmas presents was that the card should have some sort of clue on it. Most of the time, the clues didn't make much sense, and sometimes the people who wrote the clues couldn't even remember their relevance, but they all liked the tradition.

"I don't get it," Imogen said to her dad. He coughed into a handkerchief and tilted his head.

"Imo—come on now, think. You can get this one," he said.

He wore a red cashmere sweater that her mother had given him about a decade earlier. He brought it out from the cedar closet only for the week before December twenty-fifth and the day after, then folded it up for the next year. He hadn't dry-cleaned it last year— all the holiday washing, balled up and wrinkled, had sat untouched. Dad had coughed blood into his linen napkin at the Petersons'

Christmas Eve party and went the next day to the emergency
room, where he was diagnosed. The red sweater, blotched with
crab cake bits and lines of eggnog on the sleeve, was folded and put
away sometime in late January by Greta, the housekeeper, who
seemed to be less into cleaning the apartment than into rearrang-
ing items to give the appearance of order.

Her dad sat watching his daughter open his present, and Imogen wanted to go over and pick at the year-old food stains. They'd
just toasted the year anniversary of his diagnosis with a bottle of
Château d'Yquem from 1973 that they'd been saving until her college graduation. Now they all quietly understood he wouldn't be
around for that. But her mother had gone to each person and labeled all their glasses so they'd know whose was whose when
they toasted with the cancer wine, trying not to let it dominate
everything.

"I can't open it without a knife," Imogen said, picking at the
package.

"Here." Her dad handed her a pen from his breast pocket. "Use
the tip."

She sliced along the tape seam with the pen point and opened
the box. The cat came right over to bat at the packing kernels.
Greta would later shake her head at the mess the family'd made—
crumbs and Styrofoam mashed into the Oriental, but the cat would
manage to sneak a couple Cheez-Doodle-shaped pieces away. Imogen was coughing while she took a smaller box from inside the
outer one.

"Are you getting sick?" her dad asked.

"No," she said, "I'm fine." She was smoking more, leaning out
her bedroom window at night, holding the butt in whichever place
made the smoke least likely to seep back into the room. She hated
that she did it—that she could picture the textbook image of her
father's tar-coated lungs, that she knew she'd live the rest of her
life being a fatherless daughter, but that she still looked forward to

watching the city at night with a cigarette poised between her fingers.

"Is it a vacuum cleaner?" she asked, looking at the miniature device she pulled from the box.

"Nope!" Her dad grinned. "Guess again!"

"The final frontier—Dad—I have no idea." Then she wondered if it was death—was death the final frontier, did he mean the *beyond*? She couldn't remember.

Her father looked small in his chair. No matter how many Ensure drinks he had during the day, the weight slipped off, making his clothes bag at the elbows, wrinkle like elephant knees at the waist. The shoulders lagged as if he'd borrowed his button-downs from a bigger, healthier older brother.

"It's a space saver!" he said. "Get it? Space—the final frontier." He put on a deep stage voice, as if this would get her to understand what he was saying.

On the package insert, she looked at sketches of blankets and pillows bursting from a suitcase. One picture later, postspace-saving action, each item fit perfectly, stacked and even.

"Neat," Imogen said and went over to her dad to kiss him.

He put his hands on her face, and she leaned in to his chest. She could feel his clavicle underneath the soft sweater, and before she knew it, she was crying into the cashmere, then his hands, as he palmed her head. He'd always had huge hands, and they were the one part of his whole body that hadn't changed since the radiation and the metastasizing of the cancer. They stayed like that for a while. Through the butler's pantry, Imogen could see her mother, slicking labels onto things they could already identify— regular things, like glasses, the refrigerator handle, the faucet, as if someday they'd all need reminders of what surrounded them. Imogen looked at her father's foot, where his label was, and then at the floor, where the space saver's looping snout lay waiting to suck the air right out of everything.

II. Cordelia

She'd loved her room at the country house—probably it was what
Cordelia missed most from England. Her bed was set into the
wall, curtained on the sides, with thick tapestry at the front. In
the daytime, the hunting scene on the tapestry was so fitting to
the house she wasn't bothered by the fact that it actually depicted
a dog chewing on a fox's neck, trotting the flaccid animal over to
its horse-propped master. At night you couldn't see the hunting;
the threads just looked mottled and dark. Out the window, the
second-floor terrace was covered in bird crap, artfully splotched
as if the peacocks and guinea fowl had consulted her mother on
her design sense before relieving themselves on the bluestone.

They had four peacocks that had come with the house. Since
they'd been coming on weekends, only three were left. One van-
ished the morning in spring after they'd had a reggae party for
Cordelia's sixteenth and she and Simon Hobbs had spent the night
on the tennis lawn down by the river. She didn't tell him she was
a virgin, because it was just easier that way, but a couple months
later, when they did it again and the condom broke, she wound up
explaining as they waited for an appointment at the Day Clinic.
Issued a round of morning-after pills that she took that afternoon,
Cordelia helped her mother prep for the dinner party they were
hosting that night. Simon Hobbs and Cordelia's brother, Jack,
swatted at croquet balls, just taking shots at whatever wire hoops
were already set up since their set was incomplete—they had the
red ball and the blue, but the yellow had disappeared along with a
mallet. The family joked that someone could have stolen that
mallet and used it as a murder weapon, and they practiced their
alibis during the hour-long drive back to London each Sunday
evening.

Just before they gave the Berkshire house up and got ready to move to the States, most of the guinea fowl turned up dead on the lawn near the metal table and chair set. They'd gotten into the fertilizer Cordelia's father spread on the back shrubs and pecked holes in the tarpaulin he'd put over the poisonous mulch compound. The remaining three birds hissed, screeching out into the gray morning light. The sounds were so loud that Cordelia had to open the windows and yell at them the shut up until her brother came into her room and told Cordelia to do the same. She couldn't sleep. The former owner of the house had told them that peacocks went through cycles like this when they were sexually frustrated.

Simon Hobbs found Cordelia before summer term started and kissed her right in front of her parents, who pressed the car horn and finally sent Jack out to pull Cordelia away. The peacocks weren't fucking, and apparently neither were her mother and father, which was one reason they were moving back to the States. Either way, it was time to go.

III. Beatrice

Beatrice is the girl who won the Mary Trudeau Prize in seventh grade. Given once every five years, the award is in honor of a student who best exemplifies the Trudeau Way: honesty, generosity of spirit, and academic thoroughness. In a yellow skirt and matching short-sleeved top, she gives a short acceptance speech and takes a seat next to her trustee mother, who is already positive she will attend Princeton, like the rest of the family, even though college is remote and all she can think about is wanting to kiss someone before high school starts.

Bea will, of course, but it won't be the boy at camp, Jed or Jet—a name out of a musical—or Quinn at dancing school, who pulls her to the Social Hall. The room is dark and filled with empty folding chairs all facing a podium where no one is standing. Quinn's breath smells like cheese and Binaca spray, and when he leans in to put his lips on her, Beatrice will push him away and snag one of the brass buttons of his blue blazer on her dress-sleeve cuff.

In the locker room at school during sophomore winter, she will overhear Lindsay Wilton talk about how she had sex with Quinn at some party, and she will take longer to lace her Tretorns just to hear the end of the story, how Quinn fumbled and passed, thanked her at the end, but left her, hair matted and skin hickeyed, to emerge from the room alone. Later, by the One Day maxipad machine in the girls' room, Lauren Malloy will watch Beatrice comb her hair into a ponytail and ask to borrow Latin notes. Before Bea knows it, the two of them will be studying every day together in the library, then jogging in the park on the weekends, then sleeping over when her parents go to Europe and St. Bart's and she opts to stay home. When Lauren finally kisses her, gentle and on the mouth, Bea feels huge relief, thrill, as if she's won the best prize ever, until Lauren's parents catch her, pants down, in Lauren's room one afternoon and they ship Lauren to Lucerne for boarding school and instruct the school to confiscate any correspondence to and from Bea.

Princeton will accept Bea, and Harvard, too. Bethany Meyers— who played Helena in *A Midsummer Night's Dream* and winked at Beatrice from under a cardboard tree during rehearsal—is going to Crimson—and Beatrice might, too. She's just not sure.

At Kelter's Deli, everything was somehow neutralized. They were girls. They were girls with odd names who smoked after school together and maybe sometimes alone. Beatrice was thinking of her old camp crush, Lucy, a pinnacle in memory of all the unaction, the unspokenness of her situation. Imogen was thinking about her father and the wideness of the city below, Cordelia of Simon Hobbs and what she might have had if they'd never gone to that clinic. But the girls never spoke of these thoughts.

Possibly they would be bridesmaids for one another, or then, too, they might never speak after graduation. Most likely was that they would drift, like cast-off breath, away from one another. Dissipated, they would recall not so much the details shared over the plastic-covered menus that they studied but never ordered from as the way their young mouths held the smoke, how the wide windows would fog over until drops of condensation began their descent to the floor. How unhappy they were in their own isolated way—and, if they had somehow found the breaking point out of it, if they would have been more than smoking friends.

Imogen and Beatrice trace the small pyramids on the Camel box, and Cordelia, in her half lilt, tells some war story from England, about how you're never supposed to light three cigarettes on one match. They've all done this at some stage, since they are three girls, since they all smoke now; but today Cordelia's words seem darker, make them feel like something—everything—needs to change.

"With the first match, the enemy sees you're there. With the second, they aim. And with the third"—Cordelia gun-points her finger—"you're done for."

Community Service

Seven in the morning on Sunday and the boys are gathered on the Warwick town green. In their bright orange vests, Justin thinks the kids look like hunters or convicts, or—after last weekend—both.

Justin is the likable teacher at an uptight last-resort school. In the catalog they don't say fuckups, just troubled teens, but everyone knows that's the subtext. The kids are of two camps: either they are determined to rise from the sludge of drugs (selling and taking), defunct friendships, familial despair, and academic waste, or else they've given up.

Wells Zanger is the king of the latter camp, self-stuck in the high-walled troth after being kicked out of St. George's, Prindle, Markston Hall, and finally admitted to Country Cove, the last shot before juvenile detention. Justin and Wells have a greeting, "Hey, Dewar," for the cap Justin took from Wells (no slogans of drugs or alcohol permitted on clothing, accessories, or dorm walls). Justin knows Wells says "Dewar" but means "do her."

In the early October air, Wells has been squatting so long in the cold, wet grass that his buddies ask if he's about to take a crap. Justin goes to investigate, kicking through the slick maple leaves that blanket the green. Ghosts, witches, and gourds dot the perimeter of the kite-shaped lawn, and like the good citizens they either wish they were or deny being, the boys pick up trash and deposit the wrappers, newspapers, and cups into industrial-sized black bags. This was part of the deal; at Country Cove everyone did community service, whether it interested them or not.

"Hey, Dewar." Justin stops to the right of Wells, who is still crouching. Justin thinks that if these were regular kids on a science trip, say, Wells could be looking for an earthworm, or a special moss. Justin finds that he feels more for the kids when he imagines them this way, younger somehow, or alone. Often, he finds himself picturing his dead sister, Alice, with the boys. That she might have been better at saving the boys than he is, how good she was at rescuing people from their loneliness with just a touch on the forearm. How her slight physical presence gave her a gentle, otherworldly glow and calm.

"Hey, do-her," Wells says, his voice pitched off a key.

"Wells is slackin'!" shouts Jimmy Bettina from over by the bench. He has managed to position himself well—seated but near lots of trash so no one can accuse him of not pulling his weight. The kids are expected to clean the lawn of any and all debris by 9:00 A.M., when the Fall Festival starts.

Justin watches Wells and wonders if he's sick, if as the teacher he needs to do something. Situations like this are just reminders to Justin that he is the adult now, two years out of college, graduate school only a vague possibility in the distance. Even though the kids are messed up, Justin feels he could be one of them, trade in his official teacher's blazer for the roughed-up baseball cap or faded cords Wells wears. Each of the kids has an expression or gesture, the way their arms cradle their exam papers or how they sneak chewing tobacco, that reminds Justin of how he and his best friend, Matt, used to be.

"What are we looking at?" Justin asks Wells and crouches next to him. Wells faces his tribunal later at school. He is accused of forcing himself on Rebecca Stanton at the heavily chaperoned dance last week. Justin saw them kiss, knows that something happened, but can't figure out what, exactly. He wants to think Wells is innocent.

"Check out the slug," Wells says. He's ruddy-cheeked and soft around the edges still, his shoulders puffy under the orange vest. Justin thinks about Holden Caulfield and his hunting hat, and how none of the boys—even the ones who made it through most of prep school—have commented on the reference.

"Yeah, slugs are fascinating," Justin says. "You still need to pick up trash." He checks his watch.

"I know," Wells says, but when he turns to look at Justin, he stays fixed in his spot. "I didn't do it, you know." Justin doesn't say anything. "Like, I could have, but I didn't. You know, like we got to that point and I just thought of her as, like, someone's kid or something? Like if someone did that to my sister I'd want to kill them."

Justin is touched by this and filled with the rare feeling of peace that comes only when one of the last-resort kids takes a slow step up, makes some realization that will help him in the long run. Then he says, "But you don't have a sister, Wells."

Wells twists his mouth and nods. "I know. But if I did, it would matter, right?"

Justin nods and stands up before he lets himself cry. He can see Alice in the wet leaves, first as kids, when they'd jump in them, then as teenagers, when she would lie on the cold ground and he'd cover her with red, orange, and yellow fallen leaves and he would wait for her, wait for her with his heart racing, hoping he hadn't covered her up so much that she couldn't jump up, bringing them both to action.

Never Sicker

It doesn't matter whether liquor before beer is never fear or beer before liquor means never sicker—or even if it isn't the order so much as the quantity—because Jenna is going to throw up regardless. On the snow-surfaced quad, sophomores and seniors work together to slick out a sculpture. A few hours later, when the Winter Weekend has officially begun, the ground will be statued with Disney characters doing decidedly un-Disney things—smoking snow joints, hefting kegs; Ms. White and her vacant prince will be ice-picked in an embrace.

On Frat Row, Jenna and her freshman-year roommate, Cordelia, stand with their hands pulled into their jacket arms, trying to keep warm. Jenna pulls her scarf up so it covers her mouth.

"You're going to get chapped lips, Jemma," Cordelia says, slicking her own with roll-on gloss and anglicizing Jenna's name as she likes to do. Jenna has stopped correcting her. "Here." Cordelia hands the tube to Jenna, who shakes her head.

"That's okay," Jenna says. She thinks maybe she would be happier if she would do things like wear lipstick and blow out her hair so the ends didn't curl, if she wore skirts and knee-length boots as Cordelia does, even though it's below freezing. But Jenna's in jeans and hiking boots, with a down vest over her Patagonia fleece.

"So, where should we go? Deek? Theta?" Cordelia rattles off frat names as if she's ordering food at a diner, and with her lilt, the run-down houses come off as elegant, wines Jenna isn't familiar with. "There's always Alpha. Not that I want to go back there."

Jenna shakes her head and thinks about that first weekend of the fall, when they'd returned from their freshman outdoor orientation. Each member of the class had been assigned a two-day trip, rafting or hiking, or camping in the dewy grass by Marker's Pond, in order to commune with nature and—apparently—hook up with various people before the official semester started. On Jenna's Trust Adventure, which consisted of a ropes course and allowing yourself to fall back into someone's arms, hoping he or she caught you, Jenna had spent the evenings talking in his tent to some guy who later turned out to have a long-distance girlfriend. She'd felt the rush of connection, the warmth that seeped from her chest out to her fingertips when she'd made the guy laugh without trying, when he'd complimented her on her muscle tone. Such a specific thing to notice, she was sure that meant he liked her, and maybe he did, but the night ended like so many others, kissless and surprisingly alone.

Cordelia had come back from her hiking trip with stories of campfires and s'mores, and the senior—Scott—who'd scooped her up and kissed her, how she knew it would be a great relationship because he'd kissed her in broad daylight, just as people were pitching tents and chewing handfuls of gorp. Cordelia said you could always tell that a guy was really interested in you when he did more than just make out with you at a party, or in the dark, if he did one of those hands-on-your-neck kisses in front of his friends, or on the steps of the dining hall.

Then, that first weekend on campus, as the "official freshman,"

Jenna had followed Cordelia to Alpha House, where Scott lived, promising to keep her company. Cordelia left Jenna by the pool table holding a flimsy cup of warm beer, while upstairs Cordelia learned that the rumors she'd overlooked about Scott's penchant for date rape were true.

"It didn't happen all the way," Cordelia said later that night, crying at the foot of Jenna's bed. "But it was so close, Jemma. Sorry—Jenna." Jenna touched Cordelia's wrist, an awkward sort of hand-holding, while outside, the shouts of late partyers swarmed through the dark air. "I thought Scott was—you know—that he'd be my boyfriend. I'd be the freshman who got the hot senior guy."

It occurred to Jenna then, watching her not-quite-raped room-mate, that the myths of love—the music-over movie montages of beach walks and carnival rides, of fall apple picking where the guy leans over and brushes the fallen leaf off your shirt and then kisses you—that all those images could be just that, distant film cels that you could only imagine. In middle school Jenna had thought it would happen in high school, and then when that went flat, she figured for sure it would happen in college. But it hasn't—not yet—and freshman year has half slipped by.

Over the summer, while her parents vacationed in Tuscany, Jenna had met a boy at The Baker's Dozen, where she'd worked at the counter selling blueberry muffins and lattes. His name was Nick, and they'd kissed in the back room by the warm beehive oven. Jenna could smell bread browning, the sugary heat from the cinnamon buns, and Nick's clean soapiness when they were to-gether. But Nick was around for only two weeks before heading off to train across Europe with two friends from school. When he'd left, Jenna had missed not just the way he'd made her laugh by holding up sticky buns to his head to resemble Princess Leia but how warm the bread oven made everything seem. It cast a glow over the whole room. Jenna had felt sexy-funny, like Lucille Ball with flour streaks on her face, a crumb-covered apron that didn't exactly flatter her, and yet Nick had kissed her like a prom king falling for the reinvented girl in a movie.

Out on Frat Row, in the winter-empty cold, Jenna quietly hopes that there's the possibility of love somewhere on this campus, in this world. Cordelia waves her hands in the air as if she hears music Jenna can't and says, "Come on, girl. Let's go find us some fratties."

They head to Deek House, home of the hot swimmers and off-season lacrosse boys. Inside, Christmas lights wink from the ceilings and green foliage wraps the banister, as if someone's mother had visited to prep for a holiday party at which adults would mingle and chatter, instead of drunken underage college students having beer-funneling contests in the common room.

"Watch how drunk I get tonight, Jems." Cordelia smiles at Jenna, but it comes out sort of threatening. "You just watch me."

Since the events of that first weekend, when Cordelia had returned to their room with Scott's fingerprints bruising her thigh, Jenna had lost count of how many times she'd held Cordelia's long hair back while the remnants of binge drinking went into the toilet.

"You should loosen up tonight." Cordelia nudges her. "I want to see you drunk." She says "drunk" as if she means "happy."

Jenna and Cordelia make the rounds in all the rooms. Since it's an Around the World party, each room has different appetizers and drinks on offer—Red Stripe and jerk chicken, nachos and lime-tinted Coronas, pepperoni slices and jug-poured red wine. Jenna pokes into one room and the next, counting L.L. Bean blue-and-white-flecked sweaters, silly sombreros worn by broad-backed boys. One room is empty except for its host.

"How lame," Cordelia says. "That guy is all alone. Let's go to a different room." But Jenna says she wants to stay. She thinks that if she hosted a room party, if she were Ecuador or China, maybe she'd be like this guy, standing by herself in an unpeopled room; alone but for trays of egg rolls or whatever Ecuadorian food consists of.

It's a relief to be in a room that's not crowded with beer slosh and Polarfleece, that doesn't smell like perfumes wafting from various girls. Cordelia shrugs as she walks to the next room, where there's a vat of raw cookie dough and spiked eggnog—which isn't really any specific country but is sweet nonetheless.

Jenna looks at the blue-lighted room in front of her—an aquarium for people. Plastic fish attached to lines hang from the ceiling. The cooler in the middle of the room is decorated like a treasure trunk.

"What country is this?" she asks the host, whom she's seen before—on campus somewhere or downstairs in the poolroom. She thinks his name is Glen or Jon, something with an *n*.

"Yeah—I know. I couldn't figure out what to do. And we had all these fish." He motions to the point-nosed gar and barracudas, pushing them until they swing and smack against one another.

"You could say it's Atlantis," Jenna says. "That's kind of a country."

The guy smiles and says, "True. Good idea." He sticks out his hand for her to shake it. "I'm Wren—not like the bird. It's short for Wrentham—it's a family name." He says this smoothly, and Jenna realizes he's probably explained his name a hundred times in the past, to teachers, his friends, other girls.

He offers her an iced blue drink. Jenna hesitates and then accepts, thinking of the way Cordelia sways when she's been drinking, how fluid life seems for her, how love lurks around every corner—in freshman lit, at the dining hall, by the abductor in the gym. Jenna sips her drink. It tastes like chlorinated Kool-Aid.

"When you puke tonight," he says, "it'll be this color." He

points to the electric blue liquid and sounds proud, that Jenna's puking is a sure bet.

Wren is cute, though—brown hair tinged with blond, like a beach kid's, and slim, not bulky like most of the Deeks. Jenna can just see it: she and Wren will kiss under the blue lights as if the bulbs are stars—like in that song—and Jenna will tell her parents over winter break that she's really settled in at college. That she has a boyfriend with a name that's cool enough for her but formal enough for them, that classes are okay, she likes her roommate, that she has put aside her thoughts of becoming a professional baker or chef. All of this would be a great relief to her parents, especially the chef part. Jenna hadn't wanted to go to regular college—but culinary school was not acceptable according to her mother, who'd been married at twenty-two and never even had to think about what to become.

"Hello? Did you hear what I asked you?" Wren says and uses a ladle to spoon more icy blue drink into Jenna's cup.

"Sorry," Jenna says. "I was thinking about break."

"That's okay," Wren says. "I'm so totally ready for vacation. This place . . ." He gestures with his hands as if that says enough and takes a big swallow from his cup. From the doorway, a frat brother says, "Hey, Wren—you coming down for the costume thing?"

Wren shrugs and makes some signal to the brother, who winks and leaves. Wearing country-specific clothing was an option at the night's party. You could wear a kimono for the sushi-sake-Japan room, or a sarong and fake tan in one of the Caribbean rooms, and then be part of the costume contest and maybe win a gift certificate to Chili's or a frat brother back rub.

"Isn't the costume part of this just an excuse to see girls in bikinis?" Jenna laughs to Wren. She can feel the alcohol swirling inside her.

"You might just be onto something." Wren hoists himself up on a stool, dodging the ceiling-hung fish. Jenna begins to wonder what the boy would look like in real light, in the daytime, or at least not blue. Then she wonders if blue is one of those colors—like the greenish hue of highway tunnels—that instantly reveals your flaws, pimples or flaking winter skin.

"I've never seen you here before," Wren says. Jenna stands near him. Near enough to lean on his legs, but she doesn't, despite feeling a bit wobbly.

"Yeah?" she says and wonders why it came out as a question. "I guess I'm not much of a party girl."

"I find that kind of hard to believe," Wren says, looking at her drink. "You sure you haven't been here before? On a regular night?"

She had been, but Jenna shakes her head and tries for coy—like a cute movie personality, tipsy but not messy. Downstairs in the basement on other nights, the brothers played Ping-Pong, pissed in the corners of the room as if no one was there, and rated girls when they came down the stairs. "Tits, 10, ass, 8—but, dude, lose the pouch!" That was what Cordelia had gotten one Thursday night in October, but since she'd slept with two of the brothers, they'd stopped rating her and basically ignored her presence in the house. Jenna didn't know which was worse. She didn't even get a rating—somehow she was always unnoticed, not always in a bad way, just more as if she was a holographic image, sometimes see-able, other times gone.

Wren slugs the last of his drink down and reaches for a gummy worm. He shows Jenna the pile of gummy things available—worms, red Swedish fish that look purple in the light, strawberries.

"Ah—the famous berries of the sea—what do strawberries have to do with the ocean?" Jenna laughs and takes one from the tray.

"I don't know." Wren smiles back. "They just looked good, so I got a bunch of them, even though they're not exactly part of the theme."

Wren offers Jenna a gummy worm, dangling it in front of her, taking it away each time she reaches for it. Finally, Jenna bobs for it, grabbing at it with her mouth.

"Look," Wren says, "I'm fishing for you."

Jenna thinks about how this could be the story of how they met, how their underwater romance began at a frat party, how she'd found true love in a fish tank. Wren takes his hands and puts them on Jenna's shoulders, moves her closer to him. He feels the back of her neck, lifting up the loose hair. He moves in and lets his lips go to her ear, then her mouth. When he kisses her, she can taste the bits of gummy worm; the fragments of chewed strawberry get caught behind her lower lip. She wonders if Wren notices.

"Want to go upstairs?" he asks in a heavy whisper.

"Aren't we already upstairs?" She pulls back and looks at his face.

She goes to the windowsill and looks out toward the quad. The distant glow of the campus winter bonfire flickers and fades; people dance around it. They look tiny down there, students the size of rice grains, all ruddy-cheeked and flushed, looking for something or someone in the expanse of snow.

Wren comes up behind Jenna and hugs her from behind. "You okay?" he asks.

"I feel a little sick," she says. She turns to look at Wren, to search him for signs of disgust or kindness.

"Yeah, these drinks are pretty strong."

She wonders if he'll walk her home, if she should find Cordelia first and tell her Wren will see that she gets home safely.

"I think I should probably head out," Jenna says and swallows. The blue Kool-Aid taste is right at the back of her throat.

"Okay—if you gotta go, you gotta go," Wren says and sounds like a poster boy for a bathroom product.

"Yeah." Jenna waits for him to accompany her, to hold her hand, to put an ending on her "how they met" story. She wants to be able to say to Cordelia, to future grandchildren, to herself, that then Wren walked her back to the dorm. That, hand in hand, they crunched over the snow, and though she felt a little nauseated, she smiled when Wren put her palm over his heart, just to feel how fast it pounded as they stood outside her dorm room door.

"Well," Wren says and hops off the stool. "I'm going to check out this costume thing. Man cannot live a whole winter without the bikini."

"Maybe I'll see you around?" Jenna asks.

"You never know." Wren winks at her.

Jenna feels herself floating in the blue room, feels that she is a sea creature needing hooking of some kind. She goes to the doorway and looks at the room, the vat of drinks, the plate of gummy candy, and wonders if she left something back there.

Halfway to the dorm, Jenna pukes blue on a snow heave. She can taste it all, the whole mess—all the bits of world cuisine as they come up. She wonders where Cordelia is, if she'll come back to the room later or sleep somewhere else. Ahead, the last trace of bonfire embers glows against the white ground. Emptied of the drink, Jenna heads across the quad.

Near the sculpted ice princess is a towering snow castle with a Beefeater guy standing guard. Jenna stops walking to see if she is still dizzy or just cold. She tilts, the snow massing around her and she sees that someone has relieved himself on the castle, and that there's a slash of yellow just where the guard's mouth should have been. She thinks about that guy, Nick, from the summer, and maybe getting in touch with him. Or maybe love is summed up in moments—that day in the park, the time you had Chinese food by candlelight, when the boy you liked left a message, finally, on your machine. Maybe the telling of these moments is even better than the moments themselves. But then there is Wren—who could have been the love of her life or a stray kiss that will go unremembered later. You never knew where it would all lead.

Jenna stares at the ice sculptures around her. She leans on that Disney mermaid, the one who wishes for legs then wants to go back to the sea, unsure which world she's part of. Why couldn't life be like it was in the fifties, like in the black-and-white photos that lined the fraternity walls? Boys wore sweaters and courted girls in skirts and invited them places. Or like in the movies; some hot-roller-haired blonde in a dress sat next to her suited man, and they smiled because they knew, they knew what would happen. Jenna wishes for this even though part of her suspects that it was never as simple as it looks in the black-and-white film reels. But she wants it. She wants Cordelia to stop calling her Jemma, wants to huddle with her roommate, toes touching in the dark of their tiny box room. She thinks of kissing Nick in the warmth of the bakery, and then of the sticky, sweet drink taste on Wren's lips— those moments when love seemed highway-wide, and sure.

Kindling

$\mathcal{U}$ntil she dated Justin, who had one, Kyla wanted a wood-burning stove. Justin had nine whole and one half fingers, and a yellow Lab named Polly, who barked every time a car drove by the cabin on Lake Winnipesaukee where Justin lived for free in exchange for off-season carpentry repairs. Fall evenings after class at the graduate school, Justin left the lecture hall quickly, sidestepping the rest of the students as they leaned on the wall or stood in the doorway talking and feeling much younger than their years declared. Most of the time, Kyla stood around picturing what everyone would have been like in high school. Was Erin a field hockey girl then, her blond-topped hair bright as she swatted at the ball in the short pleat of an orange skirt? Did short Gregory try out for every play, only to be cast as Man in Suit or chorus/understudy, hoping each night that someone onstage in costume would call in with strep? Kyla's jeans needed washing, she wore her roommate's blue sweater, and she nodded at the conversation around her, smiling at Erin so she wouldn't think Kyla was the quiet, hidden bitch in high school who later tried to side-check her on the field.

A gasp of wind came in when someone opened the front door, fallen leaves blew in the doorway—the crumpled, dry kind, not the bright red or syrup-colored ones from the first foliage—and Kyla followed Justin outside one night. Catalog pretty in his fleece-lined canvas coat, he had dark hair that fell over his forehead. Kyla thought about how he'd slick it back with his full-fingered hand before answering questions in statistics class.

Her car nosed up to the back of Justin's, and she figured she'd get a good look at him as she pulled out of her space. He'd caught everyone's attention the first day of class, when he'd come in toting a gangly boy Kyla thought might be his brother. Justin explained that he had been a teacher at a boys' high school in Rhode Island, one of those last-shot places Manhattan parents send their children before giving up, and the kid was a former student who'd graduated and gone on to prove he turned out okay. After that, Kyla found herself wondering who or what else Justin might bring to class, or even what she could make surface for show-and-tell, if there was such a thing in a master's program.

Baby pumpkins dotted the windowsills outside Grange Hall, where Justin was fishing something out from his trunk. Kyla wondered if anyone ever carved miniature pumpkins, how they'd look knifed into triangled eyes and jag-toothed mouths. Justin gave a wave as he sat behind the wheel and watched her until she stuck her arm out the window and pulled out into the blurry street light toward home.

She was heading back to the rented house she shared with Jenna and Jenna's boyfriend, Hull, who didn't pay rent but planned on staying until he patched his kayak with epoxy and chopped-strand fiberglass and set back into the Connecticut River, this time southward. Hull claimed he couldn't take on regular work because the hours would cut into his kayaking hours. Jenna baked bread at Clear Flour, the bakery and restaurant supplier in Hanover, and often came home carrying canvas bags filled with misshapen loaves of honey wheat or seven-grain maple. Her hair and skin smelled of yeast and vanilla, and the loose strands that framed her face stayed flour-dusted and seemed gray in the light. She was just the sort of friend Kyla had hoped to make after leaving the city. Jenna knew how to caulk a bathtub or hinge a door, how to knit a cable stitch and where to inject epinephrine if you suddenly found out you had an allergy to bees while hiking.

Jenna made Kyla feel even more strongly that there was a side to herself she'd yet to understand, the one that found calm in knitting or enjoyed camping, that somewhere in her lurked a nicer, more centered person, that she just hadn't found an environment in which that person could begin to emerge.

Two nights a week, Jenna worked the early shift at the bakery and woke up at half past two to open the store at 3:00 A.M. and fire up the oven. Hull woke to her alarm and made hickory coffee mixed with hot soy milk for Jenna to take in her travel thermos. Kyla was sure Hull didn't contribute to the rent or food; Jenna's name was on the check they gave to the landlord each month.

Lying in her basement bedroom, Kyla could hear the rush and pull of Jenna's car as she drove the length of the dirt driveway. In the wall behind her bed, squirrels and other unseen night creatures scratched at the insulation, and Kyla would lie there, silently disgusted with her living conditions, until Hull appeared in the hallway outside her room. He'd pause, rubbing the cold soles of his feet against his calves, waiting for Kyla to pull the comforter cover back the way a hotel turndown service would.

Kyla's flannel sheets were old, inherited from her sister after she'd gotten married the previous spring and given out her unmatched dinner plates and the linens she'd slept on with men other than her husband. Lying between the red-and-green plaid covers, Kyla would imagine she and Hull were sealed into a gift, boxed up for some treeless morning. Hull would reach over his head and pound the wall with his palm to get the scurrying to stop. The animals would scatter, and the quiet would spread out until the only sounds left were the hiss of fruit bats leftover from summer, night-slung against the pines, and Hull's breath as he lay facing her, ready. She had formed a gulch in her mind; on one side were the times she had heard Jenna and Hull having sex—and on the other side were the slur of times she had had Hull all to herself. With stunning clarity she had divided herself into sections, so she could watch the part of her that felt kicked and discarded while the other part of her said "tsk tsk" for caring. In this way, she could make yellow split pea soup with Jenna, having had sex with Hull only an hour or so earlier, and not feel bad. Neither of them was the other woman.

On the back deck with coffee in the morning, the steam from Hull's shower puffed from the open bathroom window and Kyla pictured the bar of soap sliding down his stomach and listened to the woodpecker who insisted on trying to jab at the metal antenna near the chimney. As the hollow tin peckings sounded out into the small yard, the shower shut off, and Jenna's car turned onto the drive. She wore her hair in braids, and when Hull went out to greet her on the dirt and leafed gravel, he held the towel around his waist with one hand and one of the plaits in the other as he kissed her.

Kyla's coffee was cold, but she sipped at it and thought about statistics class; regression to the mean, probability, medians, modes, and the swan's-neck curve of Justin's left hand and forearm as he charted cluster graphs or took notes. Usually, she arrived late to class and sat near the door. The chairs were modern versions of the ones in all classrooms—the tiny seat that connected to an even smaller cartoon-cloud-shaped desk. The first day Justin had made a remark about the desks being impossible for left-handed people, and she noticed he sat at an angle in the chair in order to keep his notebook supported.

Kyla decided that she would talk to Justin after class that night and stop wondering about the voice that went with the person, so she put on a skirt and black turtleneck to remind herself to do it. As Professor Michelson wrote problems on the board, Erin passed around the photocopied handouts that detailed false statistics in medicine. Kyla had arrived on time and taken a seat in the middle of the arch of chairs. The would-have-been-class-president Chris sat to her right, rechecking his homework. Slumped down, the stoner boy Roger slipped an unfinished American Spirit butt into a soft pack and let one of his sandals flop to the rug.

Even though Justin, who came in late and with his dog, sat next to her, Kyla was thinking about chickening out of talking to him. Her hair felt knotted at the back. The lights made even Erin's ruddy cheeks glow the color of mold and highlighted each facial scar, making Kyla finger the pockmark near her left eye.

She knew if she stayed too long after class—or if Justin happened to invite her for a beer at Dougal's Pub and she agreed— that she'd miss seeing Hull the entire week, since he and Jenna were driving to Burlington for the long weekend. She'd shrugged out of going with them, unable to cope with watching the small moments that reverberated their couplehood.

Right after Chris passed the photocopied sheets to her, she handed them on to Justin, who handed some to his left and took the extras to the professor's desk and then dropped a quartered piece of yellow legal pad paper in her lap. The note read: "Since this is all so high school—want to meet me at the lockers after class?—J." Kyla was sure the teacher had seen her open the letter, so she slipped it into her notebook and swiveled to let her feet rest on the rung of Justin's chair; a wordless yes. Kyla's back bumped up to the metal bar that connected her desk to the seat, and she pretended to share Justin's textbook so he could lean in and whisper, "So, are you up for spending some time together?"

He let his lips graze her ear, or maybe she just wished they did, but she nodded in any case.

In the parking lot outside Dougal's, they could hear the music from inside. Justin's breath smelled like the hard cider they'd finished a few minutes before. He watched her, smiling as she lifted her hair from under the collar of her suede jacket. As if she needed to explain, she said, "It wants brushing." As the words came out, she remembered Alice in Wonderland saying something similar and felt for a second like a verbal plagiarist, with Justin being none the wiser. She held up a lock of hair and then let it drop.

"Maybe I could do that for you sometime," he said. His yellow Lab, Polly, pawed at his knees. From the glove compartment, Kyla produced a dog biscuit and fed it to Polly as she nosed up to her window. Jenna had baked organic dog treats for her customers several weeks before, and when she'd listed the ingredients, Kyla and Hull had tried them out, nibbling at the dense, oaty rectangles until their mouths felt gritty. Kyla'd kept the unfinished ends in the glove compartment, thinking that, if she ever broke down, the biscuits would get her through a couple of hours of waiting for a tow truck or a jump start.

Justin's hands splayed out across the empty ridge where the window glass disappeared into the door, and Kyla looked to the empty spot where the top of his right pointer finger would have been.

"Got it stuck between a fishing boat and a piling," he said when he noticed where her glance rested.

"Where?" Kyla asked. It was all she could think to say, having immediately decided that "ouch" was unsuitable, then regretted commenting at all, now slightly haunted by the image of an ocean-bound floating digit.

"Newport," Justin said and put his hands in his pockets. Bending from the knees, he moved his face near hers. Kyla sat idling, hand on the gearshift, foot automatically set to press on the clutch, thinking he would kiss her, but he didn't. He touched her face and

asked if he could call her and if her number on the class list was
correct. She nodded, and he backed away.

At seven the next morning, she helped Hull and Jenna load up
Jenna's car, slinging two duffel bags and a knapsack into the
backseat while Hull bungee-roped the kayak to the roof rack and
Jenna fixed toast for the ride. Hull insisted on taking his boat
everywhere, envisioning time and motivation to fix it, but the
thing remained unpatched and useless.

"You sure you don't want to come?" Jenna asked. She looked at
Kyla's socked feet and added, "Hey—do you mind if I pack those
socks? I was looking for them before." The house had such a communal method to it, Kyla was surprised that Jenna wanted the
exact socks she had on her feet, but she obliged anyway.

Kyla rolled the purple wool of them and handed the sock ball
to Jenna, who played a game of minicatch with herself while Hull
laced his hiking boots and brought his travel mug to the car. Her
feet were now freezing.

"Have fun," Kyla said.

"Did *you?*" Hull asked; his tone was casual enough that Jenna
wouldn't find anything suspicious. "Last night," Hull clarified
while Jenna shut the trunk of the car, mainly out of earshot. He
took a sip of the coffee, then undid the lid to pour some out. Once
they'd driven to pick Jenna up at the bakery and Hull had pulled
to the side of the road to do the same thing just before hitting the
brake and palming the back of Kyla's head. A puddle of milky coffee ditched roadside, he'd kissed her hard, his tongue still coffee-
warm. It was the only time they'd kissed outside the house, and
Kyla kept the still shot of it in her mind like a page from a yearbook, faded.

Kyla held her hands up to encourage Jenna to throw the sock
ball to her, but she didn't. Jenna threw it high and then higher
until she missed the catch and went to retrieve the socks from

where they'd landed near the compost. Kyla dug her bare big toe into the dirt and thought of Justin's lost finger.

Hull clasped his hands together and gave a small squeal like an excited girl. "Oh, my gosh—does he like you? What's his name?"

"I did." She reached over to pull a twig from Hull's chest. "And his name is Justin." She gave one foot a break from the cold by balancing in a yoga pose, one sole on the opposite calf.

"If you're done prying into Kyla's dating life, we should go," Jenna said and got in the driver's side door. Hull made a fake toast to Kyla with his mug.

"Here's to a good weekend," he said and then, "Jenna left fresh bread on the counter."

Inside, Kyla tapped the bottom of the loaf. Jenna had taught her how the bread was supposed to sound hollow when it was done, and Kyla continued to knock on the loaf after she'd put two pieces into the oven to brown. They didn't have a toaster; they used the oven broiler and placed the toast in a metal basket left over from the old barbecue that came with the house. Square with an envelope flap, the basket held the thick-cut bread perfectly. When one side was done, Kyla grabbed the wooden basket handle and flipped the whole thing over so the underside crisped, too.

She ate up on the counter with her feet in the sink basin. The tap dripped onto the top of her foot as she looked out at the tracks Jenna's car had made on the driveway. On one side of the bread, she'd slathered vanilla honey from Jenna's brother's bees. Everyone in Jenna's family seemed to make or raise something useful. Either Jenna returned from her parents' country house in Vermont with a flat of fresh-laid brown eggs or her sister-in-law would have made a new quilt for the back of their ugly beige sofa, or else Jenna would have created a whole new kind of bread—honeyed sesame walnut—and Hull would be tearing pieces off for himself and for Jenna as they parked out front. Kyla ate the honey bread first and left the buttery other piece for after she showered.

The roommates had chipped in for one of those magnetic boards to keep in the shower as well as two sets of word magnets with which to create bad poetry while they lathered. Kyla stood letting the water hit the side of her face and shoulders while she looked at the stray words—*mountain, heave, pink, drunk, frantic, moans, burn, my, ly, gifts, ed, bitter, away, boys, drive*—trying to put them into a sentence. She dragged the other tiny, wet pieces until they read: *rust burned frantic moans my pink gifts drive away bitter boys.*

Hull was always leaving dirty poems that she and Jenna would find, sometimes together as Jenna showered and Kyla brushed her teeth or if Kyla came in to pee while Jenna washed her face. They'd laugh and try to make even dirtier ones, but usually Jenna just ended up finding Hull on the couch or in their room and reciting his own words back to him while Kyla stood, damp and clothed, holding on to the shower curtain.

Hull found the magnet poems Kyla left cryptic or sad or both, and he would ask her about them. She never meant the words to have a double meaning, she just tried to string them together to be coherent, but Hull—even once when he was inside her—wanted a closer analysis. Thrusting, he'd said again and again, "What are you trying to say?" Kyla repeated the phrase now and wished Hull were with her, up against her in the water, the magnet words scrambled, dispersed like sparks.

The phone rang while Kyla was drying off, and Justin asked if she wanted to go for a hike up Mount Chocorua. They could take the Liberty Trail from the west and stay overnight in the cabin just south of the summit. She hung up the phone and shoved the rest of the bread loaf in a bag with some squeezable jam and a hunk of cheddar from the fridge, dressed herself, and rode out to meet him at the parking lot near the Paugus Mill parking area.

They ended up hiking the Brook Trail, with Justin carrying his daypack filled with the food she'd brought, a collapsible dog bowl for Polly, who followed them, and his water bottle, which clinked and swung as he moved. Kyla had her own water, and she'd stop with the pretense of taking a long drink, but really she just wanted to stare at the jut of ledges, the steep incline ahead, to think about the way Justin seemed to go through the hike as if he were part of the trees or stone slabs that edged out toward the nothing on the other side.

With her water bottle held between her knees, Kyla looked at Justin, who had the pack sandwiched under him for a cushion. Polly smelled something and went off in search of it, flaky moss clinging to her wet nose.

"Pumpkin seeds?" Justin handed some over to her, and Kyla ate them one by one, licking the salted coating off first and then chewing the husky outside. They talked about weather, about statistics and weather, and then, after he'd put the packet of seeds down, Justin wrapped his arms around her and they kissed. When Polly came back, they stopped and decided to head down, fairly rushing back to the cars in order to drive to his house to spend the night together.

Justin's rented house perched lakeside, butting up against the other cabins, which were empty during the off-season. Gingerbread-style trim outlined the steep angles of the roof, and they entered through a sliding glass door on the side. In the entryway, Kyla kissed him and figured he'd race her up the stairs to his room or carry her there, desperate as in movie lovemaking, but instead Justin cut the kiss short and pointed her up to the living room while he put the hiking pack down and loaded his arms with cut wood.

Upstairs, set to the corner of the open-plan kitchen and living space, was a large cast-iron stove with a pan of water on top of it. The cabin was shaded and cold enough so Kyla's breath showed in the air. Justin piled the wood next to the stove and lighted a twisted roll of newspaper with a match before sticking it inside with a log or two. Once he'd gotten the log to catch, he blew gently into the oven door to rise the flames.

Kyla watched with her jacket still on until she saw the refrigerator had one of those pull-down handles and wandered over to try it out and look inside. Aside from the beer, there was mustard, sliced deli meats sealed up in thin plastic bags, some asparagus, a cut butternut squash ill-wrapped in tinfoil, and several coffee creamers in different flavors: hazelnut, mint, and coffee.

"Coffee-flavored coffee?" she asked, pulling the carton out to smell the contents while gesturing with it to Justin. He sat crouched in front of the stove, looking out past the room toward the deck, where the torn backing of a folding chair flitted up and back with the wind.

"Hey—what can I say? It tastes like ice cream."

"It's funny that you have creamer here," Kyla said and then tried to figure out how to explain why. She thought of Justin standing in the refrigerator aisle at the Foodliner, debating the merits of hazelnut over mint, and felt tender toward him, toward his ability to know what he wanted, if what he wanted was just fake dairy.

She smirked at him, closed the fridge, and went to where he was so she could crouch, too.

"My sister got me into it—the creamer," Justin said. "She liked to drink it straight up."

Kyla watched the log edge burn and made a face. "Yuck. Does she still?"

Justin poked at the fire with an iron rod, toppling one piece of wood onto another. "No. Not anymore." Kyla waited for him to say more, but he didn't. He just tightened his grip on her hand and stayed like that until more logs caught, and Justin closed the small door at the stove's front.

Justin's sleeve still had jelly on it from when he'd squeezed some onto his finger during the hike, and she touched the sticky wool to her mouth. He took off her jacket and then led her to his room, where, when she looked up, she saw there wasn't any ceiling— topless walls just sectioned off one room from the next.

In the morning, she peed knowing Justin could hear her in the next room and tried to do it softly, as if the act were somehow more secretive and intimate than the way he'd slept with his hand on her breast and his eyes not quite shut. When she came out of the bathroom, he was turned to the television, watching a man in camouflage unhook a fish from a pronged lure.

"What's the point of the fisherman being in camouflage?" she asked.

Justin shrugged. "Smart fish?"

"Or really dumb—I mean, shouldn't the guy be wearing blue or green, something that looks like water?"

She was a passenger in Justin's car as he drove them toward Weirs Beach. Kyla had never been there but had been sent a postcard once from someone who had—a Tilt-a-Whirl spun its riders dizzy near a cotton candy booth while views of the Ossipee mountains were painted and airbrushed behind. She described the card to Justin as they drove into the almost empty parking lot.

Out across the bay was Stonedam Island, toward which Justin gestured and said, "I first kissed a girl out there."

He took her pointer finger into his hand and outlined near the horizon as if he could show her the exact point where his boy lips met the girl's, and Kyla leaned back into his chest until he moved them on toward the fried dough stand. The vendor wore a wool hat and sifted icing sugar onto the top of the dough before he handed it through the small window. Kyla took the first bite and walked while chewing. Near the dry waterslide, some kids played tag and chased one another with bright-hued tongues, the color left over from a flavored ice drink.

At the end of the boardwalk was the dark rise of Mount Chocurua. Kyla tried to picture the hikers they'd been yesterday—far away in miniature form like figurines in a battle display at a museum—while Justin ate the rest of the fried dough, crumpled the waxed paper in his fist, and pocketed it. They spent the morning there, and before Justin could suggest getting a bowl of clam chowder or playing another round of Skee-Ball, Kyla told him she needed to get back.

Kissing outside his house, they stood near her car. Kyla noticed that when they'd come back Polly hadn't barked, and though she felt bad for thinking about his dog while Justin bit and tongued at her mouth, the thought that Polly already knew who she was amazed her.

"When will I see you?" he asked.

Kyla thought for a second about asking him to come over, how he could probably fix Hull's kayak in a matter of hours. Then she thought about having Justin in her room, how he would see the dust layer on her bureau, the fine coating on the shells Hull had brought back for her from a beach trip with Jenna. Kyla wished then she were overwhelmed by Justin. He was kind and attractive and tall, all the items she'd listed on paper in seventh grade with her semi-best friend, Lucy—Lucy had even added "has a dog" to her list of desirable qualities, words they copied from a magazine cover.

"I don't know when I'll see you," Kyla said and tongued her molar, feeling where the cap met her gum, the warm gap of it. She liked not feeling needy for him. "In class?"

"Well, I'm here if you want me," he said and turned to go inside. She could see him in the entryway, sticking a log under each arm and tucking one under his chin as he went up the stairs.

Back home, Kyla settled in to work for the rest of the weekend, finishing statistical homework and the paper due the following week. She worked in her damp room, mainly, but since it was in the basement and had only one window, she'd sometimes take her ruffle-edged papers out to her desk.

Cornered in the common space where skis and poles leaned against the walls, her desk had one photograph on it that Jenna had placed there to welcome her. In the picture, Jenna and Hull stood back-to-back, hillside, with a green view behind them. She'd penned in "Hey, Kyla! Welcome home!" in the clear expanse of sky behind them and left the picture for Kyla to find the hot summer weekend she moved in when the others had been away at Jenna's brother's farm in Vermont.

Sometimes Kyla thought it was the order of Hull's and Jenna's arrivals that had decided the connections. In the university housing bulletin, Jenna had described herself as outdoor-oriented and kind, and without looking anywhere else, Kyla'd called her the winter before and arranged to move in when her other roommate moved out. Maybe if Jenna'd been baking miniature tarte tatins or cutting back the hydrangeas when Kyla arrived, they would have sat with sweating iced teas on the porch until something boiled up in the kitchen and they went inside to eat.

Instead, Hull had come back earlier, leaving Jenna in Vermont while he and Kyla stayed up late drinking sugar-rimmed vodka tonics with crushed lime. For two days, they'd walked around town, hiked up the hill behind the house, and lain in snow angel position near Grant's Pond. Unseen from the dirt road that tracked up to the water, Hull hummed a tune Kyla knew from years before while the long grass swayed above them. Hull's attentiveness was subtle, pulling Kyla in though she hadn't been attracted to him right away. After he'd called her out to look at a luna moth, its wings large as palms and iridescent, she tallied up the small gestures he made toward her and then pictured his hands on her breasts, her ass, his physical being somehow incredibly important to her.

Even after those thoughts, rather than wishing that Jenna would never return, Kyla found herself filled with grade school

anticipation. When Jenna had come back, carrying loaves of double wheat in a canvas sack slung over her shoulder, she'd smiled
and hugged Kyla. They'd never met, just spoken on the phone, and
Jenna was prettier than Kyla had pictured, with hair the color of
undissolved instant coffee and green eyes.

"I'm so glad you're here!" she'd said. That night, they'd had peach
curry chicken salad on the bread she'd brought home, and after the
dishes were done, the three of them took a flashlight and walked up
to Marsh Field, where a local band played for free. Stoned teenagers
sat, one leaning onto the next, sweatshirted and dew-damp, while a
few young families packed up picnic items and headed for their cars
with their sleep-drugged children. Hull and Jenna held hands, and
Jenna rubbed Kyla's arm to ask if she was warm enough. Bug swat-
ting and hazy from curry, Kyla wiped the sweat from her upper lip
and nodded. She watched the way Hull thumbed the back of Jenna's
neck and knew that he was performing for her somehow, showing
her how he could touch and where and how well.

One side of the common room was taken up by Hull's kayak, and
the sawhorses he'd set up to hold it. Various hiking boots lined the
doorway wall, as well as muddied running shoes and plastic clogs
called Plogs that some surgical intern from the hospital had left
there after a dinner party. They all wore the Plogs now—they
were perfect for a quick trip to the compost heap out back, or
when someone came home from the co-op and needed help un-
packing the groceries. Often, the shoes were in a jumble, as if
they'd broken from the order imposed on them in the bimonthly
cleanups and were socializing. It made Kyla think of dancing
school in seventh grade, how the girls were told to take off one
shoe and put it in the middle of the floor, and when they'd done
that, each boy reached into the heap and danced with whichever
girl went with the chosen leather pump or flat.

The first time Hull had appeared in her doorway was after he and Kyla had said good night upstairs as if Jenna had been there to witness and gone to their separate rooms. Later, after waiting what Kyla considered to be a respectable amount of time, he'd come down to the basement, switched the dehumidifier on, and stood looking into her room as Kyla tucked a pillow into its new case. She held the bulk of it under her chin until Hull came in and finished the job for her. In one swift motion that pillow and the next were cased, and soon they were on them, lying unseen the way they had in the reeds, only this time their arms touched and then legs until he rolled her onto him and she turned out the light.

Kicking through the leaves out back once, in a halfhearted attempt at cleaning the yard before the snow came, Kyla thought about how little she'd struggled with the decision to start up with Hull. She leaned on the rake until the rusted metal tines of it buckled and tried to conjure up a feeling of guilt, but couldn't.

When she figured Jenna and Hull were due back, Kyla went upstairs for something to eat. Near White River Junction there was a dented can shop where students went before their loan checks came through. On display in cheerleader pyramids were cans of creamed corn, salty green beans, and fiddleheads—each tin with a torn label or pushed-in side. By the checkout large barrels of cans without any labels were marked five cents a piece. They'd buy six for a quarter and take them home for times they felt like a culinary surprise or if they came in late from night skiing or a party. Today, the can opener revealed a tin of baked beans and ham that she slumped into a pot and stirred with a wooden spoon. Something, a raccoon or a neighboring dog, was trying for a dig in the compost outside, and Kyla could hear the scratch of paws on the sheet of wood they kept on top.

She took the beans and a hunk of bread for dipping into the living room. Since she'd lived in the house, Kyla had never been the one to light the fire. Usually, Jenna woke up first and did it, or

Hull, who was home all afternoon, brought in wood and folded newspapers as one of his unspoken chores. By the fireplace a copper bucket was filled with starter sticks and various kindling, including old shingles Jenna had found in a crate behind the bakery. She said they made the best kindling ever, since the shingles were easily split and very dry. Each thin plank was half-weathered gray with a more pristine top, from where another piece had been layered on. Kyla broke a couple lengthwise and Lincoln Log stacked them on some newspaper knots, put a match to them, and a few minutes later, added a small log. She sat watching the fire take, picking out one bean at a time from her mug with her fingers as her face grew warm and she waited to see the swing of headlights turning onto the drive. Alone in front of the fire, Kyla wondered if Justin was in his cottage, maybe lighting the stove or drinking mint-flavored coffee, or if he was with someone else, too. For a second, she imagined him with Jenna, what a good couple they'd make in the wilderness, and then shook off the image and threw a cube of ham into the fire, where it burned and made the room smell like bacon.

Justin wasn't in class the next week, and Kyla missed the week after that. Then it was winter break, and they had a house party with cookie decorating and naughty magnetic poetry and mistletoe kisses that left Kyla with a rim of eggnog around her mouth and the buzz-drunk she'd felt at tenth-grade parties, thrilled but slightly sick.

When the phone rang in early January, Kyla pushed Hull off of her and was still laughing at the weight of him as Justin's voice came through the receiver.

"Hey," he said, and when she said the same back he continued with "Did I dream those couple of days back in the fall, or do you really exist?"

"Oh, I'm for real," she said, suddenly aware and blushing as she flirted in front of Hull, who lay on the bed in long underwear bottoms, hands folded on his belly.

"Well, good. How about being real right now and driving over to my place?"

She could hear the television in the background and thought of his dog, Polly, in a snail coil by the stove. Justin shifted the phone and said, "Hang on, I'm just stepping outside to the porch." She could hear him inhale.

"I didn't know you smoked," she said. Kyla gave Hull a one-minute sign, and he shrugged.

"Once in a while," Justin said.

Suddenly, Kyla wanted nothing more than to be barefooted and freezing in the coming snow, smoking with Justin on his porch. He'd probably make her coffee in the morning and add whatever flavor creamer he had going, and maybe then they'd watch a matinee in town.

"So, can I see you?" he asked.

"I'm not imaginary, if that's what you mean," she said and laughed louder than the comment warranted so that Hull would know the conversation was good. Was it vampires or ghosts that didn't show on film? Or maybe neither showed up in a mirror.

"Well, I'll keep the front light on for another couple of hours. Or, if you're coming and want me to meet you in the commuter lot, just let me know. The roads are pretty icy over here—I'd be happy to drive you."

"Thanks," she said and then, "Maybe I'll see you."

Hull only raised his eyebrows at her as she sat on the side of her bed and debated putting her clothes on and heading out. With both hands, he pulled her to him so close their lips touched as he talked.

"Wherever you're thinking about going, don't."

He ran a finger from her ear down to her arm, then bent her head to the side so he could put his face into the curve of her neck.

The next morning, as Hull and Jenna cross-country-skied in

the front of the house, Kyla found a simple line of words waiting for her in the shower: "pantless boy whispers pink spring." She carried the sentence with her around campus all day, and when she went to class and saw Justin, who gave a small smile but didn't come over, she wrote the words in very small letters on her notebook.

The Wednesday before St. Patrick's Day, Jenna brought home green focaccia. The emerald-tinted bagels had sold particularly well already, but no one seemed to want the onion-specked flat dough, so they made it into pizza and sat in the living room eating. Jenna leaned back onto the middle of the couch and tilted her head so she looked up and backward at Hull, who sat to her left. He had eaten the center of his piece and nibbled the crust into an arch, and he held it over his mouth like a smiley face. When he leaned down to kiss Jenna, he kept the bread there and she bit it.

As they twitched and giggled, Kyla felt hot and itchy in her wool sweater. Hull had said he liked it once when she first moved in, and she'd gotten in the habit of wearing it on nights Jenna was going to work. Jenna's cousin had been to Iceland to hike glaciers, and along with the sheets Jenna'd inherited, the cousin had handed down the sweater. She'd pointed to the weave of yarn and the silver buttons and explained the traditions of Icelandic knitting, how unpeopled the landscape had been on her trip, and how her friend had chosen this particular gift instead of healing bath salts because she hoped the sweater would last and be handed down to a child someday. Bursts of deep red, blue ridges, and black trails made a near-mountain pattern across the front of the sweater, and the sleeves, neck, and waistline were hemmed in white. Sometimes Kyla would watch herself walk past the large windows of the bookstore in the town center and feel as if she wore a map, the veins of stitching and rise of her breasts their own topography.

The fire logs were damp from the rain that had made its way down the chimney, and they smoked as Hull tried to light them.

In the kitchen Jenna scrubbed the cookie sheet clean of oil and cheese strands while Kyla wrapped the leftovers in a recycled grocery bag and knotted the handles before freezing the whole package. Kyla looked at her watch and thought about the way Hull massaged her calves after the sweat had dried and they told stories from high school or crushes they'd had on people who worked at the photocopy place in town or the Bagel Basement. As she lay on her stomach, Hull on his back would press his heel into the back of her calf and drag the length of it over and over. Sometimes Kyla fell asleep and woke to hear Hull midsentence, and other times he'd doze in the middle of her calf—he'd stop talking before his heel halted, like an insect leg that moves after being severed.

Jenna looked at Kyla as she wiped the counter. It occurred to Kyla that, while she did not feel guilt about Hull, she felt the same anxiety about being discovered that she had as a child, taking five dollars from her grandmother's wallet, then as a teenager, showing up stoned to her ill cousin's Bat Mitzvah, aware that her actions were grossly out of place, the betrayal sickeningly sour.

Kyla continued to clean the counter. The sponge was in the shape of a fish, and Kyla held her hand over the tail, letting the pointed head do all the scrubbing.

"I don't have to work tonight," Jenna said. She'd been putting in extra hours as the bakery owner planned on opening a second shop twenty minutes away. Imagining that Jenna would end up running that place, Kyla thought of Jenna's extra commuting time and how that would factor into the plans Hull and she could make in the damp mornings come spring.

Hull came in and looked for something in the fridge while Jenna rubbed the soles of her feet free from crumbs. Kyla put the sponge on the sink ledge and sat down in one of the kitchen chairs they rarely used except as perches for lacing or undoing boots or when Jenna had sprained her ankle and Kyla'd had her sit there as she wrapped the injury in tape before the daily run. At the time,

Jenna had started to say something but then was interrupted by the fire alarm, which panicked every so often because of a low battery no one bothered to change.

"What are you guys going to do then? With your bonus night here, I mean?" Kyla asked.

Hull rummaged in the drawer they used to store the fresh herbs from the garden before hanging them on the drying rack. He stuck his fingers in and then put them to his nose.

"That's the basil from this morning," Jenna said to him and put her hand on Hull's face to show Kyla the new ring on her wedding finger. Kyla opened her mouth to say something about it, but Jenna spoke first. Hull kept his fingers by his nose, sniffing at the remains of his foraging. Jenna turned to her and said, her voice steady and detached, as though she were reading from an instructional manual, "Well, what are *you* going to do, Kyla?"

Just from the way Jenna said it, and how she held her head at an angle like that dog on the record label, Kyla knew she knew.

Hull looked at Kyla and said, "Jenna has to work tomorrow, you know, so it's not really a bonus night. Anyway, I'm going to try to do some kayak repair." He kissed Jenna's palm and added, "If that's okay with you, of course."

"Of course it's okay," Jenna said.

"Well, congratulations, anyway," Kyla said. She felt the dips in the webbing between her fingers where Hull liked to put his tongue and stood up. Watching Jenna, she tried to picture her in high school, how she would have dressed or if she ever threw up drunk, or if she'd been head of the church society or speech team, if she'd always been the kind of girl other girls wanted to befriend. Kyla couldn't tell. She wondered how Jenna had found out, if Hull had come clean, or if she'd suspected all along and confronted him. Shamed to the point where the room seemed fun-house tilted, Kyla suddenly saw herself alone and unringed, without even a dog to call her own.

On the table near where Jenna and Hull stood was the scratch pad on which Kyla had written Justin's number. She dialed it, and fifty minutes later they were having sex for the first time in a tent he'd pitched lakeside a quarter of a mile down from his house.

Justin shooed Polly away and finally collar-dragged her back to the cabin, where Matt, some drinking buddy of his, lay sweating bourbon and smoking Winstons while the stove churned out damp heat and a *M*A*S*H* rerun flickered in the darkened room.

After they made love, they sipped water from a metal canteen and shared cubes of mango Justin had brought before smoking a couple of cigarettes each and unzipping the front flap to let in the breeze. Through the netted side window, Kyla could see something flying and landing. Justin breathed deeply and reached back to touch her face before he stood up and went into the woods to pee.

Kyla thought of Polly stretched out in front of the cast-iron stove, of the winter that had passed in hers and in Justin's rented houses, and of honeyed bread. She thought about Hull and wondered if he'd actually patch his boat. Kyla held her hands together as if Justin's were in there, too, and she could somehow replace the digit he had lost to water. Kyla was sorry and ashamed that she'd never kissed his hands. She saw Justin looking out at the lake and tried to average out how many logs his wood-burning stove used up in the cold months, how many times he must have gotten up during the one night she'd spent with him just to stoke the thing. Then Kyla imagined him coming back to his bed that night to watch her, waiting to see if she would wake up.

when to plant,
weed, and harvest *

The Justin and Matt Show

They were trolling tube and worm combos, hooking blues one after the other when Matt told Justin he'd almost kissed some girl the night before as they'd had a couple beers on the dock at Jetterman's Pier. Justin had played pool with the other off-seasoners while Matt held post at the outdoor bar with some early summer people.

"Hey, Justin. What about those parachute jigs—you know, the wire line outfits?" Matt asked, as if he'd been quiet until then.

"Yeah—those work well, too," Justin answered and curled his toes over the stern edge for balance. "But why would you do that? Kiss someone else, I mean."

"Cheat on Lucy, that's what you mean?" he asked. "It was an *almost.*"

Justin nodded. Matt had met Lucy only when Justin had invited her down to Block Island a couple years back. They'd hooked up that first night, and Matt had proposed maybe five months later. Justin had only met Lucy twice himself before that, but he liked her soft voice and the way her green eyes always looked watery, as if she'd been crying recently or thought of something sad and was trying to push the idea away.

Matt didn't answer the question until later, when they were moored in the harbor, *Sally's Wish* slapping the water every time a wake came their way. Justin grabbed two beers from the port-side icebox and handed one to Matt, who was up at the bow, leaning into the rail like the kid in that movie.

"Hey, King of the World, take a breather," Justin said so Matt would sit down. He did, letting his legs go loose on either side of the bowsprit.

Matt pushed the sleeves of his T-shirt up and jerked his head back to get his hair out of his eyes. "It's like—Lucy is the best. Everything I ever wanted," he said.

Justin didn't say anything back, since Matt had a tendency to trail off and then pick up talking again. Matt sipped his drink, wiping the bottle's condensation with his palms and slicking his hair back for good. Justin thought his friend looked younger that way, like he had in the autumns when they'd returned to school freshly shorn. They'd first met when they were both fifteen, caddying for the summer at Oyster Harbors, and sometimes it still felt the same, except taller.

"Lucy." Matt said her name and then turned around so he faced Justin, his back to the water. "It's so good with her that I wonder if maybe I'm missing something."

"You mean too good?" Justin asked.

"Yeah. Something like that. It's no work—and I guess until now all my relationships or whatever have required at least some effort."

Matt's an organic farmer and sometimes when he speaks—whether it's about women or about which bar to go to on a given night—he sounds like he's tending crops.

"Who knows?" Justin said. "But I bet Lucy isn't the kind of girl who'll stick around if you do fuck up."

"Oh yeah?" Matt stood up and looked down to the water. "And you think you know this better than I do?"

"Did I say that?" Justin asked. Then, the way they usually did when they were about to get pissed off with each other, they started their game.

"Hello!" Matt wide-smiled out to an invisible, water-bound audience. "And welcome to The Justin and Matt Show!"

"Hi, folks. I'm Justin, the smart one. This here's Matt." Justin thumbed to him and stood up. "Matt's the dumb-ass who has never been faithful to anyone in his life! *Watch* as he skillfully fucks up yet another relationship! *See* the way he lets Lucy down like Bryn, Kelly, and Melissa before her! *Hear* the crying—experience the surround-sound sobs. *Witness* the drinking jags. But watch your shoes, folks—this could get messy."

"Or—take a look at Justin." Matt held on to the rail as a Boston Whaler ignored the speed limit and produced a large wake that made the boat roll. "Could Justin be any nicer? Probably not! But—could he be any more of a mooch? A grand life-loser? I don't think so!"

They continued on like this as they went into the galley to slap some sandwiches together before they were due to be onshore to meet some friends of Justin's at Dories Cove, where the shore angling was as good as at the breakwater. They'd toss live eels or big swimmers in at night, since dark fishing worked best that time of year; there was already too much action in the daylight. The summer crowds were filtering in on the ferry, traffic from the dock up into town already worse than a week ago, the beaches dotted with khaki-clad men and their bright-sweatered spouses city-breaking for the weekends.

Matt knifed some cheddar from the plastic-wrapped hunk on

the counter and ate it as he waved his free hand toward Justin as if he was a new car or a museum exhibit and said, "Justin is the perfect example of what happens when motivation doesn't just fade but completely dies."

Justin rolled up some turkey and shoved it into the gaping pita bread mouth in his hands. "At least I treat women well," he said.

"See, folks, he can't even defend his ineptitude for job or life stability!"

"Thanks for joining us for our brief but enlightening show today!" Justin said. "Tune in next week, when we discuss how many times Matt has been treated at the STD clinic."

"And for our in-depth interview with Justin, world champion couch surfer and least likely to plan for retirement, since—let's all say it together now—he already is retired!" Matt added, winking at the pretend camera.

What was great about having known Matt so long, though, Justin thought, was how they could go right from the game into easy conversation about sea depth and the upkeep of wooden boats as they rode in the inflatable and motored to shore. Justin carried the tackle box, and they both had their rods. Matt was barefoot still, and Justin looked at his friend's feet propped up on the side of the boat; Matt still had a toe ring from the trip they'd taken to Spain after college, but his feet had grown so the silver loop slid just over the nail of his second toe. Justin waited for Matt to catch up; then they walked up Water Street into town before catching a shuttle out to the other side of the island, where friends sat around drinking Bud and smoking Salems.

None of them talked much while they waited for the sun to go down. They watched the water shift with the wind, and Justin silently replayed what Matt had said during the game. The Justin and Matt Show had started around sophomore year of high school, when they'd both been busted for drinking in the dorms and, later, for taking the school golf carts out and playing dodgem in the quad. While they'd waited in the headmaster's office for their punishment, they'd acted out their story to an unseen camera, and from then on, they'd brought out The Show when one suspected the other of being an idiot, or if it were obvious to both. Today had been different, though, since it wasn't a particular incident they'd poked fun at—more a general critique of each other's lives, and Justin wondered if the nature of the jabs had changed for good.

Justin's island friends were over by the waterline, prodding at the dark patches of sand with driftwood, halfheartedly digging for clams, when the sun finally sank. Matt stood on a big rock by the jetty, balancing with his feet as he kept his hands pocketed.

"Hey—lonely guy on the rock—are you fishing or what?" Justin asked.

Matt shrugged and motioned for him to come over. "I think I'm going to head back to town and call Lucy," he said.

"Why don't you stay for a little while, and then I'll go with you?" Justin asked. Over at the shore they'd already reeled in three striped bass and set the fish, puff-gilled and panicked, in an empty cooler.

"Don't bother." Matt shook his head. "I'll walk to town and call, then just hitch a ride back to the boat."

"Don't do anything stupid, like run aground or something," Justin said. He watched the boat during the off-season, living rent-free on *Sally's Wish* in return for maintenance and brass polishing for Sanders Pirth, a New Yorker who came to the island only twice a season, when Justin vacated his boat and stayed with friends on land or went to see his daughterless father in Connecticut.

"I have no intention of doing anything other than talking to my lovely fiancée and then drinking myself to sleep in my tiny berth," he said, "while you get the captain's quarters."

"Yep," Justin said. "Well, I'll see you back there. Tell Lucy I said hi."

Lucy was a watertight example of what Matt had pointed out:
Justin suffered from his own hesitancy to pursue anything fer-
vently. Justin pictured Matt forgetting to send Lucy a hello and
then felt annoyed with himself that Matt had made a move on
Lucy before Justin had even come to terms with his desire for her.
Maybe that was part of the problem: Justin's pace was glacial;
often by the time he realized what he felt within a moment—a
confrontation or flirting or potential career interaction—the slice
of minutes had passed and he was right back where he started,
with only the dim notion that he'd failed himself.

Matt loped off onto the paved road to call Lucy, and Justin
could see him walk with his arms outstretched, touching the soft
reeds that grew tall at the ocean side of the tarmac. Justin headed
out to the water to see what there was to catch.

"Where'd your buddy go?" Flinch asked. He was a year-
rounder and was nice enough to Matt, tolerant, but didn't trust
anyone who devoted himself to land as opposed to the sea.

"To call his fiancée," Justin said. "Back in town."

Flinch nudged Mark, and they laughed. "Bet he goes back to
the Pier," Flinch said.

"Why do you say that?"

"Oh, Mr. Innocent over here." Mark gestured to Justin with
his head as he fished.

"What do you mean?" Justin said. Under his feet, the wet sand
gritted and slipped between his toes each time a wave moved in
and back.

"You're telling me you didn't see your buddy there—Matt—
with Heather by the bathroom last night?"

Justin shook his head. Heather was one of the Beautiful but
Damaged girls who periodically showed up on the island—some-
times staying for a year, other times a season or only a month.
Heather had already moved to Block Island when Justin had landed

the boat job. She ran a pottery studio in town and never dated any-body, even though they had all tried their luck at some point.

"Everybody else saw them," Flinch said, his lips wet. "They put on a fuckin' show back there."

"Yeah," Mark said. "If I was him, I'd be going back for more of that. Never mind calling home."

When they got back into town, one of the guys came down to the dock and ferried Justin back to *Sally's Wish*. Justin put the tackle and gear on the deck before he stood and pulled himself up to the railing. He used the head and then brushed his teeth before going down to the crew's quarters to find Matt, who was passed out in his bunk snoring; Justin didn't wake him to ask whether he'd talked to Lucy or gone home with Heather or both.

Up early the next morning, before Matt was awake, Justin took the inflatable to shore to stock up on food and beer. Heather was by the checkout, and when he slumped the case of Sam Adams up on the counter, she gave him a quiet hello and stood there watching the grocer print each item on the charge slip before ask-ing where his friend was.

"Back at the boat," Justin said. He thought again about Lucy, her wide mouth he'd never had the luck or motivation to kiss.

"Oh," she said. "Well, maybe I'll see you both later. I'll be at the Pier tonight—or you could come by the studio." She twisted her hair up so it stayed off her neck, and Justin thought if Matt were there, he'd have reached over to touch the stray bits that came free, an admission of guilt.

"Maybe," Justin said.

He loaded the groceries into the boat and started the motor before noticing that *Sally's Wish* wasn't on her mooring. Justin said "fuck" a bunch of times before he cut the engine and went to the dock house, where Flinch, who was part-time master there,

sat reading the paper. He tried calling *Sally's Wish* on the radio but
didn't get an answer, so he got someone to cover the harbor and
came with Justin in the inflatable to look around Grace's Cove and
in the shallows behind Marsh's Landing, where the stripers are
plentiful.

He imagined The Justin and Matt Show that would come of
this morning—how Matt had probably grounded the boat or broken the anchor chain and was drifting at the current's mercy. Justin had a vision of Matt sitting on top of the captain's house staring
out at the sea with a beer in hand, tipping his hat when he saw Justin approaching in the still water by the shore as if nothing had
happened, and all the fuss had been fake.

Instead, when he saw *Sally's Wish*, properly set on a public
mooring, Justin knew something wasn't right. He and Flinch
rounded the cove side and could see Matt's rod and reel dangling
from the railing, and just make out something beneath the surface. Justin waited for Matt to flip up from the sea, talking in his
exaggerated show voice, but instead Matt was waterlogged, flesh
pouched and nearly the color of the reeds he was tangled in. With
Justin spotting him in case he got stuck, Flinch dove in. He hefted
Matt's body up to Justin, where it landed with a squelch on his
chest, heavy and loose. There wasn't even any point in calling for
help; Matt'd been down so long, and they motored back with Matt
slumped over onto Justin's lap until they reached the shore, by
which point a small crowd had gathered.

Justin's hand cupped Matt's shoulder, and after a moment he
realized he was pawing at Matt, trying still for some response.
This was different than when he'd watched his sister go—she'd
been half out of life for so long that her demise felt more as if she'd
seeped away. He made his hand rest on Matt's wet, wrinkled shirt
and tried to remember his calling card number; he would have to
call Lucy.

Justin could see Heather off to one side of the dock, watching as an ambulance crew stretchered the body to the vehicle and left Justin there with Flinch, both of them soaked and shaken. Two of the other guys went back to bring *Sally's Wish* over to the harbor, and Justin went to the pay phones to call Lucy. He dialed the numbers and stared at the tiny metal squares on the phone's face.

Aware that he was in shock, and that this might explain why he wasn't crying, Justin thought about what Matt had said and how maybe it was time for him to find a home, even if it meant paying rent or owning furniture. He thought about senior year of high school in the dorms and how Matt had lied for him, saying whatever Justin had done was Matt's fault so Justin wouldn't get kicked out for his third offense. Then Justin heard Lucy's voice and thought he might be sick. Matt was gone. He could taste ocean water in his mouth, the imprint of Matt's dead back was still watermarked on his shirt, and he kept on having to swallow as he told her what had happened. He thought of saying "I have no best friend" and tried out the sentence in his head as Lucy turned down the music where she was so she could hear Justin. Instead, as Lucy asked again, "What, what happened?" Justin offered up the obituary this way: "You can't marry Matt."

Back at the beach, the local police were shooing people away to their day jobs, telling folks that the show was over and, more than once, insisting it was time for Justin to speak on record, to come to the station and file a report.

The Math of the Fourth Child

At the Purple Room tea is a spread of cheeses ranging from comforting, known Brie to the less familiar though creamier Pierre Robert. To accompany the dairy products are crackers shaped like butterflies, reminders of the reason for the party: the three-year-olds left upstairs with babysitters as the parents mingle and confer about preschool progress. While pecking at hors d'oeuvres, parents offer grins and hellos, sidling up to the teachers to ask about their toddlers' first six weeks of school: finesse at the manipulatives table, where puzzles and beads work the fine motors; circle time, where early ADHD symptoms might be in question; storytime attentiveness tested; dramatic play, with its shawls and fake kitchens, stoves that don't heat, doll babies that can be skull-dropped and picked up unchanged.

Gabrielle has her tiny soy and broccoli nuggets plated alongside other baby vegetables; slim carrots, zucchini slices, knobby cauliflower, testimony to the healthy eating habits the parents, as a collective, try to encourage, though they often give in, offering up fries and chicken fingers. Laura, whose name Gabrielle knows only from the rectangular sticker tag, inquires about Gabrielle's child—if he is the one who asks daily to hug her daughter, Grace.

"Yes, that'd be Danny." Gabrielle sips at the carbonated water, scans the room for someone, the husband she does not have. She has brought, instead, Danny's ailing father, her ailing father, Randall, the kind-faced hospitalist who is cornered at these events with talk of ears, conjunctivitis, sleep issues. Gabrielle tries to explain her boy's hugs. "Danny's very—you know—he likes to touch people." All the chatter out of context sounds off, inappropriate somehow, but Laura only nods.

"He seems very sweet." She inserts a small square of brownie into her mouth, then apologizes for it. "I didn't have any dinner." Excuses for eating the desserts on offer constitute half of the mothering population's conversation, Gabrielle notes, dismayed. She is determined to eat full meals with Danny.

"No, no, eat away—they're good. I would, but I'm allergic to walnuts." Gabrielle adds this last part even though she's sure only about peanuts. Not all nuts. Not legumes—probably not, the RAST tests were inconclusive.

This comment is all it takes to spur on talk of pediatric food issues, safety. "Is Danny allergic, too?" Laura asks. She tucks a sprig of her curly yellow hair behind an ear, where it refuses to stay. Gabrielle understands why Danny wants to touch Grace, Laura's daughter, who has the same hair. It looks so soft and enveloping. Then she remembers Laura is waiting for Danny's allergy report.

"I . . . we . . . don't know . . ." Gabrielle pauses, knowing the *we* is misleading—Danny is not her son, not her stepson. What is he, in fact? "We—I mean, my father and I—we thought he was fine, but then Danny went into anaphylactic shock, actually, a couple of weeks ago . . ."

To Gabrielle's relief, Laura skips over the whose father is whose issue and just gasps. This is among the worst scenarios she can imagine. "God—what did you do?"

Gabrielle has instant guilt that the severity of Danny's allergic reaction has deflected questions regarding her parental status. She does not have to explain that Danny is her father's boy, her half brother, younger by three decades, whom she now treats as her own son. She does not have to mention Randall's relapse, Diane, the wife who left him with a ten-month-old and poor prognosis.

Gabrielle tells Laura the abbreviated story of Danny's shock, the coincidental visit to the pediatrician's office, how the hives started on Danny's neck, spread to his belly, legs, the lips enlarged, eyes completely red, Dr. Dellosa's yell for epinephrine, the ER visit. She has told the details enough times now (to Randall, to the ER docs, to school, playgroup) that compressing the tale is easy. The pattern then is sympathetic nod, worried exchange of "hopefully not again," and a quick show of the EpiPen Jr. as proof Gabrielle's got the situation under control.

Gabrielle switches the topic the way she does when her obstetric patients—or anyone, she has realized—gets too personal. She is a master at guiding the conversation away from herself, investigating someone else. She says to Laura, "So—how many kids do *you* have?"

The women find themselves part of the continental shift; clumps of parents have clustered around the bar, and Gabrielle and Laura are now corner-bound, sitting on a love seat with a silver tray of miniature nut-free labeled brownies in front of them. Gabrielle eats the one from the center of the plate, hollowing the daisy flower shape of its middle.

"How many kids?" Laura pauses as if she has to check, picks up a square cocktail napkin, and drapes it over her leg. "Three— Grace is the middle." She points to the darkness of the study off the dining room, where her third child, the three-month-old, is sleeping. "You can go look at him," Laura offers, and Gabrielle peeks at the baby and comes back. This is a change since she has become Danny's mother. Before all this, Gabrielle would have looked at the sleeping baby to be polite, to reinforce that she is a good obstetrician—she brings babies into the world, for Christ's sake, shouldn't she want to gawk at them any chance she gets? As she settles back onto the love seat, Gabrielle realizes she wanted to see that baby, see if she noticed anything that made it specifically belong to Laura. Then, either way, she finds a fragment of peace there; amid the hustle and collective parental voices, the sleeping baby is still tethered somehow to his mother.

"Do you want more children?" Laura asks.

Gabrielle thinks of her patients, the ones who try for more and fail or come back every couple of years, spacing their children out evenly, appearing before her front-weighted, hands on their bellies. "I'm not sure," she says. She almost offers the fact of how she never thought she'd have one child of her own, and then winces, knowing Danny really didn't start out as hers.

Laura studies Gabrielle's face and smiles as if she's found out an answer. "Oh . . . was Danny a surprise, then?"

"You could say that, yes." Gabrielle rises from the love seat for a second to check on her father's whereabouts. Just before panic sets in because she's unable to locate him, Natasha Meade-Martin, head of the parent volunteers and the hostess, comes over to lay a reassuring hand on Gabrielle's shoulder, pressing her back onto the love seat.

"Hi!" Natasha's teeth are aligned and white as new bathroom tiles. "Randall wanted me to tell you he's gone to check on Danny in the playroom." The parent association has hired a team of sitters for the evening to watch the children upstairs so the parents can relate unrestrained below.

"Oh, well, thanks so much for letting me know," Gabrielle says.

To Laura, Natasha asks, "Are you getting advice from our resident ob-gyn?" Gabrielle knows that this is not out of true curiosity, rather it is to prove how much information Natasha has about each parent, profession, nanny name, geographical status. "Anyway, I'm just the messenger—back to the masses!"

Natasha leaves, her plum-scented perfume remains, and Gabrielle wonders if she will ever know the code of mothers, the unspoken way of categorizing: chic mothers on one side, natural fibers on the other. She does not know where she fits in, if she is considered a real mother yet, if her finger-painting techniques or snacks or clothing are done the right way. Gabrielle feels at turns full of herself, that her parenting skills come easily, and then suddenly, for no reason—a whiff of Natasha's perfume—that she will never get it right.

"We want another," Laura says, meeting Gabrielle's gaze. "Another baby."

"Four kids . . ." Gabrielle starts. "That would be . . ." She prepares for her next stock phrase, the one about how all her patients tell her transitioning from two to three children or even three to four is not nearly as dramatic as from one to two. But Laura doesn't let Gabrielle go there.

Instead Laura offers, "We—or I—really want another one. But—you know—my brother died when we were kids, so . . ." Then she waits for Gabrielle to complete the thought.

Gabrielle feels too awkward to say anything, so she waits for Laura to go on. Both women are out of Lilliputian vegetables, and Gabrielle feels she's eaten enough brownies and can't defer any longer. "So obviously his death makes it much harder?" She tries to play verbal detective—was it leukemia? Car wreck? Drowning?

"It's just—when you look at the possibilities." Laura wipes her mouth on her napkin square and sets the paper down on the glass coffee table. "It seems like the more kids you have, the more things that can happen, right?"

Randall is back. Gabrielle can spot his maroon sweater far off in the jumble of parents. He gives her a wave from across the room. He has said something to some people, made his audience laugh, probably with a joke she has heard before—an anecdote from a patient. Gabrielle waves back and instantly misses the future that he will not be in; then, before she gets sucked into those thoughts, she thinks about the math of what Laura has said.

"Well, I don't know," Gabrielle says. "All the bad things that are out there could still happen to just one kid, though."

"And then you wouldn't have any," Laura says.

In the bathroom, a powder room really, Gabrielle's knees nearly touch the sink, and she allows her posture to flag as she pees. Outside, the Purple Room parents and teachers are talking scheduling and boundaries, year goals. After washing her hands, Gabrielle retreats to the quiet of the study and looks at Laura's baby.

Laura appears next to her, unbuckles him from the portable car seat, and brings the baby to an oversized chair to nurse. "Want to keep me company?"

Gabrielle nods and then wonders if, in the half-light, Laura can see her gesture, so she adds, "Sure."

Laura says, "With the first one, I nursed alone. I just loved that time with her, you know? And now . . . by the third one it's like, hello? This is sweet and all—but it's boring." She laughs slightly, then adjusts her breast, propping the baby up on a cushion. "But then—I feel like it's all going so quickly that I should appreciate every second of it, since it might be the last time I do this."

Gabrielle sighs and tries to verbalize something she's thought of a lot recently. "I never know whether I celebrate the first time of things enough—like when Danny walked or said 'quack' when we fed those Canada geese in back of the library." She waves her arm as if the fowl are actually clustered around her. "Or if I'm too busy mourning each passage, the end of the bottle, or . . . Danny can't say 'Connecticut,' and we went for my college reunion and he said 'Connekatit' the whole time." She pauses and listens to the quiet gulping from the baby. "And I just know he'll grow out of that and that I'll miss it."

"Yeah." Laura nods. "You always do miss it, and then they're suddenly into the next thing, like they can hit a ball with a bat or use a fork or go to the bathroom without your help and you forget what you just lost."

The word *lost* stays in the air between them, and together Laura and Gabrielle go back to their earlier conversation. They make a list of all the bad things they can think of. Gabrielle has written in her all-caps doctor font on Natasha Meade-Martin's personalized stationery. Now it looks like this:

A Special note from Natasha Meade-Martin!

BIRTH DEFECT

BIOLOGICAL PROBLEMS
THAT PRESENT LATER IN LIFE

MECONIUM BIRTH

CAR ACCIDENT

ILLNESS

Then they get more specific, Gabrielle's writing degenerating into scrawl as they talk.

"We have a trampoline," Laura admits. "It's already a danger . . . and this one—we got it used, and the mesh siding is torn. Even worse."

They list genes from one side of the family with the brain tumor of unknown origin, inheritable depression from the other.

"Plus," Gabrielle adds, shaking her head, "there was that article in the *Times* about drugs to treat depression in kids and how those might cause more suicides." She chews on her upper lip and adds, "But I'm not sure how skewed those statistics were."

As Laura's baby suckles, both women imagine a parade of less specific, general yet horrible things: kids getting snatched from yards, malls, teenagers chatting online and winding up assaulted, bikes skidding off the sidewalk and winding up under SUV tires. Then, further, what kinds of accidents: if the trampoline causes the high bounce into a fall, that could lead to the broken arm, leg—a sprain and scare, concussion or fatality, the broken neck. Gabrielle does not press Laura for information about her brother's death but silently thinks the genetics from the brother could already be there in Laura's children. But then maybe multiplying more could just create further opportunities for terror, death? Never mind the good life, the siblings, the laughs, learning—

"So, you see why we have the struggle," Laura says. She has finished nursing, and Gabrielle can sense the party reaching its apex. She checks her watch—it is two and a half hours past Danny's bedtime. She is of the camp that kids need schedules and lots of rest, and her prior announcement that Danny goes to bed at seven every night was met by envy and disbelief, a few mothers clucking about kids having freedom to choose their own schedules.

"I guess if you want more kids, you have to figure out the math of the fourth child and go from there," Gabrielle suggests and wishes it had come out funny. Instead, it sounds like doctorly advice.

"Will you?" Laura puts the baby back in his seat and waits in front of Gabrielle, who still has pen and paper. Gabrielle thinks Laura is serious and starts to write. Laura says, "I'm just kidding. Kind of. I mean, if you happen to stumble on the answer, let me know. We could meet for coffee sometime—after drop-off?" This is the first time Gabrielle has been invited to do anything one-on-one with another preschool parent, and she blushes like it's a prom date.

"That'd be great."

"Dad," Gabrielle says. She finds him leaning on the kitchen counter, slumping slightly. "You okay?"

"Fine," he says to her over his shoulder. "But I need to go to sleep. I'm tired."

Gabrielle puts her arm around her father's shoulder, then reconsiders and touches his hand. "I'll go get Danny and meet you in the car?" She wants to guide her father outside, make sure he navigates the steps without falling, but knows this will frustrate him, so she leaves him to thank the hosts and finds Danny snail-coiled and asleep at the top of the stairs.

"We tried to move him," one of the sitters says, "but he just wouldn't let us."

Gabrielle knows it's not worth a speech about how she thinks adults are losing control of their kids, how a three-year-old shouldn't decide where he sleeps, particularly if that place is at the top of a precariously high staircase, but instead she folds Danny into her arms and hefts all thirty-two pounds of him downstairs. She looks to say good-bye to Natasha, to the teachers, or to Laura, but they are otherwise engaged and she has a heavy toddler on her shoulder.

"Come sit," Randall says to her outside, where he's taken a seat on a small stone bench in the landscaped yard. There is room for both of them, and they lay Danny out so he's spread evenly on their laps, his head on Randall's thigh. "Nice night."

Gabrielle fills her father in on what she and Laura spoke about.

"She's basing her decision about having another baby on the chance of bad things happening," Gabrielle says and then suddenly is aware of how her vocal tone reverts to sounding thirteen, or younger—nine—around her father. This feels comforting to her now, probably to him, too. Gabrielle will be a child until Randall is gone.

"Let's work it out," Randall says. He launches into his breakdown of the situation. And Gabrielle records it on the back of a long gas receipt, knowing she will keep the thing forever. She writes:

IF YOU BELIEVE THAT THE CHANCE OF SOMETHING BAD HAPPENING TO A PERSON IN HIS OR HER LIFETIME IS X (WHERE X IS A NUMBER BETWEEN 0, MEANING NOTHING BAD EVER HAPPENS, AND 1, MEANING SOMETHING BAD IS GUARANTEED TO HAPPEN, THEN THE CHANCE OF SOMETHING BAD *NOT* HAPPENING IS $1 - X$. IF YOU HAVE Y CHILDREN, THE CHANCE OF HAVING NOTHING BAD HAPPEN TO *ANY* OF THEM IS $(1 - X)^Y$, WHICH MEANS TAKE 1 MINUS X AND RAISE IT TO THE POWER OF Y. WHAT YOU WILL FIND IS THAT NO MATTER WHAT YOU THINK X IS, THE CHANCE OF *ALL* OF YOUR KIDS NOT HAVING SOMETHING BAD HAPPEN TO THEM GETS SMALLER AS YOU HAVE MORE KIDS.

"So Laura's correct," Randall says.

Gabrielle nods but then goes on, "There's an important caveat to this, though."

Randall touches his daughter's face with his cold hand. He can imagine her in any of the settings in which he's seen her: Iceland, Texas, her childhood bedroom, its walls covered with miniature bouquets of blue flowers. "What's that?"

"The argument assumes that the occurrences of bad things in different people's lives are uncorrelated. It's an assumption that makes the statistics easier, but it's not necessarily true. It would be true if your kids all grew up in different states and never had any contact with one another. But if they live together—which is pretty likely, right?—there may be a greater chance of something bad happening to all of them . . ."

"Like a plane crash with all of them onboard?" Randall suggests.

"Exactly. But, on the other hand, there might also be positive effects, like they protect each other and keep each other out of trouble."

"Okay," Randall says. "Summary time."

"Basically, if you thought that either of these effects—the mass catastrophe or the cooperative security—was important, then it could outweigh the purely statistical effect, the $(1 - x)^y$ rule."

Danny shifts, turning so his face is skyward, his lips wet. Gabrielle has her arms on his shins. Randall touches Danny's nose the way he used to touch Gabrielle's, running his finger down the nose like it's a ski jump. "Obviously," he says, "how much weight you give these eventualities depends a lot on your outlook. It's an illustration of the main difficulty in making accurate statistical predictions."

This is what Gabrielle—and Laura, though she doesn't know it—is left with: it is true (or at least plausible) that the number of bad things doesn't change with the increase in births; the chance of a bad thing happening to any given person is roughly the same regardless of how many people are born. This leads to the conclusion she had before, that the chance of nothing bad happening to any member of a group is smaller than the chance of nothing bad happening to a single person (except in the rather unrealistic situation in which both the number of bad things and the number of people in the world are not much bigger than 1).

"Gab," Randall says, pulling her back from her brain.

"Yeah?" She feels as though she has levitated, seen the earth as this incredibly wide thing on which she is anchored only by this bench, these two people. They have become her personal longitudinal and latitudinal markers, and for that she feels love and enormous relief.

Randall takes Gabrielle's hand and looks at her. "You're a really good mother to him," he says. Gabrielle is swept up in the praise, shrugs off the bizarre circularity that her father is praising her for mothering his child. Then she thinks that probably Danny will not remember Randall, and will know her as his only parent.

"So are you," she says.

Randall sits in the passenger side of the car and starts to nod off before Gabrielle has finished buckling Danny into the backseat. Now that he is strapped into his car seat—the one *Consumer Reports* revealed to be the safest—Danny's head lolls to one side. Gabrielle allows herself another look at him and a kiss on his pouchy cheek before she has to strap herself in a full seat away. It seems impossible that once, not long ago at all, she had never met this boy. Outside, fall is settling, the leaves wind-chucked, the air cooler now. Gabrielle catches herself taking Danny's pulse, feeling his wrist. She can hear her father breathing in the front seat. She uncurls Danny's small fist and clasps his hand to hers and notices the way even in sleep his fingers seem to know their way around hers; their hands together form their own organ, or an *x*, like on a map that insists *you are here.*

Everybody Has a Boy in Brooklyn

Order the Viennese Frosted Mocha Shake," Kyla says when they're almost to the registers.

"Are they good?" Lucy asks.

"They're supposed to be amazing," Kyla says and gives her a jab in the side so Lucy'll order first.

"What's Viennese about the drink, exactly?" Lucy says to the apron-clad coffee boy behind the counter.

"It's like, frothy, and kind of creamy, like a pastry or something," he answers and shouts Lucy's order to the guy who makes the drinks.

Kyla gets a soy macchiato, then she and Lucy wait by the side of the copper-domed espresso maker, looking up at its gleam and whir as if it's a European monument they've been sent to photograph as the summary of a five-city tour. The coffeemaking guy hands Lucy the blended drink and smiles.

At the table Kyla looks pointedly in the direction of the counter and says, "So, you had a caffeine connection?" She goes on to tell Lucy that she's sure the coffee guy likes her, that at the very least he approves of her drink choice, which she reminds Lucy is actually Kyla's drink choice, not that it matters, since Kyla doesn't think the coffee guy is that cute. At least not for her—but for Lucy, he's very attractive.

"You should write your number on a napkin and slip it to him," Kyla says, blowing through the sip hole on her cup.

"Maybe on one of those stirrers," Lucy says. She holds her fingers to her ear like a phone, saying, "Why, of course I'll go out with you." Lucy's been single on and off, mostly on, for the better part of her postcollege life. Kyla is contemplating a move to L.A., mainly, Lucy thinks, because Kyla's swatted through the dating scene in New York, Boston, and New Hampshire, and come out empty.

"Then you'd have to commute to kiss him," Kyla says and takes another glance at the coffee boy. Lucy and Kyla have come to Williamsburg just for the afternoon before the film festival starts.

"I've always wanted to have a boy in Brooklyn," Lucy says and sighs, overly wistful.

"So you can be like everyone else?" Kyla asks. "Do you know how many times I have heard people on the subway or on planes or even out in L.A. say they have boyfriends in Brooklyn? Too many times."

In their friendship, Kyla plays the role of Marlin Perkins from *Mutual of Omaha's Wild Kingdom*, motioning for Lucy to pet the cheetah or tranquilize the rhino while Kyla waits in the Jeep, talking to the camera about how dangerous each animal is. They met at birth—their mothers had met as teenagers—but hadn't become anything other than "family friends" until Mrs. Denillo's seventh-grade homeroom. Kyla had hugged Lucy—the new girl—hello, introduced her around, and then prodded Lucy to ask the teacher what the word *intercourse* meant. Lucy did, got sent into the hall, and listened as the laughter dissipated and order was restored. Kyla can convince Lucy to kiss someone, or consume caloric coffee beverages, wear her least

flattering pants to the high school reunion, or try bull's balls—
Rocky Mountain oysters—and swallow them whole.

The truth is Lucy used to think she followed Kyla's advice because Kyla knew more, that she had universal knowledge of love
or beverages that put Lucy to shame. But now Lucy's pretty sure
she does what Kyla says because she is so much happier than Kyla.
She can afford the risk. Kyla doesn't eat wheat or gluten or dairy
or meat anymore, but she smokes Camel Lights and coughs like
an eighty-year-old emphysemic. Kyla doesn't really do anything,
Lucy thinks. What Kyla enjoys most is watching Lucy do things,
especially when Lucy trips up. Kyla laughed harder than anyone
when Lucy's shorts fell down during the baton race in high school
track finals, even though Lucy crossed the finish line and her
team won. But when Billy Kingsman dumped Lucy on the big,
spongy pole-vaulting mat behind the gym, Kyla'd been heroic,
blowing off play practice to let Lucy cry on her Fiorucci shirt. The
winged cherub decal on Kyla's chest looked up at Lucy and smiled
while she snotted and sobbed until the skin around her eyes was
enflamed, swollen as if she'd been stung.

The friendship worked best when they saw each other infre-
quently, when Kyla had no real idea what was happening in Lucy's
day-to-day life. The year Kyla was away at graduate school in New
Hampshire was closest they'd ever been, talking on the phone
nearly every day. Kyla told Lucy all about the boys and the woods,
the food she'd learned to cook, the affairs she'd had. This was before Kyla'd been diagnosed with celiac disease and cut out so much
from her diet; back then she'd seemed fuller, more content.

When Lucy had visited her up there, Kyla hadn't suggested she
do anything to make an ass out of herself, not even when they'd
gone to the bar in town or when she'd brought Lucy to class with
her. Kyla sat Lucy at the desk next to hers and wrote her notes
about her classmates, then, afterward, introduced her as if she'd
lugged her in for show-and-tell. One guy, whom Kyla had a crush

on, Justin, had come out for a beer with them, regaling the girls
with stories about fishing, about his dream of being the teacher
everyone loves at some boarding school. He even had the right dog
for a boarding school position, a yellow Lab who panted, tongue
lolling on the bar floor, as the girls drank pumpkin ales and tried
to chuck stale popcorn into each other's mouths.

Lucy thought Kyla might have ended up with Justin, but they'd
lost touch after Kyla'd returned to the city, leaving the foliage and
few friends she'd made in New Hampshire behind. Justin and Lucy,
however, had exchanged addresses, and every so often she'd get a
postcard from him that she didn't show Kyla, just in case she felt
funny about it. Now Kyla talked about going to L.A., to be a production assistant or a party planner—something with accessories—
and Lucy couldn't for a second picture her with Justin. Sometimes,
Lucy found herself silently narrating her life to Justin, waiting for
his response; she couldn't tell if this meant psychologically she was
trying to be closer to him, or if this was her mind's way of wrestling
with Kyla's slow shrugging out of her life.

"Wait, don't look," Kyla says, tilting her head down toward the table
but making her eyes go to the coffee bar. "He's looking over here."

Lucy looks. The coffee guy ignores her. "I don't think so," she
says.

"Yeah, he was, I just saw him," Kyla whips back. She undoes
the coffee lid and licks the foam from the cup edge. "This drink
sucks. How's yours?"

"Really good," Lucy says, then feels bad and adds, "But in that
sickening way."

She wonders if Kyla misses bread, if she has dreams about
pizza dough, or muffins. When Lucy asks, Kyla says, "No. There's
plenty of stuff I can have—rice flour. Fairway sells wheat-free,
gluten-free mixes. I'm not going hungry, believe me."

On the way to the bathroom, Lucy surreptitiously pockets a

handful of wooden stirrers. The action goes unseen by Kyla, who is too busy studying her own reflection in the wall-anchored mirror to her left.

By the bathroom door, Kyla waits for Lucy. Inside, Lucy does a thigh lunge, an ode to her mother's germ worries, so she won't touch the urine-speckled seat. Even though Lucy is not an employee and therefore not required by law to do so, she washes her hands for a long time, dries them on her shirt, and prepares to leave the room looking even more crumpled than before. Before she changes her mind, Lucy takes a wooden coffee stirrer from her jacket pocket and dashes her number onto it. When she's out of the restroom, she slides the stick across the counter to the coffee guy. He raises his eyebrows at Lucy and hands her a mint from a pile on a cake plate, as if this is his way of saying, Yes, he will call her, they will go out, and they won't tell Kyla.

"What were you doing?" Kyla asks, having wandered around the store picking up free flyers, then leaving them on the counter near the trash bins.

"Getting a mint," she says, holding it up for proof. "My breath smells."

"Yeah, probably from that fattening drink you had," Kyla says.

Outside, they walk a half block without talking and then pause at the corner at one of those pizza places that claims to be the original. They look at the wrung-out dough, the thin disks of pepperoni, and the red sauce being ladled onto some deep dish.

"And you're telling me you don't miss that?" Lucy puts her pointer finger to the window glass. In the reflection she watches the blurred cars and people disappearing from view as the pedestrians walk past and slip around the corner of the window. Lucy can feel the extra stirrers in her pocket, how the tiny corners are already poking her thigh. Kyla turns, looks at Lucy, and says, "I don't miss anything."

A Map of the Area

From the back of the yurt, a clapping of hands.

"Okay, now," the leader says. His name is Tim, but he goes by Titian these days, knotty auburn hair and goatee to match.

Jenna looks around and notices that the Emotives Mates have gathered in a circle, standing. One dangles a hand down to her, but she backs up, does not accept the dewy palm.

"Life is a circle," Titian bellows, then he whispers the same thing. The whisper hushes the Emotives and inspires a couple of people—Jenna thinks of them as the Sandalman and Breasty—to repeat the leaderspeak.

Out the flap door, Jenna can see the yellow dome of the kitchen hut, where she is employed for two months, and then, farther, the cabin where her father has subsidized her board so she doesn't have to sleep under the blue tarp with the Emotives. Just the cook, Jenna is neither part of the leadership nor one of the hemp-clad enrollees who've signed up to learn how to express themselves better while communing in natural fibers. Jenna, in her off hours, is allowed to watch the exercises but not to speak.

"Emotion is fluid, powerful like water. Harness the energy force of the current." Titian's female counterpart, Andrea, nods and rubs hers hands together. She's come in from the late September cold, and her cheeks prove it; they are red and shiny as a tricycle.

Andrea has been the only one so far to pay any attention to Jenna. Now, even during the Emotivation Circle, the two seek each other out. Jenna does not yet know why. She has vague notions of Titian's desire for a threesome in the yurt after the newly expressive folks have gone to bed, tired from trust games and talking. But Jenna's lack of physical impulses is stunning; she doesn't remember a time in her life when she wanted less contact.

Jenna has lost her twenties, two pregnancies, the handful of friends she'd kept clustered around her at various points, and, most recently, her mother. Her father litigates, grows asparagus in the warmer months, allows himself a teaspoon at a time of the jam and canned foods her mother left. Shelved in the pantry are syrupy apricots, lavender mustard, jellies ranging from fig to blackberry, and chutneys. Jenna has tired of watching the food supply dwindle at her parents' house, each month without a mother or wife marked by a missing jar of sweet pickles or pepper marmalade.

"Green Zebra, Arkansas Traveler, Box Car Willie, Caspian Pink." Jenna actually says the words out loud to herself while adding a mix of diced heirloom tomatoes to the chili. Steam rises from the enormous pot in front of her; she stirs with a spoon the length of a yardstick. Jenna can craft five-course meals on just the two burners provided by the Emotives. By now she's got the menu down, so she cooks by rote; Monday's meal is brown raisin bread, purple coleslaw, and baked beans. Tuesday brings bread pudding fashioned from the leftover bread, Andrea's honey, and suspension of the pan over an open fire, which caramelizes the sugary bottom. Chili day signals the middle of the week, though the Emotives brochure rallied against set days, avoided "common terminologies like hump day," feeling that too much structure makes for emotional blockage.

"Basically," Andrea had confided in Jenna when Titian had sauntered off with a wad of paper and headed for the outhouse, "we're dealing with some serious emotional constipation." Jenna smiled, then waited for Andrea to finish. "But the money's good."

Most of the people on Emotive Missions are dot-commers, the suddenly wealthy, or the bored in crisis. "You'll get your fair share of BICs—but also some true soul searchers; those are the ones you feel bad for, they're still kind of lost when they leave," Andrea had explained as she'd shown Jenna the cabin Titian had built for their guests—in Jenna's case, the hired help.

"When my mother visits"—Andrea propped open a shutter to let in the milky afternoon light—"I have to decorate." She showed Jenna the closet where matching dishes, a Ralph Lauren comforter, various appliances, and wedding registry items were stacked one to the next. "You know how mothers can be, right? Mine's . . ." Andrea thought for a minute. "Mine's pretty much deaf, you know? But, I just— I like her to have a good thread count." Jenna wasn't sure whether Andrea meant her mother was literally unable to hear or just a poor listener, but she didn't ask for clarification; maybe Andrea meant both.

Jenna couldn't compare mother stories, preferences for down or Quallofil, because she still can't get her head around the grammar of her mother's death. In the past tense, her mother is too long gone—wasn't she just standing in front of Jenna, explaining the utility of twine, how to pinch her cheeks should rouge not be available? But then, there is no present tense for her mother, either. The recall of her mother's mouth, the small bursts of bosom that escaped the top part of the bra—in effect creating four breasts—feel still-present.

"Titian says mothers are born to criticize, that it's through their eyes that we see not what we are but what we could be." Andrea took Jenna's duffel from her shoulder and dropped it at the foot of the bed.

"Isn't that a famous quotation?" Jenna asked. Andrea shrugged and pointed out a tiny portable television stashed away under the comforter in the closet.

"Just in case," Andrea said. "The batteries are fresh."

Jenna crinkled her nose and touched the small knobs, the folded antenna. "In case what?"

"I don't know, maybe if you get . . ." Outside, the gong sounded. Andrea started to head out the door. "Sometimes, if I can't sleep or Titian's bugging the crap out of me, I come down here and watch whatever station comes in. Try channel twelve—you might get one of those skin care infomercials. Or *M*A*S*H*." Andrea waved and backed out the cabin's door. Over her shoulder she called, "I almost ordered one—that cream that makes your face glow? Do you think it'd work?"

Jenna ladles chili into the wide brown bowls and sets each place with a spoon Titian has carved from wood scraps. She makes sure to add a scarce amount of bleach to the rinse water after meals, and when Titian protests, Jenna says, "Do you know how much bacteria love to live in wooden utensils?"

At lunch, quiet chatter. Breakfast is silent, dinner is a discussion led by Titian, Andrea, or a guest speaker, but lunch is a regular affair. Jenna picks at a breadstick, dips it into her chili mug, and eavesdrops. One man's lost his millions—Jenna questions how he can afford the three-thousand-dollar fee for roughing it as an Emotive. Another younger one came at the request of his new wife—"She says I don't talk enough. But I do. I just don't talk about what she wants me to talk about." A few nods. Titian checks his watch. He will go into town later to pick up Avi, the single-named scholar turned mystic. A young woman adds to the conversation and touches the shoulder of the woman next to her. "Since the IPO—my mom and I—we fight all the time. Not here so much. But at home. Or wherever. So we don't want to do that. We want to learn . . ." Her voice gets lost in the chili mouthful. Then the mother reapplies her lipstick, to the obvious disdain of most of the group. "Plus," the mother adds, "the Golden Door spa was full."

On her bed that night, a camper without bunkmate or counselor, Jenna tries to pick an imaginary fight with her own mother. Do her criticisms still exist? She remembers some, maybe a weight-loss issue here, a certain college acceptance there, relationship advice from a woman who'd married her eighth-grade boyfriend.

"Hair back at the table," Jenna says to her invisible mother. "And stop fidgeting."

"Why don't you loosen up?" Fake Mother nudges back as Jenna's teenage self.

"I'm loose enough already," Jenna says, then laughs a little, both at what she knows her mother would have said about the word *loose* and about the whole scene—who thinks she'll wind up cooking at an overpriced outdoor shithole, pseudocommune, unable to mourn her dead mother?

Jenna's laugh is abruptly cut off by a sound outside. She sticks her head out the front door and sees if she can identify the noise. Bird? Dog? Coyote maybe. These were things parents taught their children: how to identify animal sounds, tips on becoming financially stable, the proper way to snip a flower stalk at an angle. It occurs to Jenna that whatever knowledge she has right at this moment—whatever her mother has passed on at this point—is it. If she doesn't already understand how best to prune or pickle, she won't get any further clues. At least, not the way her mother had. And Jenna doesn't want to learn by a book, an Internet course; she just wants the knowledge of everything her mother had stored up imparted to her mystically—the way she doesn't remember learning to make a bow, wrap a present neatly, or give in at just the right time in an argument to get her way; these are things she just knows.

The next day, Titian leads group yoga, each Emotive on a thin blue mat that slides on the cold, dewy ground. Jenna follows the poses, puts her elbows to her thighs, and when he instructs them to do Balasana, the child's pose, wonders if she'll ever give birth. So far, she's made it through the nausea stage of pregnancy, but not to the stretch-mark phase. She knows in another couple of months she and Jay will try again. She will wake with a start each morning, checking underwear or thighs, toilet paper—obsessively—for blood. She will hope her period won't start, and then, when she tests positive, worry she'll spot then cramp, lose the heartbeat. Jay will tell her not to think about it. To go about the day as if nothing is happening so that if next summer they stroll a newborn, it will be a pleasant surprise. But Jenna remembers seeing the first clot, the sweat on her lip, the phone call to the resident on call, who'd said, briskly, "If it's not a miscarriage, you'll be fine. And if it is, there's nothing we can do about it anyway." That was the first time.

The second time, nearly three months ago, Jenna had been induced; the cervix ripened with prostaglandin rods, then into labor, push, delivering something—someone. She'd left the hospital in her pouchy maternity jeans but with nothing in her arms, no new car seat swinging from Jay's hand. At home, with no mother to pack up the nursery, Jenna had sifted through the layette clothing herself, packing into plastic tubs the forearm-sized outfits, the gender-neutral yellow-and-white caps, the waffled cotton receiving blankets.

"And bless the sun and the stars, moon and light." Titian exhales audibly. The Emotives sit up, stretch, go to their tents. Sometimes

Jenna thinks Titian could spew whatever words he felt like and he'd have an appreciative audience. The Emotives are so needy that they latch on to anything Titian says as if it's prayer.

Titian approaches Jenna and puts both hands on her shoulders. She flinches, then feels guilty, then annoyed at both the touching and her response.

"You're too tense," he says. "You're not sneaking processed flour and sugar, are you?"

"Actually, I have a stash of Milky Ways and red licorice in my bunk," Jenna says, straight-mouthed so he can't figure if she's serious.

"Cabin," Titian corrects. Jenna shrugs, noting how early the competition for Andrea's attention has started.

"I'm a sucker for Good & Plentys," Andrea says when she comes over. Titian shoots her a look. "Before—I mean, I used to love them."

"Ah, yes, in her Premotives life, Andrea was quite the sugar hound."

"Well, it wasn't like I was hoarding a stash of Snickers or something." Andrea gives Titian a flick on the arm. When he doesn't respond, she pulls his goatee. Then, to Jenna, she adds, "Tim thinks he saved me from a life without whole grains."

Andrea invites Jenna to their house for late-night drinks, and she accepts. Titian puts one hand on each of their backs. "Not too late, though," Jenna says. "Tomorrow is granola and yogurt, which adds a half hour to my prep time." Titian nods, and Andrea rubs her belly as if Jenna's already offered her the food. Jenna tries hard not to tummy-rub anymore; it's such a second-trimester pose, protective and proud at the same time.

"I love your granola," Andrea says. She puts her hand on Jenna's cheek the way a grandmother might; the gesture strikes Jenna less as one of tenderness than as one of wonder.

"You could even use our goat's yogurt, if you want," Titian adds. When he turns to walk away, Andrea sticks her finger into her mouth, fake-gagging, and Jenna silently concurs.

In the late afternoon, Avi the guruesque leader climbs a lifeguard-high chair and speaks down to the Emotives, who sit on spread blankets on the yurt floor below. Avi starts with a nondenomina-tional prayer, even though he's introduced himself as a Jewish atheist. He keeps his hair clipped very close to the head, silvers flecking the sides while the top is relatively dark. When the prayer ends, a couple *amens*, some stretching. Avi continues.

"Man . . . knows only when he is satisfied and when he suffers, and only his sufferings and his satisfactions instruct him concern-ing himself, teach him what to seek and what to avoid. For the rest, man is a confused creature; he knows not whence he comes or whither he goes, he knows little of the world, and above all, he knows little of himself . . ." Avi climbs down from his chair-pulpit and adds, "Not my words, by the way. Johann Wolfgang von Goethe."

He repeats the name as many of the Emotives search their pockets for pens. For a program based on verbal expression, Jenna thinks, they write incessantly. Each time Titian mumbles a key phrase—and he'll even announce "I'm about to utter a Key Phrase"—they copy it into the tiny notebooks administered at registration. They're meant to take them home, back to their cit-ies and work pods for review, but Jenna can already see them slipped underneath paper piles, ready for recycling. She stands up, ready to leave, but makes it only as far as the yurt's door when Avi addresses her.

"Wait," he says. He moves through the seated minions and stands two feet away from her. "Don't go, we're only just start-ing—I'm not going to spew quotes all day." A few encouraging murmurs from the Emotives.

"Oh," says Jenna, her hands up, fingers spread as if she's steril-ized and ready to scrub in for surgery, "I'm not one of them."

"Oh," Avi says, exaggerated now. He eyes the crowd and then Jenna, then speaks to the crowd. "She says she's not one of you!" He doesn't give them a chance to say that she's not, really. That she wears her own clothes, not the Emotives T-shirts, that she has her own cabin, that she can't speak in this forum. But Avi goes on. "Are we not all part of everything?"

Jenna wants to back up, wants to say, "No, seriously, I am not part of this," but instead finds her body too tired to keep moving, so she slumps onto a chair. Still, she figures, she's not huddled with the masses on the floor, she's sitting quite ladylike in a straight-backed chair like the one her mother had kept by the phone in the hall, so people could hold their conversations with focus. While Avi groups the Emotives, Jenna remembers how her mother disliked talking on the telephone when the person on the other end seemed otherwise engaged. "I wouldn't even think of cooking or paying bills while conversing," her mother had said once, when she'd heard Jenna's fingers on the computer keyboard. "I certainly don't want to share you with a machine." She'd meant the computer, something her mother had never had interest in— even though Jenna's father could scan, download; he'd print her e-mails out so her mother would feel included.

"Where are you?" Avi whispers to her as he's about to go back to his leader position.

His verbal nudge wakes her up. "Here," Jenna says. "Here."

An hour later, they've completed tongue twisters and role-played, dealt with Anger Scenarios and Comfort Confrontations. They've paired off and volleyed single words to each other. Then they choose phrases from a hat. Jenna feels suspiciously the way she'd done decades before in drama class but agrees to the exercise to avoid further admonishment from Avi.

"But I don't want to let go," Jenna's phrase-partner says.

"But you have to," Jenna says.

"Great!" Avi intervenes. "Now switch the tone of phrases." Each pair repeat themselves in happy, sad, frustrated, indignant tones of voice.

"Now swap phrases," Avi says.

"But I don't want to let go," Jenna says, still riled up from her indignant "have to" before. She hasn't spoken this much in weeks, maybe months. Not so many words, not in a row. There'd been a couple of phone calls, just to say her mother'd gone, to arrange flights, a meeting with the lawyer, a few spare meals with her father, the OB follow-up.

"But you have to," her partner says.

"But I don't want to let go," Jenna says, and it comes out so desperate she can feel too much in her chest and wonders if she might faint or something equally dramatic. But she doesn't.

"That's enough," Avi says.

Andrea comes to fetch Jenna from her cabin and walk her up in the total blackness to the main house.

Andrea's boots crackle the dried leaves underfoot, and Jenna holds her arms out in front of her, aware of scurrying nocturnals, the cold wind chapping her face.

"Sorry about Titian," Andrea says, as if they've just been discussing him.

"That's okay," Jenna says and then, "What do you mean?"

"He's just trying to break you," Andrea says. In the dark, in the late fall, suddenly Jenna thinks she could be in a thriller; Andrea and Titian could murder her, make her disappear completely. "What I'm saying is, he's not kidding. He really buys everything he's saying out there." Jenna can't see but senses that Andrea has gestured to *out there*, the rest of the complex. "And he wants everyone else to get inspired. And he's jealous of you, I think."

Andrea stops where she is and reaches out for Jenna. Jenna thinks about Titian's jealousy and is glad of it, then protective of Andrea. "Are you okay?" Jenna asks. "Can I do something for you?" She touches Andrea's thin arms through the bulky jumble of her sweater and blanket wrap.

"Oh, sure, I'm good," Andrea says. "Tired is all." They stand there, quiet a minute, until Andrea adds, "Don't get me wrong. I like my life here. And even though I'm not the most expressive person in the world—which is why I signed up here in the first place—I'm getting better."

"You're an Emotive?" Jenna asks, aware how bizarre her language has become, also aware of a sudden other side to Andrea.

"Nearly three years ago," Andrea says. "How a girl from Texas got here is anyone's guess—but I'll tell you what. Where I grew up, no one talked." She does not mention her deaf mother, her father and his liquor, the brothers who—except for one—all linger at her parents' tumbling house.

"How'd you even find out about it?" Jenna asks.

"My mother. She saw a flyer—or a pamphlet." The two women move now, trudging through the freezing mud toward the very distant glow of the house. "Tim had just started out then; you know, he hadn't perfected his spiel. But he was this—just a comforting force for me. I came for the two-week program, but I never left."

"Wow," Jenna says. Somehow she'd figured Andrea and Tim had started the place together. But now she can see it, Andrea slowly pulled over to the Emotive way of life.

"You're probably thinking, *How the hell does she do it?* and I'll tell you—it's not easy. Part of me just hates this shit—the talking and the talking and the talking. That's why the TV in your cabin. But then, there is a good part of all this. Really."

Jenna bites the middle of her upper lip, nibbling where there's a tiny itch. "Will you stay here?" She's not quite sure why she asks, just lets the question out and waits.

"If Titian has his way. But fuck me if I raise kids here. And I want them, but he gives the same old fight: too many people on this earth, too much of a drain on natural resources."

"You've got time, though, right?" Jenna's mother had always said that, sounding biblical or like that Byrds' song.

Andrea responds, "Turn, turn, turn. Yeah. But I'd be pregnant right now if he'd agree to it. But not until then. So maybe not ever."

Jenna wishes she could see Andrea's face. Then she wonders about who did the cooking before her arrival, who'll come the next season after the winter shutdown. She wonders if everywhere she has been, in each connection, she is replaceable. Jenna touches Andrea's hair and feels her own dry hands. She wonders if the woman is teary or more complacent, like her mother had been when Jenna'd reported news of her first miscarriage.

"Don't you even feel bad for me?" she had wailed at her mother. "It would have been your grandchild—don't you get it?" Her mother had let Jenna scream at her, cry and shriek until her face was raw and blotchy, but she hadn't responded. Jenna could see the relief on her mother's face.

"Lots of people miscarry," her mother had said finally.

"People?" Jenna liked to pick at her mother's grammar, her word choice.

"Women. Women, then." Her mother corrected herself.

"You didn't."

"No," her mother said. "But after you have children, you won't look back at this the same way. It simply won't mean as much. You'll see."

Now Jenna thinks this is true. The first one paled in comparison with the second—wasn't even with the same person. For the first time, Jenna realizes her mother died thinking Jenna would have had the baby. Her mother never knew about the hospital, the limp form that emerged and was shuttled away from Jenna, the genetic tests administered to the fetus. Jenna is comforted and sick, too, that her mother believed herself a grandmother-to-be right up until the end. Jenna feels the stomach roll she still has, then follows Andrea up the porch steps. Jenna thinks about how she's found a place empty of strollers, vacant of cooing—how she doesn't even have to go to the grocery store and skip the baby items aisle. Then she suddenly has an image of all of them as adult-sized infants, and before she can laugh, she feels like crying—who would pick up the big babies, who could possibly take care of them all?

"The thing is," Andrea whispers back to Jenna, "I think Tim's just scared. If he has a kid, he'll have to talk to it, and do all the things he does with these people he never sees again. And then— one day—that kid will leave. And then where'll he be?"

Avi adds a splash of Jameson's to his coffee and doesn't bother to explain himself to Titian, who dramatically gestures no when offered a spill from Avi's flask. Jenna accepts and likes the burning slide of liquor in her throat. The drink also gives her a break from talking, from answering questions: where from, married to whom, doing what, why here, what next.

It's Avi's turn. "Three down, one to go," he says and produces school photos from his wallet. Jenna blushes; somehow she doesn't picture spiritual leaders even having wallets, let alone two-by-two snapshots of Jesse, Danielle, Davy. "Our fourth's due in three weeks."

Jenna clears her drink to the sink's edge. "Don't go," Titian says. "We can play games."

With pleasure, Jenna notes that the salsa and chips Titian slumps into bowls are nonorganic. He catches her noticing this and

says, "They ran out. In town—they don't always carry everything we want." It's the first time Jenna has heard Titian sound
apologetic, embarrassed.

The four crunch and dip, eat and chew audibly until Avi offers,
"Let's play a game."

"Not some psychological shit, right?" Andrea asks. She turns
to Jenna and talks while thumbing to Avi. "This guy interprets
everything: dreams, what color you like best, the way you
wipe—"

He cuts her off. "It's true—whether you're a folder or toilet
paper crumpler says a lot."

Titian laughs hard, Andrea follows, and Avi checks to see
what Jenna's reaction is. She says, "But—doesn't it make a difference that women have to wipe a lot more, and maybe that influ-
ences their style?"

They wait for her to say more. "I had a roommate who used to
wrap up her whole hand like a glove, then go front to back."

Avi says, "From a bacterial standpoint, front to back is important. For women."

The chip bowl nearly depleted, Andrea swigs liquor from Avi's
flask while Titian brings out paper and pencils. They all write the
names of famous people on tiny scraps, and then each plucks one
from a bowl and acts it out.

"Verbal charades," Avi explains.

"And why is this psychologically exploitive?" Jenna asks.

Andrea's eyes are wide, her top lip flecked with salsa. Avi's
mouth is slack from the drinking, his nose red. "Not exploitive,"
he says. "Revealing. Not exploitive." It is clear to Jenna that now
Avi thinks she's damaged or troubled, that she picked the wrong
word.

After Jenna gestures Elizabeth Taylor, Bob Dylan, Richard
Nixon, the game slows down. Titian is tired. He pulls Andrea into

the kitchen, and Jenna can see him snake a hand up her shirtfront. Andrea kisses him.

"So," Avi says to Jenna. "You gonna end up staying here like the rest of the cooks?"

That night, Jenna listens for the nameless scurrying—the squirrels or possum, a distant howl—but hears nothing. She fetches the tiny TV from the closet and sticks it at the foot of her bed while she slithers into her sleeping bag. Each night when she gets inside, she thinks about sleeping with Jay in the first months of their courtship. Outside on the deck, they'd zipped their bags together—it had seemed so intimate. Jenna hadn't even ever thought zippers to be universal, to fit one in the other. Until Jay had told her, she'd thought that only their sleeping bags would link up— that their fate together was determined by their mutual affection for Patagonia gear.

On the little screen, the reception is surprisingly clear. News, reruns, a science fiction program Jenna's never seen before. She watches with the sound off as a three-headed warlock attempts to woo—or slay?—a shrunken yet buxom beauty. Jenna thinks about what Avi said. She could stay. It seems so simple suddenly; she could leave Jay, their cottage with the unfinished built-ins, her bread pans neatly stacked near the stove, the ovulation kits packaged in the bathroom. Jenna imagines living in the cabin through the winter, into the spring; maybe longer. With her two sweaters, one pair of jeans, the red long underwear—an entire wardrobe in one drawer—the same foods week after week. She falls asleep with a dragon, two little people, and the warlock toasting something, her feet rustling inside her bag.

At one of the camps Jenna's mother had forced her to attend at age eleven—a day camp, for "girls on the verge of becoming young women"—Jenna'd been taught how to cross her legs at the ankles, play kickball, practice tongue-kissing on the back of her hand. This last was revealed by her mother, who'd found her daughter sitting at the breakfast table practically gnawing on her right hand. Jenna had not been embarrassed, the act was aimless on her part—she'd felt disconnected from her body, dreamy—until her mother had swatted her hand away.

Later, to try to apologize, Jenna had found her mother in the flower garden and told her about the trust circle she'd been a part of at camp.

"You get in a circle," Jenna said. Her mother had a basket over her wrist and was laying dahlias, foxglove, and snapdragons, alternating the stalks so the blooms wouldn't tangle.

"A circle, okay," her mother said.

"And, well, you all crowd around? Like this." She moved closer to her mother. "No, wait, Mom—put the basket down." Her mother set the flowers and basket on the grass. Jenna pulled her mother by the hands and turned her around. "So, you need to sort of sit in my lap." They tried that, but Jenna nearly toppled over.

"What's the point of this exactly?" her mother asked. She wiped her mouth, tasted the salt slick.

"You're the one who makes me go to that stupid place." Jenna suddenly whipped around so they were face-to-face. "Now, you have to let me sit like this." Jenna's mother, still standing, felt the weight of her slim daughter. Jenna bent her knees slightly but didn't sit all the way. They stood there, semisuspended, for a few minutes.

Jenna's mother kissed the back of her daughter's neck.

"I guess it doesn't work very well with just two people," Jenna said. "There was a whole bunch of us, you know. And, well, you could really sit—like relax and everything, but still be standing."

"Because the circle supported you?" Jenna's mother asked.

Jenna brightened. "Yeah. Because of that."

* * *

After the granola and sheep's yogurt, Jenna finds Avi in the yurt. He's separating various colors and lengths of silk strips.

"Another game?"

"Of course. And a lecture. About openness." He smiles at Jenna, who smiles back. "And closure."

Jenna picks up a green strand. Then she notices Avi staring at her. "Oh, God, don't analyze me, okay?" He laughs. She imitates him. "Hmmm . . . she picked green, she must be missing something, deprived." He laughs, but Jenna then wonders—why would she say that? She drops the green one and picks red.

"You're not going to make us do a trust circle, are you?" she asks.

"No. No. And you won't have to fall back into someone's arms, either."

"Oh," Jenna says. She can see Titian and Andrea walking toward the yurt, followed by the Emotives, all clad in their special T-shirts. "That sounds kind of nice, actually."

Avi lets her fall back into his arms with her eyes closed—quickly, before anyone else sees and thinks it's the opening exercise. Jenna sits near the door again, in her chair, but feels good, as if she's got something none of the others has. Andrea crouches next to her.

"Titian and I wanted to ask you something," she says. Titian gives her a thumbs-up from his position near Avi. The two men are addressing smaller groups on the appropriate way to be open in a nonemotional setting. Jenna nods. She thinks Andrea will ask her to stay. They want her to live with them, maybe Avi, too—and his wife and tons of children. She won't need her own, she could just help with Avi's, and maybe try to sway Titian into wanting one. Jenna thinks that maybe she will say yes, that then she will have to call Jay, then her father.

"Now," Andrea says, "don't be freaked out, okay? We've never asked any of the cooks this before."

Avi starts a new game in the middle of the room. He's giving directions, but Jenna can't hear them clearly.

"I'm ready," Jenna says, looks at Andrea.

"We'd really like it if you'd consider making pumpkin soup."

Jenna has to have her say it again.

"Pumpkin soup," Jenna repeats. The words sound foreign, feel twisted on her tongue, as if they're gibberish.

"It's labor intensive, but we had real positive feedback last year—especially with some organic cinnamon—and maybe one of the Emotives would help you with the scooping."

Jenna just stares at her. "Oh."

"Oh, don't be upset. Really. You can even use our kitchen."

Jenna has not heard the directions of Avi's game, but she and Andrea are herded over to join.

"Kangaroo," an Emotive says, then says various words that Jenna hears only some of. She can't live here. She has to see Jay. Did she ever tell him what it felt like to be kicked—pleasantly— from the inside? Did she give or just think of giving her father the recipe for the asparagus dip? Jenna can feel herself about to cry. She holds back, listening to "Apple, bracelet, canned corn, dreams, elephant, friends, Gregorian chants . . ."

She figures the alphabetical aspect of the game out. "I'm going on a trip and I'm bringing . . ." she starts. She has to come up with an *m* word, then trace back, remembering everyone else's choices. "I'm going on a trip and I'm bringing . . ." She falters, then says, "A map of the area." It's the first thing that came to her mouth; it won over *melons, marshmallows, mice, mother.*

One of the Emotives interrupts. "Wait, Avi, I thought you said it has to start with the actual letter."

Avi looks at Jenna. "Yes, well, technically, it would be 'map of the area,'" he says.

"But that doesn't make sense," Jenna says. "Grammatically. No one says 'map of the area.' It's *a* map of the area." She begins to cry, hard. "Isn't it?"

They all sit there. The whole group of Emotives, and Titian, Andrea, Avi, and Jenna. Who will explain it? The talking, the fine points of speech, the looseness of something leaving you?

By the Time You Read This,
I'll Be Gone

Refilling the ketchup bottles takes the most time. After hours, Heather sits with her hair lolling onto the tabletops, not minding that she will later reek of spilled beer, ash, and garlic from the Dockside Italian-style happy hour that came with appetizer scampi and rolls delivered frozen, shipped by the hundred crate.

By the bar, two late-night drinkers alternate watching Heather's methodical squeezing of the ketchup and keeping track of the news on television. One of the drinkers is checking her out; she's aware that either he recognizes her from her prior child stardom or he wants to get her number, or—most likely—both.

The television is hoisted in the air, attached to the ceiling by L-bolts, angled like one in a hospital room. A week after the event and the local news flaps back on itself, revisiting the drowning. Heather remembers the way Matt hugged her while he kissed her, how sure he seemed that they had something worth keeping, how he said he hadn't seen her movies but he'd rent them if she wanted him to. After Matt had left her, bra still undone, out back by the loading dock, she'd repeated a line from one of the movies. The scene had earned her national praise for comedic timing and wordless emotive skills; in it she is sneaking away from a summer camp, leaving the other girls asleep in their bunks, the counselors unaware; she cannot find her shoes.

Now, as Heather wipes the sticky condiment residue on her apron, she remembers the original title of that film: *By the Time You Read This, I'll Be Gone.* The producers had trimmed it to *Read This*, then changed it completely once the theme song was written. The movie was released as *Summer's Gold*.

"My character's name is Gold," Heather said time and again in press interviews.

After the ketchup, she starts in on the salt, unscrewing the shaker tops and filling them from the salt box with the little girl on the front. Heather recalls wanting to be that girl, the one kicking through the rain, but as she looks at the girl now, she wonders what the rain has to do with salt and why they didn't think to put the girl by the ocean. Then she thinks how she is by the ocean, how Matt drowned in it, and how she wound up here, far from the film sets on which she grew up. The lighting is the thing that people don't understand, how on set actors glow, how flawless they appear thanks to reflecting panels and a team of people to tend to them.

All the salts and peppers are massed together, condiments ready for action. Heather imagines herself among them sitting, legless but full up, just waiting with an army of glass objects, hoping to be held.

What She Was Doing
at His Parents' House While
He Was in the Bathroom

In Matt's bedroom are copies of *Let's Go Europe* dating back to when there were still an East and a West Germany. Paging through one while she waits for him to finish flossing and flushing, Lucy notices circled cafés, a youth hostel marked by an *X*, jottings made years ago. Where was she when the book was new? Was that the high school summer in France, the immersion program in the tumbling abbey meant to increase fluency that resulted mainly in kissing the ponytailed Canadian gardener? Did he fall asleep on the night train from Barcelona with his pack secured between his legs, passport and money slicked to his belly under the rugby shirt she'd found in his closet? She tries to picture each of them younger, in their separate lives and places. Maybe he stared at the Bridge of Sighs in Venice at the same time she served waffle cones and double scoops at J.P. Licks and stared, drip-coated and aproned, at the painting of a cow on the wall.

Maybe they both longed for each other then. Or maybe he'd pressed some girl, an American Alpha Gamma Epsilon girl, up against the side of that fountain in Budapest one night and kissed her. Or was he the sort to go for a local, the unnatural blonde in Prague who had a no-shoes-in-the-house rule since she didn't own a vacuum, the Parisian who then told her boyfriend, the quiet girl from Edinburgh who'd made him consider, briefly, doing a semester abroad there?

When Matt comes out of the bathroom, he finds her crouching, still examining the *Let's Go* pages, looking for something.

"Those are my brother's," he says and sits shirtless in his flannel boxers on the futon.

Imagined images of him with his T-shirt tan lines and baguettes torn in two, the smooth stones collected from the river in County Cork, the skin-thin airmail letters, all disintegrate before she can think of what to say. She had thought there might be a travel journal somewhere, with sketches or funny incidents, phone numbers of girls he would never call, an address where he should send the five pounds he borrowed from the kind gentleman in the South Kensington tube. Lucy looks a few more minutes at the shelf, hoping to locate this book, a manual somehow, of what Matt or his brother—someone—was like before she got there.

43 Lake View Avenue, South

Upstairs it's the second night for sitting Shiva. Kyla's mother, Trishelle, died: pancreatic cancer that kept her housebound, tethered to a rolling IV pole. Heather is the middle neighbor, and downstairs Brian and his new girlfriend are watching porn. Every couple of minutes someone bearing a fruit basket or box of hard candies will come in the communal front door and head upstairs, past Heather's entryway.

When Heather takes her Shepherd-Lab mix, Suspicion—Susie—out for a walk, the leash gets tangled, caught between back leg and fore, and the dog pees on it. Heather's too busy watching the splaying of naked bodies through Brian's front window to notice until it's too late, and back inside she has to rinse the leash in the sink and loop it on the railing outside to dry in the fall air.

Part of her wants to take something upstairs, a carton of cookies, or a quiche, just to show she understands: that they are neighbors and that someone has died. Kyla, who has now lost her mother and father—is she a daughter anymore?—explained that the mourning ritual will last seven days. Since Heather is apartment-sandwiched between Kyla and Brian, who works the late shift at Conbrin Electric, Kyla told Heather first about the mother's passing, then went downstairs to tell Brian. This week Brian's got a girl staying with him from out of town. Heather was there when the taxi pulled up to the house. Suspicion ate dinner—leftover mushroom lasagna—late and had to go out for her night walk close to eleven, just when Brain's girl rolled her window down and motioned for him to come outside to her. He paid the driver and carried the suitcase up the stairs while the girl steadied herself on the banister. Heather saw that the case was one of those fake tapestry kinds, and even in the dim street-light, it looked new. Somehow, this depressed her, thinking of this girl buying a new set of luggage just to come see Brian—Brian who watched porn every night and didn't bother to shut his blinds, Brian whose recycling container was filled with empty plastic nonfat ice-cream sandwich boxes. Why nonfat? Heather wondered. Did he not burn off the calories watching the movies?

Suspicion liked better to lick the washed tins from Kyla's recycling, the pinto beans and organic vegetarian soups that came in oversized cans. Kyla was even thoughtful enough to put the sharp severed can tops in a separate container so Suspicion wouldn't slice her tongue and paw the way she did on Brian's reduced-calorie mexican macaroni mix once. Heather'd had to rush the dog to Blakely Memorial and have them stitch the mouth and foot, which made her late for work at the courthouse. Heather had to keep Suspicion in the car, head funneled off from the rest of her body so she wouldn't tear at the sutures, while she took her pads and supplies inside.

Heather has a degree in graphic design, and this is the first time she's put it to use, having been waitress, potter, live-in girl-friend, actress, part-time pet groomer, manicurist in training, barista. Now she works as a courtroom sketch artist and has to get to work very early when there's a case that's closed to the cameras. Tucked into some detail of her pictures—a briefcase corner, a fingernail—you could see "Heather" written in tight letters; evidence she'd been there.

One time Heather had to do a road rage case—a guy who'd had a woman pull over on the interstate and then shot her. It was better for Heather just to draw, to concentrate on the charcoal and the way she could get the sticks to move across the colored paper, than to think about the people she depicted. One man testified, looked right at her, and Heather'd had to duck down, shielding herself behind her hair.

The past couple weeks she'd been hired for a case involving a white man who killed some black girls back in the sixties. She'd wanted to tell Brian about it in the entryway but couldn't really say much for legal reasons, but she could say that she enjoyed the work. To her mother Heather explained what the job made her feel: that she'd become a good judge of when people looked sorry— maybe they were remorseful or maybe just excellent at pretending, but true sorrow pulled at the mouth, the muscles at the tops of the cheeks near the ears, and, Heather said, you can't fake that.

The first night of Shiva, Heather went up just to bring Kyla some flowers that had been delivered and set on the front stoop. Even though she was only a neighbor, not a friend, it seemed the right thing to do. Heather held the pot of mums as she took the stairs two at a time and wondered if couldn't they have sent a different kind of flower to someone who just lost her mother. Heather wondered if Kyla knew about flowers, if she'd analyze the delivery that much. Kyla's front door was open, and she was sitting off in the corner on a low stool while people picked at the side-table food and talked. Kyla nodded to Heather but didn't get up, so Heather left the plant on the kitchen counter and looked again at the food. Bald white eggs gathered together on a platter like old men, sticky breads sheared of their ends were ready for slicing, and bowls of cashews and nectarines were at the back. Heather didn't want to take any of the food and didn't know what to do, so she left and went to her apartment, where she could hear people sounds: a baby fussing, some crying, a cough. Two teenage boys—the dead woman's grandchildren?—took a seat on the stairs near Heather's doorway and ate candied pecans. She could see them holding handfuls of the nuts while they talked first about sports and then about a party that had occurred or maybe would occur.

At work, Heather had to produce a drawing about every ten minutes, and she was pretty good at guessing when people might move or rearrange themselves, so she knew beforehand that one of the boys was getting ready to stand up. Before he did, though, he looked over at her, peering from around the corner. He told the other boy to get a look. They both stood up and watched her watching them until some old lady came down and told them to get ready to go. One of them winked at Heather, and the other made some gesture that excited her even though she didn't want it to.

Once the mourners left, the front hall had only Brian's boots, a couple of umbrellas none of the tenants used much, and Kyla's blue raincoat, which was missing its sash. Heather stood out there, listening to the sounds coming from Brian's apartment. It was difficult to tell the real moans from the televised. She took Suspicion outside and let her have a good dig in the brush, nosing into the fallen leaves, so Heather could look through Brian's window. Naked on TV, a man held a bare woman upside down so her face was to the bed. Heather wondered if Brian ate the nonfat ice-cream sandwiches while he watched this kind of thing, or if he waited until later. Suspicion barked at a mole or a mouse hunching under the piled dirt by the curb. Heather wasn't sure how long she'd stayed out there. Each time a car came by, she patted Suspicion or looked to the sky as if she was searching for a meteor shower or was about to comment on the weather.

Today, she saw Brian's new girl towel-wrap her hair and head across to the market to buy their supper: cod cakes and coleslaw, and more ice cream. The girl went right over there in her robe as if that was what people did, paraded around in their underwear or house clothes, and then came back to where Heather stood sorting the mail. The postman just shoved a rubber-banded pile of letters and flyers into the black box on the side of the house and left them to figure out what pieces went where. Heather handed the girl Brian's pile, and the girl smiled without showing any teeth before slinging the plastic grocery bag over her shoulder and going inside to watch something on television.

Thursdays, Heather works late. She drives to the courthouse at two in the afternoon and she doesn't come home until eight, and she's not allowed to eat while people are testifying. Sometimes as she draws she creates sandwiches in her head, envisioning egg salad on rye with lettuce, or restructuring the whole thing on a sub, swapping tuna for egg. Then she feels guilty for thinking about food while someone's trying to tell his story to the court.

Sometimes, she's still sketching in her head when she's trying to sleep, the way, after having been skiing or on a waterslide, the body keeps doing it even after the activity is gone. Heather feels much of life is like that, already repeating itself. Smells overlap— grape soda from childhood, someone's garlic breath, low tide— and people's gestures do, too. The way a May Day parade queen had raised a hand to her in a wave, her mother's single raised brow, a guy she'd slept with who'd drowned the next day—he'd raised his mouth to the soft spot under her chin. Daily, Heather feels the familiarity of gestures, smells, words is so common it seems eerie; isn't *lukewarm* a grotesque word? The act of hair growing, isn't that slightly revolting? And touch—comforting and sickening, both. That guy she'd had sex with had drowned the next day; she'd watched as his body was hauled to shore and hadn't known where to go or what to do afterward, shattered not so much at his death as at the realization that there was no future with him, that he would never even have the chance to miss her or wonder about her.

In drawing, she'd learned some people are harder to draw than others. Attorneys had certain gestures they did a lot; the hard part was when they wouldn't face her. It made it tough to get a good sketch. When Heather got to the courtroom super early, and they were already at their tables, taking notes, she'd sometimes do quick sketches of their faces so she could capture them before they turned around. Heather always liked making the judge—she never had to draw below the chest, and the arms were plainly visible.

Through the ceiling, clomping and dragging—of furniture, though maybe it's a body? It occurs to Heather that she doesn't even know what they did with the mother's body. The mother, Trishelle, had died while Heather was working, and she'd come home to a quiet house. Brian slept during the day after he'd had his breakfast sandwich and left the crumpled waxed paper wrapped in the leg hole of his boot. Kyla was upstairs, Heather figured, and a man— her brother, Heather thought, who had the same curly dark hair and full belly—told Heather what had happened. He said Heather should expect some noise when people came to visit for Shiva. Heather asked him what happened later, after the week had passed, and he told her about Sheloshim, the thirty days of mourning when the mourners try to get back to normal activities even though they and everyone around knows about the grieving.

As he was explaining this, Heather thought maybe she would meet someone if she went to pay respects to Kyla. Kyla had men- tioned in passing that she knew lots of nice available men, but Heather hadn't let herself be fixed up. One time Heather was asked out by a jury member after the trial ended and he'd kissed her right in front of the cement horse and soldier statue in the park, but then she didn't hear from him again. Then, as Kyla's supposed brother was talking, he started crying, and Heather felt ashamed for thinking his mother's death place could be her romantic redemption. When she blushed she felt even worse, because the brother quickly wiped his tears and said he was sorry for taking up her time.

Now that it's the second night of Shiva, Heather is getting used to the sounds from upstairs. The constant shuffle gives her a reprieve from her hollow house, the loneliness that gnaws at her until she is moth-eaten, pocked. Mourners are eating and feeling sad up there, and she's somehow recording it just like she's listening, almost wanting to press her ear to the ground to hear the girl and Brian rolling on each other. If Heather can't sleep tonight, she can always take Suspicion for a walk, or even go and sit on her stoop—they're her stairs just as much as they are anyone else's, right? And then she will put her knees under her sweatshirt, move over to let the mourners pass. Or she'll hunch herself to one side so Brian, if he can keep his pants up long enough, can get out the door. She will leave the door to her place open, in case the phone rings, in case someone needs something.

Watermark

Lucy's father, Mark, water-skies off the Florida Keys. Her mother, Ginny, watches from the shore, sees him, her fiancé, wave to her. Really Ginny can't see him, she can see only his swimsuit, bright as a cherry tomato, but she knows it when he waves. Farther out on the dock, H.C.—his name is Stanley but they call him Hard Cash, another story—starts singing Jerry Lee Lewis and miming piano. Ginny shouts, "That Jerry Lee was a crazy man!"

They are years away from conceiving her, the daughter, Lucy, and thoughts of sex or labor, the engorged breasts of early parenting, are far out of reach, tucked away like a yellowing photograph.

Trishelle sits next to Ginny, touches the taut red of her sunburned shoulders, her nose peeling, and nods. "Really, a thirteen-year-old bride. Oh, Jerry!" And then, back to the sunburn, "So much for mixing oil and Mercurochrome." They sing about shaking, shimmying their upper bodies.

Suddenly, H.C. calls out, "Oh, Jesus!" He runs to Lucy's mother, who sings "Breathless—uh" as she and Trishelle spin each other around again and again until the beach slides into the water and it's all a blur.

H.C. screams, "Ginny, look out there!" as he points to the water.

The boat pulls in circle after circle. Lucy's father gives the slow-down sign, thumbs pointing to the ocean like an upside-down hitchhiker's sign, but the boat still speeds. H.C. gets the megaphone as Ginny runs out to the dock end to tell Lucy's father, but he's already seen it racing along with him, a gray fin a yard away. He gives thumbs up, thumbs up, until the boat gears are pressed full.

Trishelle and Ginny shout, *"H.C.!"* and "Shark!" waving their hands like cheerleaders in a Y, then an X formation.

The fin is a foot away from the skis when Lucy's father closes his eyes to salt water. When he opens them, the dorsal is against his shin, the rat-tail end of it high, just below his knee. H.C. yells, "Help's coming—do something!"

The boat's drivers cut their circle fast, Lucy's father crosses the wake, doubles back over to lose the fin, the dark shadow of body belonging to it darker and longer the closer into shore they move. Thinking Lucy's father will glide out to them, the drivers cut the engine. One ski off, he meets the dock instead, crashes into wood and bolts, breaks his collarbone and three ribs.

H.C., a summer lifeguard before his gambling days, lifts Lucy's father out of the water and onto the shore end of the dock. Kneeling next to him, Ginny and Trishelle point to the fin, which has come farther out and onto the sea surface to reveal itself as a bottle-nosed dolphin.

Its beaky snout tips toward the sky. The dolphin seems to call out to Lucy's father as he is stretcher-lifted into an ambulance. Ginny, still barefooted, climbs in with him, unaware that one of her bikini straps has come undone. Lucy's father, holding Ginny's hand says, "Ginny, oh, Ginny," over and over until he passes out. Trishelle and H.C., sun-oiled and sanded, follow in their car.

Lucy's father is left with a smooth, star-shaped scar on his collarbone. Nearing summer, it is time for Lucy to bring this story out again. She seems to see the happening so plainly in her memory, it is hard to believe she knows it only from being told. Her parents were her age then, the water locked into its flow, all of it bright. Unvowed, they hadn't graduated from college, or conceived her, hadn't felt their love slacken, the dialogue sucked right out of their car rides or Sunday evenings. Lucy is sure she has seen that moment on the beach; felt the fin, the sanded blood, the ambulance that goes off into whatever night, the blue of the lights—that siren—the slipping and rising of the watermark as if for always and always.

In the Pink

$\mathcal{M}$anoir de Mode used to be the Chapin Museum of Natural History. Now, where the stuffed yaks, Eocene fossils, and tiny bugs preserved in amber were displayed, two-hundred-dollar jeans and infant-sized women's waffle stretch shirts hang boneless from wire racks. Near the military-style coats, Lucy pauses to scratch the top of her foot and marvels at how easily the skin flakes off at summer's end. Crouching between a thick-wooled, Russian-style, double-breasted number and a cashmere blend pea-coat, Lucy can't help but wonder which army members or military personnel might actually wear these coats—fancy sailors aboard the *SS Bendel* maybe. She's about to say this to her mother, Ginny, who thumbs through the clothing as if it's someone else's laundry, but her mother beats her to speaking:

"You could try one of these." Ginny offers a maroon coat.

"War Chic?" Lucy shakes her head.

Ginny is about to respond but motions to a strollered baby, who is spitting white, cheesy drool and still managing a smile. To Ginny's horror, and the hovering salesclerk's disapproval, its mother uses her shirt cuff as a handkerchief. Lucy feels her own still flat belly, the splitting cells inside not yet showing exteriorly, and knows she will be the kind of mother who uses her clothing as a burp cloth, too. She realizes when she becomes a mother, her own mother will have a whole new territory by which to comment, judge, or admire her.

Outside, Ginny looks at her mobile phone, checking for messages even though there's been no ring, no buzz, then bends down to fix Lucy's pants hem; the seam has flipped over, an unintentional cuff.

"I'm hungry," Lucy says, thinking maybe her mother will guess just from this that Lucy's pregnant. She and Justin have waited out the first trimester, squirreling the secret between the two of them, not so much for the risk of miscarriage but for the swell of pride in knowing something so huge, so potentially public, that no one else can figure out.

"I bumped into Jillian Levy—do you remember her from that ski trip? She's a new member at the club, she's redoing the tiles in the upstairs bath and needs my help deciding between glass and marble." Ginny links her arm through Lucy's, and they walk down Newbury Street past the high-end boutiques, Ginny's newly blown out hair bobbing slightly with each step.

"I like the ones you and Jim have in the guest bathroom," Lucy says. She feels she must comment on the trivialities of Ginny's days to give more weight to them. She acknowledges within herself a certain guilt about this, that she's not having a real conversation, more just bucking informational tidbits; the tile showcase she read about in a British magazine, the wholesale fabric place, her opinion about Ginny's shoes, whether her feet look too wide in ankle boots.

"The ones in the guest bath are from Marseille." Ginny nods as if she knew all along her daughter's preference for French Country style.

"Oh," Lucy says. "Did you bring them back?"

Ginny stops to survey a window display at In the Pink, the store in which Ginny pronounces everything adorable and Lucy fights the urge to roll her eyes. In the window, the mantis-limbed mannequins stare vacantly back. "No—we shipped them. They're too heavy, especially with Jim's back. Even though he's on the new medication. He might stop it, actually, based on the research."

Lucy swears she can feel a kick inside her. But it's too early, right? She thinks back to the reading she did at the library, squatting between the book carousels to page through medical texts that depicted the embryo and fetus in every stage of development. How could it be that something, someone—a person who would make decisions, find or lose love, devour cinnamon or despise it, conquer or merely exist in the world—could be actually growing in Lucy and her own mother couldn't know it without being told? Lucy is disappointed by the lack of karmic connection, the thought that somehow, underneath the bathroom tiles, the new club members, the stunning inaccuracy Ginny has in buying pieces for Lucy's wardrobe (the fact that she would even call Lucy's closet heap of old T-shirts and jeans *a wardrobe*), that Ginny isn't magically connected enough to Lucy to just know.

"Do you want to go inside?" Lucy asks and points to a rose-colored bag that rests on the tallest mannequin's hip. "Is that the purse you were talking about before?"

Ginny doesn't move her eyes from the window. "That's the one. It would be just right for Turn Back the Clock Night at the club."

"Why, what decade is it this year?" Lucy asks, thinking about the flapper costume, the fifties sock hop, the polyester disco days outfits her mother had worn in years past.

Ginny turns to Lucy and sighs. "Oh, this year the committee

couldn't decide, so, it's the fallback one, Peace and Love." Wearily, she holds up two fingers in a peace sign.

"Hippies, you mean?" Lucy grins. "I can really see you in a paisley print top and wraparound skirt."

Ginny nods. "What's really odd, Luce, is that I did wear that." She pauses and watches the fashionable folks walk past, their tiny heels clicking on the pavement. "It feels silly to think about dressing up in clothing I actually wore—like I'm repeating my life or something."

Lucy can't think of what to do, so she puts her hands on her mother's tweed-covered shoulders. Then the gesture seems too big, so she just touches her mother's hands, pulling at the loose skin on the top, almost pinching her but not quite. "I think it's neat—it's like if I dressed in early eighties gear—it's sad kind of, because I'd be dressing like a seventh-grader and I'm so much older . . ." Lucy looks at her own hands wrapped around her mother's and then suddenly hugs her mother so tightly, clutches her so vehemently that Ginny allows her purse to slide off her shoulder, where it swings and bumps against them.

"I love you so much, Mom," Lucy says. She thinks she should say it more, wishes that between bathroom tiles and fierce proclamations there were other things to say, but then considers that maybe it's enough as it is.

"I love you, too, honey," Ginny says, and Lucy can tell she's already reeling in whatever emotions she had, already patting her back, most likely horrified by the display on Newbury Street.

"Do you want to go get the bag?" Lucy thumbs to the mannequins.

Ginny considers for a minute and then looks at Lucy straight on. "I had thought about it . . ." She raises her eyebrows at Lucy, and all the moments between them from babyhood to adolescence to Matt's funeral to wedding dress shopping a second time come

clomping back in a rush. "But I think we'd better get you something to eat. I'm guessing an Italian sub . . ."

Ginny pauses, waiting for Lucy. "Yeah, something acidic, really tomatoey."

"I thought that might hit the spot," Ginny says and, with the
wink implied but not demonstrated, tells Lucy that she has known
about her, all of her, all along.

Talk

Before his marriage, Lyle hadn't known much about food. Kyla had given him chili paste in a tube one year in his stocking, and as the tree lights flinched behind him, she shook her head as Lyle asked what purpose flavored glue might serve.

Two years in, Lyle could tell the difference between habanero peppers and cubanos, knew when Kyla had pan-fried zucchini blossoms by the sweet oil that coated the kitchen sink. Kyla was a wondrous chef despite not cooking with wheat and gluten, yet a perfunctory dishwasher, leaving slicks of garlic-infused olive oil on frying pans, melted and browned bits of pecorino on the cookie sheet they used to cook the hand-rolled dough, crumb armies in uneven lines rimming the sink.

Lyle enjoyed plunging his hands in the hot dishwater, rummaging among the unseen utensils and plates, then picking an item to soap and rinse. Reed-tall, Lyle's slim body seemed likely to bend at the waist and bow earthward as he stood barefooted over the murk and disposal-chewed dinner remains thinking about what he could possibly concoct for Kyla, who lay, nauseated and flushed, in her thirty-seventh week.

Lyle knew not to touch Kyla's back when she felt ill, so he stretched her legs out over his lap and rubbed at her knees. She turned her face away from the fan to look at him and then put her hands over his. Often this was her way of asking him to stop moving or scratching or tickling without asking outright, so he made his hands wide and flat and still.

Kyla shook her head. "You don't have to stop," she said. "This time I was just putting my hands on yours."

They looked at each other a minute, and then Kyla motioned for Lyle to put his face near the belly-swell to feel the baby who swirled and flipped inside.

"I'm thinking about later, you know, afterward," Lyle said with his cheek against Kyla's stomach skin.

"Really?" She rubbed at the sparse hairs at the very top of his head. "I'm thinking about something crunchy—not carrots, popcorn maybe. With nuts. Peanut brittle." She stood up. "That's what I need."

"What will I do if I can't think of all your funny stories to tell her?" Lyle said and made his arm into a crane, lowering it so the hand clasped Kyla's shoulder and pulled her up by the shirt.

At the Crescent Mill Mall near It's All Twisted, the pretzel stand, a candy vendor handed Kyla a sand-colored slab of peanut brittle pocked with tiny air bubbles that had burst in the process of heating and cooling. Lyle watched his wife break a piece off to hand to him and was about to let himself wonder if this was the last time they'd have peanut brittle when Kyla said, "It's not like we've had it before."

She knew where his mind went in the fluorescent lighting. "So you'd have to say, 'The first and last time your mom and I had peanut brittle . . . ' "She stopped talking to pick some gummed up candy out of a molar.

The obstetrician, Gabrielle, had consulted with the neurosurgeon and reported in the hush of the beige office that the tumor was Stage 4. Lyle looked beyond the doctor at her framed family photos on the wall: toddlers—hers? steps?—in orange water-wings in the first lap of waves on a beach somewhere, grade school kids and a man—the husband? father?—dangling from the limbs of an umbrella pine, all in matching sweaters. Then Lyle thought maybe the pictures were there for that purpose, to distract patients from their diagnoses, so he stopped looking at them and turned to his wife.

"I knew it would be," Kyla was saying to the doctor about her tumor when Lyle rejoined the conversation. "Of course it's the most aggressive kind, what else would I get?"

Prepregnancy, Kyla had been an event planner in Santa Monica and was used to big news arriving suddenly. Either the catering truck would be stuck with a flat off Montana or some second-tier celebrity would increase the guest list by fifty a day before, or they'd realize the sterling silver whistles in the baby shower gift baskets were a choking hazard—regardless, Kyla accomplished whatever event she'd planned. This time, though, what she said to Gabrielle (and thought how L.A. it was to call her surgeon by her first name), maybe for Lyle's benefit, was "I don't think I'm going to pull this one off."

Lyle let tears well up until they couldn't be contained and the overflow dripped onto his cheeks, collected into widening disks on his light blue shirt. As if they were a by-product and therefore not his fault—rather like sweat during tennis—Lyle allowed the tears to keep coming without brushing them off as the doctor went over details of Kyla's condition.

"Since the tumor is in the parietal lobe, Kyla might lose the ability to write," Gabrielle said with her hands clasped. "She could have speech disturbances. Seizures are common with tumors in this region of the brain, and talking can become very difficult."

Lyle thought about Kyla's scrawling penmanship, the way the letters slanted forward as if they had somewhere better to be. Words curved into the right-hand margin until they blended into the next line. Lyle made Kyla laugh when he navigated directions she'd written, reading what the words looked like on the page: "Left nerp flanging stream, fish miles."

"You might experience a loss of recognition of your body parts—say, where your hands are in relation to your sides—spatial disorders are sometimes a problem after surgery." The doctor paused. "I assume we're going ahead with it?"

Kyla looked at the ob's face, her name plate with the sturdy block letters spelling "Gabrielle," and tried to picture the doctor as a schoolgirl. Had she worn rainbow suspenders, or refused the crusts on her peanut butter and Fluff sandwiches? With an ephemeral blush, Kyla wondered if Gabrielle had been one of the mean girls, the rumor spreaders, the ones who shrugged off the girls who still played with plastic horses at playground time, the way she had. Once, Kyla had admitted to Lyle how cruel she'd been in seventh grade, writing fake love notes and starting the Let's Hate Jennifer B. Club after Jenny B. received too much sympathy for her emergency appendectomy. Then later, how the meanness crept back, how she'd slept with her roommate's boyfriend in graduate school, not because she needed to but because she could. Lyle had suppressed a laugh, unable to comprehend that his now empathetic, vanilla-scented wife had been hipless in seventh grade and the class bitch, and heartless in her early twenties, whereas now she had to have Lyle be the one to complain that the cleaners weren't drying the laundry well enough, and mildew was starting to appear on the hems of her shirts.

"Kyla?" Gabrielle shifted some papers around on her desk,

fidgeted with her plastic conception wheel the way the newly married finger their rings. "Statistically, the procedure is the best plan of action."

Kyla and Lyle looked at each other and then nodded.

"Let's do it." Kyla eased the words out, wishing she had agreed on something, anything else—a party theme, a *yes* to the college formal, the proposal Lyle had given her, a resounding *sure* after he'd tried earlier to sell her on the idea of having babies young. After the scheduled cesarean, she would not go home with the baby and Lyle but would remain in the hospital until Obstetrics had cleared her and Neurology had wheeled her away.

"I like the terms she uses," Kyla said to Lyle in the car on the way home. "*Aggressive*—like there's a hostile takeover in my head. And *debulking*. Good word."

"I think that's just the medical term," Lyle said. The skin under his eyes felt engorged, his shirt was still wet.

"Oh. I thought maybe Gabrielle made that up—you know, to sound poetic." Kyla thought of the aggressive girls in grade school, how her mother had used that word to describe them when what they really had been was cruel. Then she thought of onion rolls and imagined they were the shape and size of the tumor, bulbous and soft, in need of debulking.

Up ahead, bursts of red and yellow on the road median's hibiscus plants were their own stop and slow signals. Lyle pulled the car over to the roadside and put his arms around Kyla, who thought to pull the emergency brake up while the car stalled and Lyle's face burrowed into the space between her collarbone and chin. She cried a bit, and then, when Lyle kept nuzzling, she laughed.

"That tickles," she said.

"Come on," Lyle said, annoyed and not yet guilty for it.

He knew Kyla would react this way, calm and funny, her slight distance making his emotions seem garish and whiny. It had been the same when they got together—he totally knocked over by her wit, her orange-zested salmon, the way the tops of her breasts seemed to escape the netting of her bra, the way she'd loved him so suddenly. She'd been unruffled, happy but poised.

"I want to name her Rey," Kyla said, her voice soft as she looked out the window. Sparrows and a couple pigeons rummaged in the wood-chipped mulch.

"Oh, Ky." Lyle put his face in his hands. She had been insisting on naming the baby Mavis, after the great-aunt who'd taught Kyla to tell a plum tomato from a cherry, who had pickled Bolivian Rainbows and showed her how to dice them with capers for a fish sauce. But Lyle and Kyla had met in Marina del Rey and had joked then about the name, about having three kids—Marina, Del, and Rey. Now, there could be only one.

Lyle and Kyla stayed there on the side of the road letting cars and SUVs pass, sometimes honking, as they held hands. Kyla took out a sheet of paper and wrote "Rey" in various fonts, swirled and loopy like on a celebrity kid birthday invite, block-lettered stout like she'd used for the autism fund-raiser the year before, and then bubbled, like on a fifth-grader's Mother's Day card.

"Which will be more like her?" she asked Lyle. "Will we have a script girl or a capitals-only printer?"

Years later, Lyle would show the lettered paper to Rey as she tried to make a cover for her fourth-grade autobiography entitled "All About Me." She copied her mother's loops and lines and set the paper aside while Lyle glued a photograph on the cover from when Rey had been born. Rey, swaddled in a yellow cotton blanket; Kyla had held her daughter at arm's length, on display for the camera before the edema had increased. All the fluids had leaked into her veins, and Kyla's small chin had swollen, her face bulbous and smooth like the surface of an egg. She'd felt her cheeks and asked for a hand mirror.

"I may be puffy, but there's not a wrinkle in sight," she'd sa
The blue-and-green patterned gown had reminded Lyle of his a
gebra textbook's Escher-print cover, where lizards had overlapped
one another until he couldn't tell what was tail and what was
snout.

It was this image, the sweat-lined lip and johnny-clad body,
Lyle thought of while he helped Rey finish her homework.

"You can tell me something about her, if you want," Rey said.
She didn't always want to know, and Lyle closeted away details
until Rey allowed him to spill them. She put her finger on the
photographed nose of her gone mother as if expecting it to beep.

"She liked cool baths," he said. "And she ate tomatoes like
you'd eat an apple."

"Yuck," Rey said. She pictured biting and spurting seeds, drip-
ping juice. "You already told me about the bath part."

"Well." Lyle swallowed a sip of lemonade. He wondered when
he would run out of stories, when the clips of Kyla would recede,
failing him and their daughter.

"Oh—I have one!" he said. "After her surgery, she forgot lots of
stuff. You know, names of people and if milk was called milk or
something else."

Rey listened, looking up at her father's wide hands as he gestured. "Then," Lyle continued, "I made her lunch one day—grilled
cheese on potato loaf with a pickle on the side."

"That's my favorite!" Rey said. Lyle loved how Rey could make
comments like this and, having not been a witness to the actual
loss of Kyla, sound happy. It was, he realized, the same tone Kyla
had after her surgery—placid, happy, as if all the evil in the world
happened to someone else, nearby.

"I know. Mine, too, but I like Swiss and you like that processed
American goop—just like Mom," Lyle said. "But Kyla—Mom—
didn't want the pickle I'd served her on the side. Didn't even want
it on her plate. But she couldn't think of how to say that."

Lyle looked at his daughter and took her whole face in his hands as if he hadn't ever seen her until now. "And then—you know what she did? Kyla said, 'In the theater of my life, this pickle has no role!'" Lyle laughed and looked at the cover of Rey's now-pasted book.

Lyle looked at his daughter, their daughter, and tried for one moment to see her as a woman, a decade or two from now, then instantly stopped himself so the future Rey dissipated and the ten-year-old came back with too-large teeth and wide forehead. The one who didn't yet really miss her mother. The daughter whose only assignment was to write the "All About Me" that summed up only one decade.

"In the theater of my life, this pickle has no role," Lyle repeated, and Rey joined in on the last couple words.

"I know just what she meant," Rey said and nodded.

In the Herd of the Elephants

Smiling Cadillac wide, Julia Roberts stares out from the television. She's riding on top of an elephant somewhere—Thailand, maybe—and manages to look graceful, hair piled up, and unfazed by the heat. In their eighth and ninth months, Lucy and Jenna are considerably less cool; sweat dollops run their jagged course from Lucy's temple to her jaw while perspiration seeps through Jenna's bra, oozing from the underwire until she can feel it on her stretched stomach.

Bloated like a pair of bullfrog cheeks, they are nevertheless sitting right next to each other, not bothering to leave a space in between.

"I wish I had a trunk," Lucy says, putting her forearm to her nose and flinging her wrist. "I would splash myself in a water hole."

They debate the merits of a trunk versus a marsupial pouch, then drink the last of their Russian iced tea. Lucy's mother made a jug of it—loose tea tied in cheesecloth sacks submerged into hot water—and stuck it in the fridge, and they've been sipping at the ginger-orange of it until their tongue tips are slightly burning.

"What about Ella?" Jenna says to Lucy.

They still haven't settled on names for the babies—now too big to swirl inside them so they just punch and roll—and the women are desperate enough these days that they look to everyday objects or anyone they encounter to see if they can pick something suitable: Lottie was the bag packer at Shaw's market, Jinelle was the vacuum brand Lucy thought sounded good for a girl. The Baby Romaine from their salads didn't seem right for a child, but they decided it would work for the rock group they'd never form.

"Ella's nice," Lucy says. "You could have Ella and I could have Louie."

They don't know if they are carrying boys or girls or one of each, but the husbands, who both work on the farm, have a feeling they'll soon be surrounded by a herd of females. Today they sift through the harvested brussels sprouts and bunch the snap beans into crates to be shipped. When they come home, linted with cornhusks, Jenna and Lucy'll go out to the truck, see what remnants they've got in back, and fashion dinner out of the bruised tomatoes or button mushrooms.

On the television, Julia heads into the jungle to be with orangutans, leaving the heft of elephant she rode on to wait in the dusty shade.

"There's only two kinds of elephants," Jenna says. "The Asian elephant and the African—the African's the biggest, so that's me."

"Give me another couple weeks," Lucy says, still facing the screen. "Then we'll see. You'll be in labor and I'll be sitting here, sweating and packing on the pounds."

Since Jenna is due three weeks before she is, Lucy is terrified her friend might have the baby and suddenly leave her behind, back in the world of the nonparenting.

"Maybe we'll go at the same time," Jenna says to try to make her feel better, even though it's best if she is full term. The last thing she'd want is to have Lucy stuck in the NICU while Jenna's home breast-feeding on the couch.

Lucy perks up. "Maybe we will! Can't you see it? The guys running back and forth, checking on us, comparing how much dilation."

They joke about being crops the men need to tend, about wetting through the pickup's seat when their waters break, or the way Jenna's husband's face would curl up if he were rushing her to the hospital, driving with his chest pressed to the wheel the way he did when the main pipe burst and nearly flooded the cabbage crop two years ago.

Jenna flips channels for a minute to look at the weather, which annoys Lucy. "Can't you just leave it? You know it's still hot out, so why bother checking?" she asks. She fans herself with a paper towel and then says, "This isn't working."

"Hey—what about Windy or Cloudy or Cirrus?" Jenna asks, going back to their name game.

"Cirrus isn't bad—for a boy."

"Those are ice clouds," Jenna says and then, feeling the need to explain herself, "I only know this because I watch the Weather Channel too much."

She tells Lucy about thin stratus clouds, which sheet the sky; the patchy altocumulus ones, which are made of water but hardly ever produce rain, and the mammatus clouds, which have pouch-like shapes hanging out like bosoms.

"Hey—we're mammatus," Lucy says and makes Jenna turn back to the animals.

Back at the documentary, one of the orangutans is old and might not make it until the end of filming. Movie-star Julia is clearly upset and watches mothers bug-pick their children to feel better while the gray-haired one ails in the distance. Lucy starts to cry when Julia talks to the camera about her experience in the jungle, about how it changed her, how she liked watching the primates use sticks to fish a row of ants out from a hole in a log, how surprised she was by the way the group communicated.

Seeing Lucy cry makes Jenna start. When they watched a documentary about seagulls, they learned that depending on the species and where they lived, a quarter of all newly paired gulls split up. Lucy's first fiancé died in the water, and when the seabirds dove in, beaking for their dinners, alone and away from their mates, Lucy told Jenna again about how part of her still missed Matt. Here she was, married to Justin and having a baby, but the slice of her that still loved Matt would always wonder what love and children would have been with him. Maybe those feelings will trickle away, Jenna thinks, thin out and fade as Lucy gets further into life with Justin, when the baby is born.

Jenna knows what Lucy means, though, the curiosity about what might have been. This pregnancy is her fourth. The first three didn't take. Actually, Jenna knows the first one wouldn't have worked at all—it wasn't with her husband but with her first fiancé, Hull, who went off to teach an outdoor course in Colorado the summer after their engagement and never came back.

Jenna's real husband, Jay, saw her heaving behind the bakery before Hull had gone. He stopped his truck and offered help she didn't take until about a year later, when she burned an arm making rolls and he drove her to the emergency room. At their wedding, each guest left with a loaf of braided molasses, the same kind she'd been making when Jay came to her rescue.

Jenna didn't meet Lucy until a year later, when she was pregnant again and Lucy was mourning Matt, working part-time on the farm. Jenna could say Lucy is the sister she never had, but it's different than that. All her life Jenna felt she deserved a friend like Lucy, who fit the way she wanted with a husband, a woman Jenna knew she wanted to spend her life with. When she saw Lucy, crouching in the bulbous pumpkins that fall, and then later, wiping tears back as she hedged the shrubs at the farm's entryway, Jenna knew she'd found her. Jenna raked the clippings up for Lucy and listened to her talk about the engagement, about her unused law degree, about her guilty crush on Justin, who had been Matt's good friend. Only later did they realize they'd both known Kyla, a girl who'd hurt them both, who had also dated Justin, leaving him for Lucy to find later.

"Hey, look, she's back on the elephant," Lucy says, pointing to Julia Roberts, who has to leave the jungle and head back to Los Angeles, where there are people instead of orangutans.

"She looks so different without the makeup and lighting," Jenna says.

"She looks really awake," Lucy says.

She puts her hand on Jenna's baby-belly, its stretched birth-mark unseen underneath her T-shirt, and Jenna touches hers. Jenna remembers the elephant footage they saw the year they'd first met, when Jenna was miscarrying again and again and Lucy still slept in Matt's ripped T-shirts. The elephants slugged along the dry land, females remaining with females as the males went out to live independently. The bulls liked to be alone, or didn't know how not to be, and they long-distance-communicated only when it was time to mate. There wasn't a set breeding season for them, and the cows stayed in heat only three to six days at a time, so the process was tricky.

Jenna remembers Lucy saying, "Can you imagine having a pregnancy last for nearly two years?" And how that made her cry since she couldn't hold on to hers for longer than five months. But now she can imagine it: living huge and round for another couple of months, walking ill-balanced but with a whole other person inside. In the elephant documentary they watched, they saw a cow birth a too-weak calf. The herd needed to migrate toward water, and the mother elephant had to leave her baby's unmoving body to dry and disintegrate in the sun. Each year that same mother, buoyed by her female friends, revisited that place and stood for a while, remembering the baby she didn't get to have.

"Borneo," Jenna says reading the credits on-screen. "They were in Borneo, not Bali."

"Let's go make something for dinner," Lucy says and pulls Jenna up by both upper arms, the way you do when someone's drowning.

"Sounds like a plan," Jenna says and exhales hard, blowing the hairs off her forehead. They walk—hands linked like they're walking trunk to tail—into the kitchen, where there's bread rising, and stay there together, just like this.

Behind the Vines:
A Note from the Author

The people in these stories introduced themselves to me individually; I like to think of their collective stories as a map of sorts, the way that one place or person in your life pulls you to the next, then reloops you into a friendship you had that faded, or a place you'd left and now revisit.

Lucy was first—she appeared as she is in "Early Girls," at the gym, holding on to the teats of a big yoga ball—and I knew something had happened to her, but it wasn't until well into the title story, "Early Girls," that I knew exactly what her loss was. Lucy led to her mother, Ginny, and to Justin, though he came to life first in "Kindling." The way Lucy meets Justin through Kyla is how I met him, too. Later, Justin led to Matt, but before all this was Jenna, whom I first wrote about in "Voler." Originally, I had planned on the focus of "Voler" to be solely on Heather, but it turned out to be Jenna's story of coping just as much—if not more—with her friend's backstory as with the track of her own life.

Gabrielle, with her slight remove and wish for connection, presented herself clearly as a girl in "Animal Logic." As I continued to write the book, the grown-up character of Gabrielle kept pleading to be written, her relationship with her father explored, her need to keep moving coupled with a desire for permanence that is doubly threatened by Diane and her father's health, and secured in the end by Danny, her son, and by the math in which she finds relief.

I knew about Justin and his friendship with Matt before I knew Justin and Lucy would wind up together. I also wanted to see what it was like to write about someone losing a fiancé—Matt—and the loss of that love and beginning while also touching on the fact that Matt wasn't necessarily faithful. Does it change the perspective we have for Lucy? Or does it not matter because Matt's death overshadows other issues?

Gabrielle and Jenna are cousins who live apart, their parents obviously connected, and in my mind Jenna probably consulted Gabrielle about her conception problems. In fact, there are other stories: Ginny as a twenty-year-old shop clerk having an affair with her older, non-Jewish, married boss; Jenna meeting her husband Jay's parents in New Jersey while a strange news story unfolds in the background; Lucy reconnecting with James from camp years later, in London. Some of these stories were written, others sketched out, a couple not on the page at all, just fragmented in my head.

The map is endless—how we connect to people and spread, vinelike, and overlap—and yet for this book, I had to tame the growth in order to focus on the heart of this novel, Lucy and Jenna finding each other through the sprawl of adolescence, travel, love, work, loss, family, flings, and time; Kyla's personal evolution from a not very nice friend to someone whole and fully realized; and Gabrielle's quiet peace with her father and new mothering role.

If I were to draw a real-life picture of my vines, there would be just as many arrows and lines leading from one friend to the next, back to one boyfriend and on to the seventh-grade friend who later roomed with my husband at college and through whose twin I wound up meeting my spouse. There would be my husband's cousin who is married to a guy whose sister is married to a man whose sister-in-law is now one of my best friends, even though that's not how I met her (this union was performed by my first editor). Friendships, relationships, familial and otherwise, seep, the edges and overlaps spreading, and it's only when I pick through the brush of it all that I realize how tenuous some of the important connections are—what if I'd had a different editor or hadn't been friends with the twins in seventh grade. But I did—and so here am I, and in the same light, here are these girls, these women, who are tangled and untangled, their stories mapped out.

Emily Franklin

EMILY FRANKLIN

EMILY FRANKLIN is the author of the novel *Liner Notes* and a fiction series, *The Principles of Love*. She is co-editor and contributor to a two-part fiction anthology: *Before: Short Stories About Pregnancy from Our Top Writers* and *After: Short Stories About Parenting from Our Top Writers* and editor of *It's a Wonderful Lie: 26 Truths About Life in Your Twenties*. Her writing has appeared in many publications, including the *Mississippi Review* and *Boston Globe*. She lives outside of Boston with her husband and their three children.